"There is no such thing as putting off the wedding," Tilford said in a cold haughty voice. "You'd better understand that at once. Now run upstairs and put a few necessities together, you are coming home with me."

"Tilford!" gasped Maris horrified. "How could you possibly think I could be spared now? Don't you know I must care for my mother and little sister?"

"That's ridiculous," he said, his handsome face hardening. "You don't owe your family a thing! And when I put that ring on your finger it gave me the authority to insist you do as I tell you!"

"Authority?" said Maris lifting puzzled eyes to his stony offended countenance. "I thought it was a pledge of love and tenderness."

"Well, that, too. But it is all based on authority," he said coldly.

Maris stared at him for an instant longer then looked down at her spectacular diamond ring as if she had never been acquainted with it before. Then, slowly, she took it off and held it out to him.

"You had better take it back then," she said quietly. "For I could not wear a ring under those conditions." Then, pushing the ring into his hand, she turned and fairly flew up the stairs, her face ghastly white and her head whirling . . .

Tyndale House books by
Grace Livingston Hill
Check with your area bookstore
for these bestsellers.

Grace Livingston Hill

MARIS

LIVING BOOKS®
Tyndale House Publishers, Inc.
Wheaton, Illinois

This Tyndale House book
by Grace Livingston Hill
contains the complete text
of the original hard-cover edition.
NOT ONE WORD
HAS BEEN OMITTED.

Printing History
J. B. Lippincott edition published 1938
Tyndale House edition/1990

Living Books is a registered trademark of Tyndale
House Publishers, Inc.

Library of Congress Catalog Card Number 90-70056
ISBN 0-8423-4042-4
Printed in the United States of America

96 95 94 93 92 91 90
 7   6   5   4   3   2   1

MARIS Mayberry awoke slowly that Wednesday morning and even before her eyes were open she had a heavy consciousness upon her of something being wrong, just a faint uneasiness, like a small dully-tinted cloud on the horizon, that seemed to carry a sense of menace. What was it? She groped for it in her thoughts and tried to bring it to life again, that she might dispel it from her new day and prove by morning's light that it had been nothing real, and it need no longer burden her soul.

But the uneasiness continued, and she roused herself to search for it. What had she been doing last night? Where had she been? She had been out late, for even with closed eyelids she sensed that it was mid-morning, and mother must be letting her sleep late.

Oh, now she knew! She had been out with Tilford. She had been to a grand family dinner. All the Thorpes had been there, and it had been very formal. The dinner had not been served till half past eight and they had sat at the table over two hours. And then there had been a long time afterward when she had been carefully taken over by each separate member of the Thorpe connection and instructed in the history and traditions of the clan.

It had been a long process, and most depressing. When it was over she had felt very small and unworthy to enter even the fringes of such an august body.

But that had not been the real weight of her burden. It had not quite come to the surface of her mind yet, but she felt intuitively that it was going to be fully as disturbing this morning, when she did remember it, as it had been the night before.

It had been rather late when they left the Thorpe mansion, for at the last minute after some of the cousins had left they had taken her up to the gallery and shown her the old family portraits, great oil paintings by famous artists, set in huge hideous gold frames. She had realized that this was a sort of final rite that was being performed upon her before she should be considered eligible to go on with her preparations for the nuptials.

But even the great gallery with the ancestors set in gold had not depressed her. She had known about them, and been told before by Tilford of the high points in each one's biography. She had been duly impressed by the ladies in high ruffs and puffs and chignons, and the gentlemen in knee breeches and lace ruffles and wigs. She had even found some crisp original comments to make upon each, that showed she appreciated their nobility, and stood to admire in their august presence. No, it was not the picture gallery that lay heavily on her mind. They were only painted ghosts of the dead. They could not disturb her future.

They had come away at last. She had received chilly kisses from her future mother-in-law and two aunts-in-law, and formal handclasps from the men of the family. Then Tilford had brought her away in his luxurious car, and she had tried to realize that in a few days now, three brief weeks to be exact, she was going to belong in that car. She would be a part of a life of luxury. It didn't seem real yet, but the glamour of it all had carried her so far, and some day of course she would realize it, and take it as a matter of course. Still such thoughts had not disturbed her. Now she was coming to it. She could see its shadow just a few steps ahead. Ah! Here it was!

They had turned into her home street, the moonlight shining very brightly on the house. Just the plain old white house where she had been born, big and roomy and comfortable and shabby. She hadn't thought of its shabbiness before. It had just been home to her, and always very dear. But now, in sudden contrast to the luxury where she had been all the evening, it stood out sharply, there in the moonlight. *Shabby!* That was what it really was! And it was too late to do anything about it now before the wedding!

Suddenly she had spoken out her thought, interrupting Tilford's eulogy of one of the ancestors whose portrait they had seen.

"This home needs *painting!*" she said. "It ought to have been done before. It must be looked after just as soon as we get back!"

Tilford had stopped abruptly and given her a strange questioning look, as if he were seeing something in her he had never seen before, and then a quick caution came into his eyes, an amused curve about his lips.

"That will scarcely need to trouble you by that time," he said almost curtly. "You will not be there any more, you know. It will no longer be your interest what the house looks like. You will seldom see it, of course. You will belong in another world."

And she had given him a quick startled look, seeing suddenly things she had never realized before, possibilities that loomed with sharp premonition, and now, overnight, had become a burden, a heavy menacing cloud on her horizon.

As if it had been a little bundle the contents of which she suspected but had never seen, she deliberately took the fear and undid its wrappings, searching what was to be found herein.

What had that look of Tilford's meant? Had he intended to let her see it, or was it something he was concealing till afterwards? Oh, that could not be. Surely he was but trying to remind her of the beautiful house where she had been all the evening, and the beautiful life that was to be hers!

Yet she must face this thing out and get rid of it. She could not have an uneasiness hovering even on the edge of her mind through these strenuous days. What was it that had caused that sudden startled pain in her heart? A pain that she had refused to recognize that night? She had commandeered sleep to drown it away last night. Better face it now once for all.

Was it the sudden knowledge that when she was married she would be leaving forever everything else that was dear to her?

Nonsense! What a foolish idea! Her people would still be her people, and as dear as ever. They would rejoice in her good fortune. They would be pleased and proud of her, and would enjoy many things that they had not been able to enjoy before.

But stay! Would they? Would her dear quiet father, and her sweet-faced mother ever come to know and like and fit in with all those Thorpes? Even, just casually? Ever feel like holding their own along that gallery of ancestors?

She was not ashamed of her family. They were grand. They were real people, and she wouldn't have them changed a whit in any way. But would those Thorpes ever recognize that? With no great fortune behind them, and no painted ancestors, could they understand how people could be noblemen and women without possessions?

And how would some of their opinions and standards harmonize? Would they have any thoughts in common? Politically, socially, religiously, intellectually? Even morally? Their standards were all so very different.

And how about herself? Was *she* going to be able to fit in with the Thorpes? But that was another question. She could think that through afterwards. She had first to ferret out the truth about that burden on her heart.

Had it really been that Tilford's words and tone, and the very glint in his eye, had seemed to expect that of course after they were married she would be utterly separated from her dear people? That their interests and concerns and affairs would be no more hers? That she would be henceforth apart from them so utterly that she was practically leaving all she loved behind her, and coming to him and his people and his interests? As if he had bought her body and soul!

That was it! That completely desolating thought!

Not once had it entered her head that she would be cut off from her people and her home after she was married.

Of course she was expecting to live in a home of her own, she and Tilford, and she had up to this time looked upon it as a delightful adventure, something like playing house when she was a child, only on a larger scale. She had looked upon Tilford as the gilded fairy who was going to make this lovely play possible. But not once before had it entered her head that the dear people and places and things would be cut out of her life forever after. In her family marriage meant that all concerned only acquired more dear relatives, and wider realms of things and places to love. They did not give up what they already had.

Did Tilford feel that way, that he wanted to cut her off from her people? That *he* had no interest in them for themselves? She hadn't thought about it before, but now she recalled that he had seldom seemed to care to linger in the house and talk to her father and mother, or be brightly interested in her sisters and brothers. He had always some excuse to call late for her, and leave at once.

Now she recalled also that her father had asked some puzzled questions now and then about the Thorpes, had tried to be friendly in the few minutes Tilford allowed him. Was it her fault too that she and Tilford had had so many engagements that there hadn't seemed to be time for her parents and family to get really acquainted with her fiancé?

She had taken it all so for granted. She had thought all those matters would settle themselves. And now that horrid cold feeling at the bottom of her heart, in the memory of Tilford's look last night! That feeling that she was about to leave everything that had been dear.

That wasn't as it should be, was it? All girls didn't feel that way, did they? They were in a sense leaving home, but they were going to be with the man they had chosen for life. Did she love Tilford enough to make up for leaving everyone and everything?

It suddenly became clear to her that she hadn't ever faced that question. She had just gone on through the brief weeks since he had asked her to marry him, in a daze of wonder that one so rich and influential and handsome and sought after had chosen her. It had seemed almost too good fortune to be true, and his way had carried everything before it.

Rides in his gorgeous car, admiration and flattery, social affairs that had heretofore not been in her sphere, the wonder and envy of all her old friends. And then Tilford's eagerness to bring everything to a consummation, to rush her through functions and ceremonies; prepare her for requirements that had not been before in her scheme of things, and plan for a wedding far beyond her highest ambitions. There hadn't been time to think. Had there been something missing, something not quite in accordance with her dreams? Something tender and shy and precious, almost too precious to dare expect? Words? Looks? The first touch of hands, the first reverent touch of lips?

Tilford's way had not been like that. He had carried everything with a high hand, stated what he wanted, and expected her to concede. His kisses had been almost formal, like taking a bite of fruit he had just purchased. She had tried to ignore a vague disappointment. There had been no dreamed-of thrill of joy. Was that all that love meant? Perhaps there was no such thing as romance in this age of the world. Somehow, in spite of Tilford's haste to possess her, there was a coldness, a matter-of-factness about him that left no room for the ecstasy that she had always expected to feel if she ever fell in love.

Was she in love? Perhaps she was only taking love for granted and it wasn't love at all.

Suddenly she sprang up sharply.

"Oh, snap out of it!" she said angrily aloud to herself.

What were all these foolish thoughts anyway that she was allowing to wander through her mind? It was too late to consider such questions, even if there were any truth in them which of course there wasn't. She was engaged to Tilford Thorpe, and wearing the most gorgeous diamond on her engagement finger that any girl in their town ever owned. And downstairs in the library there were neat white boxes of already addressed wedding invitations, awaiting only their stamps before they were taken to the postoffice. Perhaps her sister Gwyneth was even now putting on hundreds of stamps, and she ought to hurry down and help.

And over across the hall in the guest room closet there were many lovely garments hanging that she would never have thought she could afford if she were not marrying Tilford Thorpe. Also, down on her mother's desk was a thick envelope containing estimates from the expensive caterer that Tilford had said was the only caterer in town who was fitted to handle an affair like their wedding supper in a satisfactory way. She had gasped when she caught a glimpse of the figures that were written on those heavy expensive sheets. She had cringed as her brother Merrick leaned over her shoulder and read them aloud, fairly shouted them in an indignant tone so that the whole family could not help but hear. She recalled now with a sharp breath of pain the look of almost despair in her mother's eyes as she listened. She ought to get down as quickly as possible and straighten that out. Surely they could plan some way that would not cost so much! Poor father! All this was going to be so hard on him. She hoped that when she was married she would be able to lift the financial burden from his shoulders a little.

But all these things going on, the whole machinery set in relentless order for her wedding, and she daring to spend an idle thought on whether this was really romance or not!

Those invitations had to be mailed tomorrow, the exact number of days before the wedding that fashion decreed there should be, though the heavens should fall. It was much too late to alter anything even if she found out that she was not in love with her bridegroom. Even if she found out it was all a terrible mistake, she could not turn back now. Nothing short of a miracle could undo those inexorable plans. There was no time now to check things over. It was too late for that.

Well, forget it! She had enough to occupy her mind without letting it bring up questions like that, that ought to have been settled beyond a question long ago. But *when?* It had all been so sudden! If she had made a mistake she would doubtless have plenty of time to regret it.

But of course this was all nonsense. Everything was all right. She was making a brilliant marriage, and everybody thought so. Simply *every*body. Even her mother hadn't demurred. Even her father had only said: "Are you perfectly sure he is what you want, little girl?" and then had given her his blessing. Although as she thought of it now it seemed as if it had been almost a sad-eyed blessing.

Oh, what gloomy thoughts! And she had been so gay and happy before last night! It was just the effect of that awful family party with all the eulogies and injunctions that had depressed her. She simply must snap out of it.

She arose and began to dress rapidly, dashing cold water in her face, putting on a gay little rose-colored print dress that she knew was becoming. Likely Tilford would telephone her after lunch to go out for a few holes of golf, but she must be firm about it. She must stay at home and get those invitations stamped, and do a lot of other things that she had put off from day to day.

She began to hum a gay little tune, just to keep up the illusion that she had no misgivings, and she gave a final pat to her pretty hair, trying to make her eyes sparkle as she gave herself a brief glance in the mirror. Yes, she was all right, and everything was going to be lovely of course. She would do wonderful things for mother and dad and the others when she was a married woman, with time, and plenty of money to spend! That nonsense about being separated from them all was a ghost of the nighttime. Tilford had no such idea as that. Tilford was a splendid dependable young man. He would be a good son, and would always be wanting to make her happy. And after all, what was romance? Just a figment of a silly girl's imagining. When one grew up one got to be sane and sensible, and didn't yearn to be a Cinderella. After all, wasn't she marrying a fortune, and wasn't she going to Europe for her honeymoon?

Maris had finished her dressing and had almost regained her ecstasy of yesterday over her happy lot in life, when another memory of last night that she had almost forgotten suddenly came to the surface and cast a sinister shadow in her path. The wedding dress! How could she have forgotten so important a matter! And now, what was she to do about it?

She dropped down in a chair by the door and stared at the wall with troubled eyes.

Her mother had wanted white organdy for her from the first. She had thought it so suitable for a girl with a quiet background, and no great fortune.

"I know you are going to be a grand lady, dear," she had said wistfully, "but it seems so much better taste for you to dress simply, and not try to appear that you are one before you really are."

And Maris had agreed quite happily. She had always liked white organdy herself.

So her mother had made the dress most exquisitely, for she could do wonderful work with her needle. And the beautiful Carrick-macross lace, which had been in the family for years, had seemed just perfect, as if it were made for the simple dress pattern they had selected. The dress was almost finished, and even now was hanging under a white shroud from a long hook on the inside of the guest room closet door. Maris had taken a parting look at it last night before she went out with Tilford, noting with proudly happy eyes the exquisite finish, so workmanlike, so perfect! No Paris import could possibly excel this charming dress! And it was all done but a few stitches! Just a few more inches of lace to appliqué and it would be done! Dear mother! How she had worked over it. Sometimes when she must have been very tired. That last glimpse of her wedding gown had sent Maris on her way, starry-eyed to the family gathering.

And then, one of the first things that happened after she got there was that Mrs. Thorpe took her aside, before she had fairly got her wrap laid on the bed, and asked rather imperiously:

"And now, my dear, about your wedding gown. I was going to speak to you before, but I haven't really had the opportunity. What had you planned? Because I have a suggestion."

The color flew into Maris' cheeks and she held her head proudly, "with the Mayberry tilt" as mischievous young Gwyneth would have said.

"My wedding dress is all ready,thank you. It was the first thing I planned." She said it very quietly but firmly. Her future mother-in-law eyed her thoughtfully.

"Well, you are forehanded," said Mrs. Thorpe, pleasantly. "Most girls leave that until near the end. But, my dear, I'm wondering if you quite appreciate what a formal gown would be required for this wedding? Of course whatever you pick out would be *charming,* but it could easily be used for some less formal affair. You see, I've found just the right garment for you, at a very exclusive little shop where I frequently deal, and I'm quite sure you'll like it. It is perfect for the occasion, and one that you would always be proud to remember having worn on the greatest occasion of your life. Of course it was a bit expensive, and so I secured a special price on it. If you feel it is still too high I shall be glad to pay the extra expense, for I do feel that for the honor of the family you should have it."

Maris' color had drained away at this, and her eyes had become a deeper blue as she lifted her chin a bit haughtily. She could imagine the steel in her father's eyes if he should hear of this offer to help pay for his daughter's wedding dress. She could imagine the hurt in her mother's eyes at the interference.

"I think you will be pleased with my dress," she said a bit haughtily.

"Perhaps," said the older woman, "but nevertheless I would like you to see this dress of which I speak. I'm sure after you once see it nothing else will seem the proper thing."

"Then I wouldn't want to see it," laughed Maris with a tinge of asperity beneath the laughter.

"Oh, now, my dear, you certainly are not as narrow as that! But I must insist that you see it. I really feel very strongly about the matter, and of course I'll be glad to finance it."

Maris drew the Mayberry dignity about her.

"My father would not permit that of course," she said quietly.

"Well, of course, if he feels that way. But I didn't like to make suggestions without offering to pay for them. Then you'll see it tomorrow, won't you, Maris? I told the woman to hold it, that you would likely be in sometime in the morning. Of course if you have to delay till afternoon, just phone her and say when you will be there. Here's the address, and the phone number."

She handed Maris a card.

Maris took it reluctantly, looked at it a minute, struggled with her annoyance, and then lifted a face on which she tried to hold a winning smile:

"I could *look* at it," she said pleasantly, "but it really wouldn't be worth while for the woman to take the time to show it to me, because I simply couldn't do anything about it. I have my wedding dress, and I like it very much."

"But you will see it because I ask you to," said the older woman with an underlying tone of authority in her voice. "I have spoken to Tilford about it, and he feels that you should see it. I ask it as a special favor."

More family arrivals just then prevented further talk, and left Maris, bending the little troublesome card back and forth in her fingers. She finally slipped the card into her small evening bag and the thought of it was submerged in the dull monotony of the evening. But now it rose with all the imperiousness of the Thorpe family and seemed as binding upon her as if she had signed a contract to go and look at that dress. Tilford was in it too. Really, that wasn't fair! The bridegroom was not supposed to know anything about the bridal robe till he saw her in it for the first time as she came up the aisle. But perhaps Tilford's mother didn't realize that.

Well, what should she do? Just forget it? Could she get by? She had a feeling that perhaps it might be hard to explain to Tilford why she had ignored his mother's request. And over and above all she had a little shivery feeling that this matter of marriage was assuming a grave and sinister appearance. That word "formal affair" that Mrs. Thorpe had used last night had made it seem that it wasn't just a matter between herself and Tilford, but as if she were about to marry the whole Thorpe connection and come under their authority. Was that so?

And what should she do? She didn't want to make a useless fuss about what might after all prove to be a trifling matter. Perhaps she had better go and look at the dress and say she had seen it but she still felt that her own would be more suitable. And yet, even to compromise so much seemed almost disloyal to the mother who had worked so hard, and wrought love into every stitch of that exquisite fairy dress.

She had been so sure until last night that all the Thorpes would admire and praise it. And now she had a feeling that they would look on it with scorn. And perhaps if she went to look at this other sophisticated dress it might make her dissatisfied with her own lovely dress. Oh, how she hated the thought of all this interference!

Well, what should she do? Was it thinkable that she should tell her mother, and that they should go down and look at that dress? Was it at all possible that the lovely organdy was not formal and stately enough for this wedding that the Thorpes seemed to think was their wedding and not hers?

Suddenly she sprang to her feet, opened her door and listened a minute. She could hear a distant sound of dishes in the kitchen. A pang of conscience shot through her.

Mother was washing dishes, and she ought to be downstairs helping. By this time of course Gwyneth should have gone to school. And mother had dismissed the maid yesterday! She had pretended it was because Sally was inefficient, but Maris knew in her heart that her mother was trying to save money, just now when this wedding was going to be such an expense! And here was she lingering upstairs considering whether she wouldn't add more expense by buying another wedding dress at the most exclusive shop in the city! What utter nonsense! What ingratitude! Of course her lovely organdy was the right thing. It was beautiful as a dream, and nobody, not even Mrs. Thorpe, could say it wasn't. And anyway, Tilford would have to take her as she was. If he didn't like her in her own wedding dress he needn't marry her!

With her head held high she tiptoed across the hall to lift the white cheesecloth covering and reassure herself by another glimpse of the dress which had seemed so wonderful to her just last night.

And there hung the dress in all its white cloudiness. Nothing could have been lovelier! Formal? Yes, its very simplicity gave it an air of distinction! There was something about it that even formality might not question.

Then suddenly she saw that the lace which had been hanging from the sleeve last night, hung no longer. It was all delicately in place with tiny invisible stitches, exquisite and perfect. It was done!

Then mother must have sat up till all hours last night finishing it! For she knew by having watched the rest of the lace put on what a time it took, and what infinite care her mother used. It was all wrought together so perfectly that the sewing was only a part of the artistry.

Sudden tears sprang to her eyes! *Dear* mother!

Then it *had* been a crack of light beneath the sewing room door that she had thought she saw last night down the hall as she came softly up the stairs not to disturb anybody! When she looked again it was gone and she had thought it imagination. But mother must have heard her and turned the light off quickly so that she wouldn't know what she was doing, and then turned it on again when she was sure her child was asleep. Dear mother! Precious wedding dress! Not for any new formal relatives would she hurt her mother now, by even suggesting that they look at that other formal attire that had been urged upon her!

But there would be Tilford. If he should speak of it how would she answer? Well, perhaps she could run down sometime this morning and just look at the dress and then tell him she liked her own better.

Suddenly as she stood at the head of the stairs trying to think it out there came a frightened cry. Gwyneth from the distant kitchen suddenly flung the door open.

"Maris! Maris! Come quick! Something's happened to mother!"

2

AS Maris flew down the stairs on panic-stricken feet the telephone set up a wild ringing, and on top of that the doorbell shrilled out through the house, but Maris sped on to the kitchen where her intuition told her her mother would be. And there on the floor beside the sink with the dish towel still in her grasp, and her soft brown hair that was graying at the temples, fallen down around her shoulders, lay the mother. Her face was still and white, and Maris' frightened eyes could see no sign of breathing as she stooped down with a low cry. "Oh, mother! Mother! Mother! You dear little mother!"

"Yes, *very* dear to *you!*" said the sarcastic voice of her brother Merrick as he came angrily into the room. "What's the matter here?"

He caught a glimpse of his mother prone upon the floor and his young face hardened.

"If anything's the matter with mother you've yourself to thank for it. That doggone fool wedding is at the bottom of it all. I've seen it killing her day by day! Get out of the way and let me lift her up! Get some water, can't you?

Send for the doctor! Somebody answer that telephone and tell 'em to shut up and get out!"

He gathered up his mother in his strong young arms. Such a frail little limp white mother with the dish towel still in her hand!

He strode toward the couch in the dining room.

"Gwyn, can't you stop that telephone! It's fierce! Maris, can't you bring some water? Isn't there any aromatic ammonia around?"

Merrrick was standing over his mother, frantically peering down at her white silent face.

A young man who had come in with Merrick and had up to this time stood in the doorway silently, answered the appeal in his friend's eyes and came over to the couch. He stooped over, listening, and laid his hand on the wrist.

Merrick looked at him with fear in his eyes.

"Is she—*gone?*" he murmured hoarsely.

"No, I think not," said the other. "Let's have that ammonia. Dip that towel in some water and wet her face."

Maris with white face and frightened eyes brought the bottle, and then got a wet cloth and began to bathe her mother's face. She knelt down beside the couch, and found she was trembling so that her knees would hardly support her.

The telephone had ceased and presently Gwyneth came to her brother.

"It's Tilford," she said. "He says he's got to speak to Maris."

"Well, he can't speak to Maris now. I'll tell his highness where to get off!" and Merrick strode out in the hall to the telephone.

If Maris heard at all she was too frightened to take it in. She knelt there tenderly bathing her mother's still white face, and trying to stop the trembling in her limbs, trying to keep her lips from quivering.

She was aware that somebody else, an outsider, was

kneeling beside her listening for a heartbeat, feeling for a slender evasive pulse in her mother's frail wrist, but she did not turn her head to look at him. It didn't occur to her to wonder who he was, or if she knew him. She was intent upon her mother's face. Was it too late? Was she gone from them forever? Would she never be able to tell her how she loved her? How sorry and ashamed she was that she had let her do so many hard things alone, while she had gone on her gay way having a good time and never noticing how hard she was making it for her precious mother.

She thought of many things while she knelt there so quietly bathing that white face, helping the man beside her to lift the head of the sick woman and hold the glass of restorative to her lips. She was examining herself, seeing herself as she had never seen herself before in all her happy carefree days.

Maris did not hear Merrick at the telephone, though he was shouting angrily:

"Well, you *can't* see my sister. She's busy. Our mother has been taken very ill. We aren't sure but she's dying. Get off this wire. I want to telephone for the doctor! Get off quick, I say!" Bang! Merrick hung up.

Then in a second he lifted the receiver again.

"Merrick, you must be crazy to speak to me this way. Do you realize what you are doing?" babbled forth the indignant voice of his future brother-in-law. "Tell Maris to come here at once. I must speak to her right away. I won't keep her but a moment, but I must tell her something right away!"

"Will you get out of my way?" yelled Merrick. "If my mother dies for want of a doctor we'll have you arrested for murder. Get off, I tell you! *Thunder,* have I got to go next door to get a message through to the doctor? Operator! Operator!"

"But Merrick, listen to me—"

"Oh, go to *thunder!*" roared Merrick. "No, I won't listen

to you. I'll go to the neighbor's phone and you can keep right on talking to yourself—" and Merrick banged the receiver down on the table and left Tilford protesting in dignified indignant tones. But Merrick had gone next door to telephone, and presently Tilford took it in that nobody was listening to him. A vast silence seemed to have dropped down upon the wire, and nobody was getting the benefit of his high-sounding words. Tilford was a handsome man, and usually depended a good deal on the effect of his personal appearance when he was talking, but he found himself at a great disadvantage just now, for his physical beauty had no effect whatever on the telephone wires. There didn't seem to be even an operator around to hear him. So at last he hung up in disgust. Somebody should suffer for this! Merrick of course was the greatest offender, but if Merrick were not available his sister should certainly take it. Perhaps it would be as well for him to go right around to the house now and see Maris personally, make her understand what an unforgivable thing her brother had done. He never had liked that fellow anyway. When he and Maris were married he would forbid Merrick the house! One didn't have to marry all one's wife's relatives of course. He would make her understand that thoroughly when the time came.

So Tilford Thorpe started on his way to see Maris.

Maris on her knees beside the dining room couch was holding a cloth wet in aromatic ammonia in front of her mother's face and crying in her heart: "Oh, God. Don't let her die! Oh, God, don't let my mother die!" and was coming out rapidly from the coma of gaiety into which the orgy of festivities connected with her engagement had plunged her.

As the agonized minutes passed and still that white face did not change, save for a quick catching of breath, faintly, so faintly that they weren't quite sure it had been a breath, it seemed as if the atmosphere rapidly became clear of a lot of things that had filled it for Maris in the past weeks. True values of things and people began to adjust themselves to her sharply awakened mind. Such things as special hours for wedding invitations to be mailed, and the importance of pleasing Tilford's relatives sank into insignificance. Years of tender care and sacrifice and precious love stood out in clear relief and importance. Strange sharp memories came and stood around like witnesses against her. The time when she had cut the vein in her wrist with the bread knife and mother had held it together till the doctor got there. The time when the bull had dashed into the garden from a herd that was going by on the street, and mother had sheltered her behind her own body. That was when she was only two and a half years old, yet she remembered how safe she had felt. The time when she had the whooping cough and almost died, with an unbelievable temperature, and mother had stayed up for two whole nights and days, most of the time on her knees bathing the hot little body under a blanket, trying to bring down the temperature. The time when there had had to be a blood transfusion and mother had offered her own. Such a precious mother who had guarded and served them all. Her deeds stood crowding about the couch hand in hand, silent witnesses of the past. And last of all her lovely wedding dress seemed to her troubled mind to come floating down the stairs and stand with the rest about that couch where the little gray-faced mother lay.

"Oh, mother, mother!" Maris suddenly cried, softly, and her hand paused with the wet cloth she was holding, and her head suddenly went down on her mother's breast for an instant of despair. Then up again instantly, just as strong hands lifted her and Merrick's voice, grown suddenly tender and more worried, said, "Take her in the other room. I'll look out for mother."

That roused her. She straightened up.

"No! No! I'm all right!" she whispered. "I must stay here!"

"There's the doctor!" announced Gwyneth, hurrying to open the door. And then they all made way for the doctor, and Maris felt those strong arms lifting her again and leading her to a chair.

She did not look up to see who it was. Her eyes were upon her mother's face there on the couch.

Someone brought her a glass of water and she drank it, and then went back to stand at the head of the couch and watch the doctor's face.

The strange young man was sent on an errand for the doctor, and Merrick went to telephone his father. Maris stayed to wait on the doctor and answer his questions, though she found it was fourteen-year-old Gwyneth who did most of the answering.

"I wasn't here," was all Maris could say in answer to some question about whether her mother had felt badly the day before, and what she had been doing.

"She had an awful headache yesterday," said Gwyneth sadly. "I guess she worked too hard. She would do so many things. I tried to help her but she sent me to do my home work and said she could do it all herself. But once I saw her put her hand over her heart and I asked her what was the matter, and she said, 'Oh, just a sharp pain.'"

"Had she been having pains in her heart?"

"She never complained," said Maris sadly. "I'm afraid we were all so busy with our own affairs that we didn't notice."

"She sewed a lot last night," volunteered Gwyneth. "She told me this morning she'd got it all done, what she was working on."

Tears sprang to Maris' eyes, and she turned away to hide them, and then turned back again as she heard her mother give a soft little breath of a sigh. Oh, was she coming back to them, or was she gone? She watched the grave face of the doctor anxiously, but he worked on quietly and gave no sign. Only asked for water, and a spoon, and handed the glass back to Maris.

A car drew up at the door. The young man came back and brought whatever it was that he had been sent for, but Maris took no notice of him. Some friend of Merrick's, she thought. Then a few minutes later a nurse arrived, and Maris caught her breath in hope and fear. But there was no time to ask questions. She must go upstairs and get the bed ready for the patient to be moved. There were sheets to hunt out, the good sheets. Where *were* the good sheets? Every one she unfolded seemed to be torn or badly frayed at the hems. Oh, the house was in perfect order for a wedding, but not for illness. And they had not been expecting to have any of the wedding party stay overnight with them, for they all lived in the town.

"There aren't any good sheets left, Maris," whispered Gwyneth. "Mother had me help her gather up the laundry for the man this morning, and we put the last good ones in the bag. She said she must run up some of the torn ones till the laundry got back."

Suddenly Maris took it in. Mother and Father had been scrimping on everything that there might be more to pay her wedding bills. There were beautiful garments hanging in her closet, costly garments, for her parents were sending her proudly away from their care; and her generous hope chest was full to overflowing with linen and percale sheets and pillow cases, smooth as silk, and fine of quality; and towels in abundance, rich and sumptuous as any bride might desire. But the mother of the bride must be put to bed in torn sheets!

Suddenly Maris' face went white and her lips set in a thin line of determination. She put back the torn sheets she had been unfolding hopelessly, and marched into her own room to her hope chest. She delved deep and brought out a wealth of lovely smooth sheets and pillow covers and brought them into her mother's room where Gwyneth was taking off the worn sheets that had been on the bed.

Gwyneth looked at her in startled dismay.

"But, Maris, those are your wedding things! You mustn't use those!"

"Why not?" said Maris grimly. "They're mine, aren't they? Mother bought them for me, didn't she? I have a right to use them the way I want to, don't I?"

"Yes, but mother wouldn't want you to use them up now. Not on her bed."

"I'm sure she would," said Maris, "if she knew how I feel about it. I'd rather use these now on mother's bed, Gwynnie, than on any grandest occasion that could ever come in my life. Wouldn't you feel that way, Gwyn, if they were yours?"

"Oh, yes, I would," said Gwyneth, "but then I wouldn't have the Thorpes to think about."

She said it so quaintly and so gravely that Maris would have broken down and laughed if she hadn't felt too frightened and too sad to laugh. But somehow it opened her eyes to the way her young sister felt about her future relatives.

And just then the doorbell pealed through the house.

"We must muffle that bell," said Maris. "The doctor said there mustn't be any noise. Mother starts every time she hears a sharp sound."

"I'll go," said Gwyneth.

"No, you stay here and help me. Tuck the sheets in over that side. The doctor wants to get mother in bed as soon as possible. They are going to bring her right up. Someone will go to the door, Merrick, or that young man he brought in with him. He's been very kind."

"Young man!" said Gwyneth. "Didn't you know who that was? That's Lane Maitland, the boy that used to live next door to us five years ago. Don't you remember him?"

"Lane Maitland? Why, yes, I remember him. But I

didn't know him. I guess I didn't even look at him. Gwyn, you run down and tell them we're ready. I'll wait here and put out some more towels. Maybe they'll need me to help get mother settled."

Gwyneth started, but as she passed the window she exclaimed:

"Oh, Maris! That must have been Tilford that rang the bell! There's his car out there now."

Maris looked up in dismay.

"Well, I can't see him now. You run down and tell him what's happened. Quick! Before Merrick gets there! Merrick hasn't any sense."

Gwyneth vanished, and Maris turned back the covers carefully. She could hear that they were bringing her mother up the stairs. The nurse was ahead, eyeing the arrangements with a quick keen glance. Maris had no more time to think of Tilford now. But surely he would understand.

Then there was so much to be done that Maris forgot Tilford entirely. She helped the nurse to undress her mother. There were things to be hunted for. A night dress and bed jacket. Mother just didn't seem to have anything. All her garments were worn. Maris was ashamed to hand them out. She dashed into her own room and opened the drawer where her own pretty lingerie was waiting to be packed for her trip abroad, selected a pretty gown and a little pink jacket with sprigs of embroidery scattered over it. The tears blinded her eyes as she hurried back with them to the nurse.

"Oh, haven't you something plainer, something old and worn?" said the nurse. "Keep these till she is able to sit up."

Maris felt as if her eager gift had been rejected but she hurried away and hunted again among her mother's things.

"That will do," said the nurse reaching for an old faded

gown with a tear half way up the back. "I shall want to cut it up the back anyway. It's easier to put it on without disturbing her."

Dear mother, so inert, lying there limp, while others arrayed her in her old garments. Mother who never let anyone do anything for her, and was always waiting on others! Oh, if she had only seen all this before. If mother didn't get well, would she ever be able to forgive herself and go on with life?

"Can you get me some ice?" asked the doctor crisply, breaking in on her frantic thoughts.

Maris dashed downstairs for the ice, and almost knocked over Tilford who was standing at the foot of the stairs, his handsome face snarled into an ugly frown.

"What on earth is the matter with you, Maris?" he said vexedly, reaching out his arms to prevent a collision. "You seem to be all wrought up. Can't you have a little self-control? And why have you had to keep me waiting so long when you know how busy I am this morning? I've been waiting here exactly fifteen minutes!" He glanced at his watch to be accurate. He was always accurate about details. "I sent you word that I was in a great hurry and would keep you only a moment, and yet you didn't come. I can't understand it."

He gave her a severe look as if she were a naughty child, and Maris burst into tears. Her lips quivered, but she controlled herself at once.

"Oh, hush, please," she said in a whisper. "We mustn't talk here. Mother is very sick indeed. The doctor said there must be absolute quiet. Come into the kitchen with me. I can't stop even a minute. The doctor wants some ice."

"Well, why doesn't he send the nurse after it? I saw a nurse go upstairs. Does he expect to make a pack horse of you?"

Maris flew to the refrigerator and began to work away at the ice with an ice pick and mallet. She was suddenly very angry. She had hoped for a little sympathy from Tilford, and he had only sharp words.

"Mercy! Don't you have a modern refrigerator?" he said as he followed her annoyedly and stood watching her knocking off the chunks of ice. "I thought everybody had ice cubes now."

Maris shut her lips tight. At another time she might have explained that her father had had the money saved for an electric refrigerator and was just about to get one when she announced her intention of getting married soon, and everything else had to give way to get money for that. But now she was too angry to explain anything. Tilford was being disagreeable. He knew her father wasn't wealthy.

"Well, come and sit down somewhere," he went on haughtily. "I've got to tell you one or two things before you vanish again. Are these chairs all right to sit on? Kitchen chairs are apt to have flour and grease on them," and he inspected one with a disdainful finger.

"Anything in my mother's kitchen is perfectly clean," said Maris with uplifted chin.

"Oh, certainly, of course," said Tilford perfunctorily, "but servants aren't so careful."

"We have no servant," said Maris briefly.

"You have no servant? Why, what has become of Sally?"

"She is not here any more," said Maris. "And now, Tilford, you can sit down anywhere you like but I have no time to sit down. If you have anything to say, say it quickly. I'm taking this ice right upstairs. My mother is too precious to run any risks of delay."

"Nonsense!" said Tilford. "You probably are exaggerating the whole thing. Your mother is just tired, and will be all right in a few hours. You should get a good servant at once. Two of them, in fact, while you have a nurse in the house. Would you like me to stop at an employment agency and send a couple out?"

"Certainly *not!*" said Maris firmly. "We will look after our own household. Tell me quickly what you want for I've got to go, and I may not be able to come down again for some time."

"Well, really, Maris, I never saw you in a mood like this. I'm sure I hope your mother won't be ill often."

Maris didn't answer. She was working swiftly, gathering up the pieces of ice in a bowl and closing the refrigerator door softly, still sick-room conscious, he perceived. It was evident she meant what she said and would not be there long.

"Well, Maris," he said, more pleasantly, "what about this dress mother wants you to see?"

"Well, what about it?" said Maris still haughtily.

"Why, mother said you promised her to go and see it and try it on."

"No, I didn't promise her, Tilford. She told me about the dress and I told her that I had no need for a wedding dress, that I already had one, and then some people came in and we didn't talk any more. That's all. I have no need for another dress, and if I did I would pick it out myself."

"That's not a nice spirit, Maris. You certainly don't act like yourself this morning. I don't know what has come over you. Whatever was actually said, you are perfectly aware that my mother expressed a wish for you to have that dress and asked that you go and see it at once because she had had it reserved for you. I came this morning to take you down in my car to the shop, because I wanted to save you the trip, and you act this way. Come, get your hat and we will go at once. Slip on another dress, can't you? That one looks a bit like a kitchen rig."

Maris flashed a look at her bridegroom and spoke in low decided tones.

"I cannot possibly go anywhere today, Tilford, even if I wanted to go, which I certainly do not! I have no wish for another wedding dress. When I am married I shall wear the dress my mother made for me, and no other. If people do not like it they can look the other way. But at least until I am married I am the one to say what I shall wear. My mother sewed half the night last night to finish the lovely dress she has made for me, and I certainly shall not wear any other no matter whether it pleases anybody else or not."

Maris was very angry now. She was washing the pieces of ice and lifting them into a clean bowl.

Tilford's face was a study, if she had only had time to see it. Amazement and scorn struggled for the mastery.

"Your mother *made* your wedding dress!" he exclaimed in a tone of horror. "You were going to wear a *homemade* dress to *my wedding!* You were going to do a thing like that to *our family?*"

Maris wheeled and stared at him for a half second in amazement. She had never seen Tilford like this before. His handsome face was almost disfigured with scorn. Then she said crisply:

"Why, yes, I was. You see, I thought it was my wedding, not entirely yours. At least I thought it was *ours,* not your family's. And you have always seemed to rather like my homemade clothes. It didn't occur to me that you or anybody would have anything to say about my wedding dress."

"Well, I am amazed," said the haughty youth. "It seems my mother was entirely right in feeling she ought to do something about this. A homemade dress at a Thorpe wedding!" he repeated. "Really, Maris, you and I will have to have a plain talk. Suppose you take that ice upstairs and come right down and we will settle a few things, here and now. I know of course that you are very much wrought up. You have evidently been working too hard. Your people have no right to let you get so tired when you are to be married so soon. The strain of the festivities is enough without difficulties in your home. But it is time I made a few things quite plain to you that I have been taking for granted you understood."

"You have certainly made a good many things plain to me already," said Maris cryptically, as she rescued the last lump of ice from sliding off the table and plumped it into the bowl with the rest, "but I have no time nor desire to discuss anything more with you this morning. I'm going now."

She opened the back stair door and darted away.

He arose hastily and strode after her calling up the stairs.

"Listen, Maris. Have you sent off those wedding invitations yet? Because this is the last day they should go. If they aren't done suppose you give them to me and I'll take them home. Mother will have her secretary finish them."

But Maris closed the upper stair door quietly and firmly, and when he sought the front stairs and went half way up calling her name cautiously, the white clad nurse came silently out with her finger across her lips and shook her head at him. And though he waited for some minutes Maris did not appear again.

For Maris had other things to think about. Her mother was gasping for breath, and it was apparent that it was going to take swift work to save her life.

Two hours later the worst seemed over, for the present at least. The tired heart had taken up a slow, but dependable beat again, and the mother was sleeping. She had taken a few sips of nourishment, and her hand was lying in her husband's who sat beside her, gray and worn and anxious.

The nurse was putting her domain into immaculate order, report card and pencil, thermometer and medicine on the bedside stand; starched white uniforms hanging in the guest closet in place of the hastily removed wedding garments. The house had assumed a new atmosphere. Merrick had gone to get Sally to return to the kitchen. Gwyneth had gone to the store for the list of necessities her mother had made out before she suddenly dropped out of the day. The strange young man whom her sister had said was their old neighbor Lane Maitland, had disappeared along with the doctor. The nurse was with the patient, the house was very quiet. Maris had just returned from the attic where she had hidden the addressed wedding invitations, boxes and all, wrapped carefully in many thicknesses of tissue paper and stuffed under the eaves behind an old trunk, when the doorbell pealed through the house. She must go and muffle that bell before she did anything else, she thought to herself, as she hastened to answer the ring.

There stood the Thorpe chauffeur with a letter in his hand, addressed in Tilford's handwriting.

She frowned as she looked at it. There was something so assured and almost smug about even his writing. The thought darted through her mind unbidden, and she shut it out again. She must not think things like that about the man she was going to marry, even if he had been disagreeable when she needed sympathy and help. Everybody had faults, and of course Tilford had some little things—. She looked at the chauffeur questioningly.

"Were you to wait for an answer?"

"Yes ma'am I was to wait and see if you had any message."

Maris stepped into the living room and read the letter. It was not long.

Dear Maris:

Of course I realize that you were overwrought just now and I shall not hold it against you. I would not trouble you again today but that the time is getting short and this matter of the wedding dress is somewhat insistent. My mother feels as I do that we should not let this most suitable garment go, now that we have found it. So I have taken the liberty of having it sent up to your house. I will take care of the bill myself. Call it a wedding gift if you like. I am told that it is the custom in some oriental lands for the groom to provide the wedding garment. And I am sure when you have seen it you will agree with us that it is most suitable for a formal occasion such as our wedding is to be, and that any mere homemade dress would be entirely out of place.

Let me know if I can help with the invitations. You know they should be mailed not later than this evening. The man will wait to see if you have any message.

Hoping that your mother is now feeling much better and that by tomorrow she will have fully recovered.

Yours as ever,

Affectionately,
Tilford

Maris had just reached the end of the letter when she heard the nurse calling softly, insistently:

"Miss Mayberry, could you come here a minute *quick!* I don't like the way your mother breathes and I want to telephone the doctor at the hospital."

3

LANE Maitland, as he rode away with the doctor who was going to drop him at a garage where he had left his own car for a slight repair, studied the doctor's grave face awhile before he spoke.

"Is Mrs. Mayberry going to get well, Doctor MacPherson?" he asked quietly.

The doctor gave him a keen glance.

"I'm not sure," he said thoughtfully. "If she pulls through the next day or two she may pick up. But it depends on several things even then. How well do you know the Mayberrys? You used to live next door, didn't you?"

"Yes, five years ago before we went to the west coast. I knew them pretty well. Maris was in my class in high school."

"Yes, I thought so. You and Maris used to play tennis over at the old court by the women's club, didn't you? I thought I remembered. Well, I suppose you've kept in touch with them from time to time, haven't you?"

"Well, not very closely," said Lane. "You know kids don't spend much time writing letters. But they were the first people I wanted to see when I got back. They were real people. Mrs. Mayberry was like a mother to me after my own mother died. She took care of me when I was sick once. I think a lot of her. I went around to the house with Merrick this morning, the first place I've been since I struck the town, just to see Mrs. Mayberry, and we found her lying on the floor in the kitchen. I haven't had a chance to ask any questions yet. I don't know whether she's been ill before, or this is a first attack, or what?"

"I guess it's what," said the doctor speculatively. "The whole trouble is the woman's worn out I think. She's worked too hard, and hasn't stopped to consider herself. To tell you the truth when I came in I thought she was gone. There didn't seem to be any heartbeat at all. But she was coming up wonderfully when I left. Unless there's another set-back she may pull out this time without any serious harm. And then again, the least little thing might blow her out like a candle. I'm not just sure how far her heart is involved. She's been a wonderfully wiry little woman with a lot of nerve and courage. You see, Mr. Mayberry was pretty hard struck by the depression, almost lost his business and his house, but managed to keep on his feet, and now I believe he is weathering it pretty well. But she's stood by him through thick and thin, and done more work than she should, and been up late nights. You knew the daughter, Maris, was making a grand marriage, didn't you?"

"Merrick said something about a wedding as we came in but I didn't quite catch the drift. He seemed to think it had something to do with his mother's condition."

"Yes, I shouldn't wonder. Maris is marrying into swelldom. A big snob, if you ask me. But don't say I said so. Of course he's rich, and painfully good-looking, but she's too nice a little girl to let that count for everything. Oh, I guess he's all right, decent and all that, but acts like he was frozen in the making. Wait till you meet him. However, I wouldn't wonder if it has been rather hard to keep up to the social standards of his set. Not but that the Mayberrys are every bit as good socially, and better, than the Thorpes, only they're not so afraid people won't know it. But I imagine there's been a lot of hard work and worry connected with trying to get ready all the fuss and feathers the Thorpes would expect. That's all. That good little mother is just worn out."

"But you think she could get well?"

"Yes, I think—I *hope* she could. That is, if she pulls through the next few days, she'd have a chance. But—there's more to it than that. She needs a quiet place away from everything that could possibly worry her. A place where she wouldn't hear anything but the clouds going by, and the flowers growing, and a bird or two now and then. If she could have about six months to a year in a place like that, yes, I'd say there was a good chance she might be her old self again and live out a healthy life. But I don't know how they ever could afford a thing like that."

Lane Maitland was still for a whole block, and then he said thoughtfully:

"I know a place like that, and it's standing idle. Let me know if it's needed, will you, Doctor?"

"I certainly will, son. And maybe I'll let you know soon. And then again—I might not get the chance. You can't tell. But I'll not forget."

Lane stopped at his garage and picked up his car. He drove thoughtfully back to the Mayberrys to get Merrick and take him after Sally. But he said nothing to Merrick about his talk with the doctor. He was remembering Maris when she was fourteen with her gold hair like a halo and her eyes shining. He used to carry her books home for her every day from school, that last year before he went away. He wondered why he had never kept up the correspondence with Maris. Only a Christmas card or two, and then they had lost sight of each other!

But something had to be done to help Mother Mayberry get well.

Then suddenly Merrick spoke:

"It's that doggone wedding that's got mother's goat!" he broke forth. "I don't see why Maris doesn't see it."

"What could she do about it if she did?" asked Lane gravely.

"Well, that's just it. It seems that when a girl lets herself think she's in love with a man that's the end of her. She's mesmerized, or something. She has to do just exactly what he tells her to, no matter if the whole family is going to the dogs on account of it."

Lane considered this and then he asked:

"Is Maris in love with this man? Really in love?"

"Oh, Gosh! How should I know? What is love, anyway? Thank goodness I've never been in love yet, but when I see any signs of it in myself I hope I'll have sense enough to consider whether my family that have loved me and slaved for me all my life are going to be alienated by it. It isn't right. It isn't reason."

"No," said Maitland, "it isn't right, but what are you going to do about it? The world has been going on that way pretty much ever since it was made, I guess. Of course people ought to consider, but they don't. It's just a glamour, I suppose, and you can't help yourself. But what's the matter with Maris' man? Isn't he all right?"

"All right? Well, I suppose most folks think he is. I guess he has pretty much that opinion himself, but not me! Oh, how we *don't* love one another! I tell you when this wedding is consummated he and I are going to be the most unloving brothers-in-law that ever were mismated. And I don't mean maybe. And as for my mother and his mother they're about as much alike as a wood thrush and a turkey."

"Not a very pleasant outlook," said Maitland, "but how does your sister reconcile all this?"

"My sister? Oh, she's *crazy!* That's what I say, love makes you crazy. You don't know what you're doing when you get in love. I hope I never get that way. Why, he rushed her, see? Took her out in his limousine. All the girls thinking he's grand just because he has curly eyelashes and a natural permanent wave. He got her a great hog of a diamond, and he's taking her on a trip to Europe for the honeymoon, and she's completely etherized. She doesn't know what it's all about yet. She'll wake up sometime when it's too late, and see what she's done to all of us, and to herself! I only hope our mother doesn't have to die to make her see!"

"She mustn't!" said Lane Maitland. "We mustn't let her! You know I had a kind of a share in her too. She nursed me through typhoid and I'll never forget it."

"So she did, brother. You're one of us. Mother thought a lot of you."

"Well, look here, Merrick, I want you to promise me something. I want you to give me your word of honor that you will let me help just as if I were a real son and brother, will you?"

Merrick gave him a look of appreciation, that held almost a hint of surprise.

"Why, sure, Lane, but I don't see how you could help, just now. Oh, errands, and things like that. Sure, we'll count on you, and love to do it. But—you sort of speak as if you had some inside dope. The doctor didn't say anything leery about mother, did he?"

"He said she was tired out. He said she needed a long rest. And if it comes to that I've got just the place. I want you to promise if she has to go away you'll call on me."

"Sure I will, and don't you be afraid I'll forget it, either. That's great! But here's Sally's house and I imagine we'd better get her back as soon as possible to the kitchen, for there's plenty for her to do there, I guess. Let's hope she's at home."

But just then Sally appeared at her door, curiously peering out to see what car was stopping before her place.

"Oh, there you are, Sally. Can you come along with us right away?" called Merrick. "Mother's been taken very sick, and we need you all kinds."

"Sure I'll come, Mister Merrick! Your ma sick! Now I jes' thought 'twould end up that way. I was so sure I didn't unpack my things much. I'll get my workin' cloes and come right in a little minute."

And true to her word, Sally didn't take long. She was soon out lugging a neat suitcase, and climbing into the back seat of the car.

As they turned into the home street Merrick sighted the limousine standing before the door.

"What the dickens!" he began scowling. "Why does that boob have to barge in on us when he knows we don't want him around?"

And then as the doctor's car shot around the corner and drew up behind the limousine, "Great Scott! Is that the doctor again? I thought he had to be at the hospital all the rest of the morning. He didn't tell you he was coming back, did he? You don't suppose mother's worse, do you? You don't suppose they've sent for him again, do you?" And with a white face Merrick leaned over, opened the door, and was out on the sidewalk before the car had really stopped.

"Easy, boy!" warned Maitland in a low tone. "Remember it's important there be no noise!"

Merrick nodded and flung himself silently across the lawn and in at the door, his heart beating wildly, anxiously.

The doctor was there before him though, and bending over the bed. Maris made way for him and slipped out into the hall.

"Mother wasn't breathing right and the nurse sent for him," she whispered to her brother, her white anxious face showing him that there was still cause for alarm.

Solemnly the sister and brother stood together, breathless, watching what went on in the sick room, grasping one another's hands without realizing it, as their anxiety increased.

The doctor was very grave at first. They could tell by the way he touched the pulse, by his low-toned inquiries to the nurse, by the way he listened to the heart, that this was no light matter. It seemed a long time before the tenseness around the bedside decreased, and fear seemed to be vanquished, sliding out of the room once more. It was almost as if the room itself had drawn a sigh of relief at the respite. Glancing at their father on the other side of the bed, still holding his wife's hand, they could see that the grayness was breaking about his eyes and lips once more, and hope was dawning again on his face. They hardly dared be sure till they heard the doctor's voice in a low murmur to the nurse: "That was a close shave," and saw her nodded response. They welcomed her alert hopeful movements as they watched her putting the medicine glass on the table, and writing something on the report card.

Then, and not till then, they withdrew to the hall window.

"What's the idea of that chauffeur out there?" murmured Merrick resentfully. "Is he waiting for something?"

Then suddenly Maris remembered.

"Oh!" she said, the color coming into her white face, "I forgot! He's waiting for an answer to a note."

"Well, you'd better let me go down and tell him you haven't time to write any answers now, that your mother has been near death's door again. You look fit to go to bed yourself."

"No!" said Maris quickly, "I must write it. You wouldn't understand. It won't take but a minute! Lend me your pencil."

Maris took the pencil and wrote on the back of the crumpled letter.

> Please do not send the dress. I cannot accept it on any condition. If it comes here I shall call the shop and tell them it is a mistake. You do not understand how you have hurt me. Mother is worse. I have no time to write more.
>
> Maris

She slipped it into an envelope and went down to the waiting chauffeur. "I'm sorry to have kept you waiting," she said, "but my mother was taken very sick again. I have had no time to write but a line."

But even as the chauffeur took the note and turned to go, Maris, to her dismay, saw a handsome delivery truck drive up and stop. A man in plum-colored livery with silver buttons got out and came up the walk bearing a mammoth white box tenderly.

Maris with hardening countenance stood and watched him come. She mustn't let him ring that terrible bell again, and she must remember to muffle it as soon as he was gone.

"Are you from Leon Archer's shop?" she asked. "Well, this is a mistake. You'll have to take it back. I just found out that it had been ordered, and was about to call up and tell them not to send it."

"But I was told to leave it here, ma'am!" said the man.

"Yes, but I'm telling you to take it back. I cannot receive it. It was a misunderstanding. I will call the shop immediately and explain."

Reluctantly the man turned with his magnificent box and went back to the truck, and Maris hurried to the kitchen to see what she could do to suppress the bell.

But she found Lane Maitland there ahead of her, perched on the stepladder, working away at the bell, which already showed signs of submission.

"Oh," said Maris with relief, "how did you know what I wanted?"

"Well, you see, I remembered that bell of old. You won't recall it likely, but I was sick in this house once, and I know how that bell used to go through my head when my fever was the worst."

"You're Lane Maitland, aren't you? I haven't had time to recognize you before. Of course I remember. Didn't I play picture puzzles with you when you were getting well? You've been very kind. I don't know how you happen to be here after this long absence, but I'm really grateful."

She gave him a tired little smile, and he grinned back like an old chum.

"That's all right, I'm here, and you can just count on me for anything I can do to help. I'm only too glad to get the chance to pay back some of the kindness I received. Is your mother worse that the doctor came back?"

"She was," said Maris, the trouble starting in her eyes again. "I think she is easier now. The doctor and nurse seem more cheerful. Now I must go back and see if I'm needed."

"Better lie down a bit yourself," advised Maitland. "You look rather all in."

"Perhaps I will after a little."

Then Sally eased in from the maid's room off the kitchen.

"Oh, Sally! I'm so glad you've come!" said Maris, and almost choked with tears as she said it, her relief was so great.

"That's all right, Miss Maris. You just go lay down. I'll ten' to all this," she said with a wave of her hand that included the dishevelled kitchen. "I'll have a meal ready on time. Don't you worry."

"I'll wipe dishes and set the table for you, Sally," said Lane Maitland cheerfully. "It won't be the first time I've helped in this kitchen, will it?"

"Sure, you wiped dishes fer me many a time, an' set tables too. He's a good wukker, Miss Maris. You run along. We'll get along fine!"

So Maris turned and went away, feeling suddenly that she must sit down quickly, or lie down, or she would presently crumple up on the floor the way her mother had done that morning.

She flung herself down on her own bed for a minute, trying to get rid of that whirly feeling and as her head sank into her pillow it seemed that all her troubles rushed over her at once. Mother sick, dear mother! Of course that was the worst. And the possibility that even if she should get well she would be an invalid all her life. How could the family get on without her?

For the moment her own marriage had sunk out of sight. Never once in all her gay bright plans had she considered the possibility of mother out of the picture, and herself away across the water where she couldn't help. Now it suddenly rushed over her as an impossibility to consider any such thing.

Well, she mustn't go on so far in the future. She could dare to live but one day at a time just now, perhaps only one hour. There was no telling what an hour might bring forth.

But there was the question of those invitations, and that dress! She hoped she had settled the dress, but there was no telling. Mrs. Thorpe had a very firm chin and when she wanted a thing she was in the habit of getting it. Would there have to be more battling? For she was determined on one thing. She would wear no other dress for her marriage than the one her precious mother had made. Even if it were not lovely and suitable, she would wear it anyway!

Well, she had done all she could about the dress for the present at least. If the Thorpes didn't like it they could stand it. Of course Tilford would be angry and she would have him to deal with next. She had seen him in a towering rage with other people two or three times, and she did not anticipate the experience. But it didn't matter, did it? Not anything mattered till mother got well. Why did such trifling unimportant matters have to come in and torment her now, when her heart was wrung with anxiety? And there were those invitations. What should she do about them? That all important date which the postmark was supposed to bear was rapidly passing by and could not be recalled. There would be a terrible rumpus among the Thorpes if the day went by without their being mailed. But it was unthinkable that she should invite people to her wedding when her mother lay at death's door! They surely couldn't expect that of her!

Yet, on the other hand, if mother should suddenly get well and the wedding go on as planned—though in her heart she felt this was not in the least likely, hardly possible—if the day had to be changed to please the Thorpes' ideas about when the invitations should go out, that would mean that father would have another awful expense. All those costly invitations engraved over again! Oh, she couldn't do that to father.

Well, and suppose she simply mailed them as had been planned all along, and then they had all to be recalled? Oh, it was too much of a problem for her weary mind to work out. She turned her head on her pillow and let slow tears trickle down her cheeks.

"Oh, God," she suddenly cried in her heart, "show me what to do. Please make it very plain. I don't know how to go on. I know I haven't been living very close to You these last few months. I've done nothing to deserve help. But won't You please straighten things out and bring mother back to us again?"

In the midst of her prayer she became aware of voices, children's voices outside, the boys and little Alexa, coming home from school. Alexa wasn't quite five and was only in kindergarten. Eric and Alec were in grade school. But what were they doing home at this hour? They usually took their lunch and didn't return till two o'clock. Was it a half-holiday?

She sprang up quickly. They mustn't be allowed to make a noise and disturb mother. Would Gwyneth be back from the store yet?

She hurried down and met the children as they were about to enter the house.

"Sh-h-h!" she said softly. "Mother is sick. You must be very quiet! Come around this outside way to the kitchen and Sally will give you some lunch. Why are you home at this hour?"

"Lexie has a sore throat," said Eric, the ten-year-old. "The teacher sent us home. She said we'd havta have the doctor and see if Lexie has the measles. If she has we can't any of us come back till we see if we get it too."

Maris' heart sank. Measles! More trouble!

"My froat is sore an' I want my muvver!" wailed Alexa with a quivering lip.

"That's all right, darling, sister will take care of you," said Maris, putting her arm around the little girl and drawing her close. "Come on, we'll go up to sister's room. You can get into my nice bed, and have a pretty little nightie on, and some lovely orange juice to drink," coaxed Maris, trying to think how she was to manage this new complication.

"No, I don't want ta go ta your bed. I want ta go ta muvver. I want my muvver!" Her voice had increased to a shrill roar.

Maris gathered the child up in her arms and carried her out through the garden to the hammock under a big tree, and sat down with her in her arms.

"Listen, Lexie," she said soothingly, "muvver dear had a bad fall down on the kitchen floor, and she hurted herself, and we had to send for the doctor. He put her to bed until she gets all mended up. He said she must lie very still and sleep a lot, and we mustn't try to wake her up for anything for awhile, so she would get all well."

The child looked up for a minute with great eyes filled with horror, and her baby lip puckered pitifully. Then she wailed again and two tears rolled down her pink cheeks.

"I want my muvver. I'se got a sore froat!"

"But Lexie, you don't want muvver to be sick a long, long time, do you? You want her to get well quick, don't you? You wouldn't like muvver to be so sick she couldn't ever get up again, would you?"

The child shook her head.

"Well, then, you're going to be a good, good little girl, as brave as a soldier, and let sister take care of you and make you well, till mother can get up again, aren't you?"

A slow reluctant nod.

"But my froat is sore. *Awful!*"

"Well, we'll go right upstairs and get into bed and send for our good Doctor MacPherson. He gives you nice sweet sugar pills, you know, and he'll make you well quick. Come on! Let's see how softly we can get up the stairs so we won't wake muvver."

Little by little she coaxed the child, until she finally yielded with a weak smile and said "Wes" she would be a good girl and not make a noise when sister took her up the stairs. At last Maris landed Lexie in her bed and began to undress the hot little body.

There was no question but Alexa had a fever, and it looked to Maris' inexperienced eyes as if there were some kind of faint rash beginning to appear. Oh, was this also to be added to the burdens? Measles and a wedding! A wedding and a quarantine sign on the door. Oh, what a mess! And what would Tilford say to it all?

Suddenly she began to laugh.

Alexa turned and stared at her in wonder.

"Vat is funny, Maris?" She tried to focus her heavy eyes on her sister who was laughing almost hysterically, though very quietly. It had to be either crying or laughing, and she preferred to laugh.

Suddenly she sobered. She must not let herself go like this. Too much depended upon her just now.

"I was only thinking how funny it was to have measles and a wedding at the same time."

Alexa gave a faint little giggle.

"Can't I be a fower girl?"

"Not if you have the measles."

"Is I got measles, Maris?"

"Well, maybe. We'll have to ask mother's nurse to come and look."

"Has muvver got a nurse? I want ta see her."

"I'll get her in a minute. You lie still and be a good girl."

"Awwright! Myrtle Hayes has gotted measles. She had 'em two days. She wasn't in school. Now I got 'em, mebbe! Isn't that funny?"

"Yes, very funny!" said Maris with a bitter little grin.

"When you got measles you get fowers an' paper dollies sent to you by the class. We sent some to Myrtle Hayes yestidday! Do you 'spose I got measles fum her, makin' her a paper dollie?"

"Oh, no. You have to be with people who have them to get them."

"Well, I was wif her two more yestiddays ago."

"Yes, that was it, likely. Now you lie still till I call the nurse."

Mrs. Mayberry was sleeping nicely and the nurse sitting by with a book. Maris almost envied her. She had no perplexities to settle. She had only to sit there and do her duty as it came to her hour by hour. Oh, of course there were responsibilities, but she was trained to meet them. And there was always the doctor at the end of the telephone to call upon in necessity. While here was she suddenly plunged from having a good time, into every kind of a mix-up, things she knew nothing at all about. As if it wasn't enough to be on the eve of her marriage with all sorts of new problems to deal with, without having her mother, the mainstay of the family taken down so desperately ill, and the baby of the house sick besides! And she had no training for such things, and no one to call upon in her extremity. She was the oldest child. Her father mustn't be more troubled than he was already, or he would break too. And Merrick was so hot-headed he was no help at all. As for Tilford, he had made it all too evident that none of this was his problem. She couldn't consult him, though of course she would have to tell him pretty soon the latest developments. What would Tilford say to a contagious disease? Well, she would soon find out, for there he was coming up the walk, she saw as she passed the window. His car was parked out in front.

But Maris did not run down to meet him. She followed the nurse back to the sick room and let Sally deal with the front door. One burden at once was all she could carry. Tilford would have to wait till she was free.

The nurse came in and examined the little girl. She said it looked like measles to her, but the rash wasn't coming out well. She hinted that it might even be scarlet fever.

"You know there's quite a bit of it around," she said. "Just keep her asleep till the doctor gets here if you can."

But Alexa was restless and wanted her mother, and it was some time before even a story kept her still enough to drop off to sleep.

As soon as Maris was sure the child was sound enough not to cry out and disturb their mother, she hurried down to Tilford. He met her with an angry frown.

"It seems to me, Maris, that you are very inconsiderate," he said as he glanced at his watch vexedly. "I have waited exactly sixteen minutes for you this time. And how long was it this morning? My time is valuable, you know.

Especially so just now when I am planning to be out of the
country for at least six months. Hereafter I do wish you
would try to come down promptly."

Maris was very tired, and overwhelmingly worried.
The tears were very near to the surface and she needed
comfort.

"I came as soon as I possibly could," she said trying to
keep the tremble out of her voice. "You don't realize what
has been going on here."

"Well, I certainly realize enough," he said coldly, sitting
on a straight chair opposite the couch where she had
dropped down. "I can't quite see how your family can be
so inconsiderate to you, at a time like this, with your marriage so close at hand."

"What do you mean?" said Maris sitting very straight
and flashing her eyes at him. "Do you think it was inconsiderate of my mother to drop unconscious on the floor
while she was preparing to iron some of my pretty things
for me? Do you think it was inconsiderate of my little sister
to come home very sick from school, with a sore throat
and probably a bad case of measles, or perhaps scarlet fever?"

"You don't mean that that has happened too?" said Tilford looking at her accusingly as if somehow it was all her
fault.

"The doctor hasn't seen her yet, but the nurse is sure
that it is one or the other."

"Well, for heaven's sake, Maris, have you had both of
those?"

"I'm sure I don't remember," said Maris wearily, "I
guess so. But anyway that doesn't matter. The fact re-
mains that Alexa is very sick, and I've got to go right back
to her as soon as possible."

"Not at all, Maris. You must not go near her again. You
know even if you did have them when you were a child it

is quite possible to get them a second time. I've heard of cases. And it would be simply out of the question to run the risk of you being down with measles on your wedding day, you know. You must telephone for another nurse if the one you have isn't adequate for the situation. I shouldn't think measles was much anyway. She'll probably be running around in a day or two. But you must not run any risks for the wedding."

"Wedding!" said Maris tonelessly. "We can't have a wedding if everybody is sick!"

"Nonsense!" said Tilford with his magnificent air, as if he owned the earth and would brook nobody's interference. "Sickness must not be allowed to interfere! I'm sure your mother isn't selfish enough to want you to put off your wedding just because she might not be able to attend when the day comes. And as for the child, why I can telephone my sister in Chicago to get my little niece ready to be flower girl in Alexa's place."

Maris gave her bridegroom an incredulous look. Was it possible that he was in earnest?

"I wasn't thinking of the ceremony, or the flower girl," she said coldly. "I couldn't think of getting married while my mother was lying at death's door, and my sister was so sick she needed me. You don't realize how sick mother is, or you wouldn't talk that way. Twice today we thought she was dying. The doctor said it was a miracle that she didn't. Do you suppose I could get married and go away across the ocean with my mother sick like that?"

"Well, just what would you propose to do about it?" he asked in a cold haughty voice. "Our reservations are all made for a certain day. We have the finest suite on the ship. I would have to forfeit a good deal of money to give them up now. Also you know that my sailing date is obligatory, as I have business appointments to meet which cannot be delayed. There is no such thing as putting off the wedding, and you'd better understand that at once. And now I think what you had better do is to run up and put a few necessities in a bag and come on home with me. It would be far better for you to stay at our home till the wedding day and then your nerves won't be all upset. Mother will agree with me, I know, and it will give us a chance to get all the arrangements perfected at our leisure."

"Tilford!" gasped Maris horrified. "How could you possibly think I could be spared now? Don't you know I must care for my little sister?"

"That's ridiculous, I tell you. I can get you a child specialist nurse who will handle this case much better than you can. You are just spoiling that child anyway with so much coddling. And I positively must assert my authority and put a stop to this!"

"Authority?" said Maris, and burst into a sudden hysterical giggle. "What authority have you over me?"

"The authority that that ring on your hand gives me," said the young man loftily. "You are as good as my wife now, when you are wearing that!"

"Authority!" repeated Maris slowly again, a kind of scorn creeping into her voice. "I thought it was a pledge of love and tenderness."

"Well, that, too, of course. But it is all based on authority."

"And what love and tenderness do you show when you talk in this way about my beloved family? When you want me to come away from them when they are very sick and need me. When you can suggest that I could possibly plan for a wedding with my mother at death's door!"

"Now, look here, Maris, I thought you were a sensible girl. Suppose all this had happened three weeks later, after we had been married and were half way across the ocean? Would you have insisted that the ship turn back and take you to your precious family?"

Maris caught her breath and stared at the young man

who suddenly seemed an alien, not a lover. Her face was very white. Slowly she rose from the couch and looked at him.

"It *didn't* happen three or four weeks later," she said steadily, "and we are not married yet, remember! I don't know that I ever want to be married if that is the way you feel about it."

There was a gravity in her voice that Tilford had never heard her use to him before.

"Miss Maris, your little sister is crying for you and I can't seem to stop her. I'm afraid she'll waken your mother!" came the low authoritative voice of the nurse.

Maris turned and flew up the stairs.

Tilford gave an exasperated look after her and said to the nurse, "Will you kindly ask her what she did with the wedding invitations? I can't find them where we left them yesterday."

The nurse gave him a calm glance and went upstairs without answering. But no word came from above, and Tilford presently took himself away.

Upstairs Maris was having her hands full trying to quiet the little sufferer and wishing the doctor would hurry. She had no time just now to think about weddings. It seemed to her that all the troubles of the universe had suddenly fallen into her pleasant life, and there was just nothing that could be done to right things. Everything was jumbled up. She didn't even want to think about Tilford. Just the memory of his handsome face turned her sick at heart. What was love anyway? Just a thing for fair weather?

4

MARIS lay down on the bed beside her small sister, holding the hot little hand in her own, and her heart seemed just
about as heavy as a heart could be.

But she talked on, making up a ridiculous story about a
canary bird who wore rubber boots and got the measles
and had nice orange juice to drink out of a silver spoon,
and all the time her sub-conscious mind was aware of the
little boys outside playing ball and yelling to each other at
the top of their lungs. Oh, dear! She had tried to tell them
their mother was sick, but they probably hadn't taken it in.
It was good they were on this side of the house and not the
other. Her mother perhaps could not hear them.

But then they drew nearer, close to the house, and began shouting some altercation about whether the ball had
been out or not, and suddenly bang! bang! bang! came the
ball against the wall of her room, close by the window.

The little girl started from her sleep.

"What's that, Maris?" she asked opening startled eyes.

"It's only Eric and Alec throwing their ball against the
house." She tried to answer in a sleepy tone. "I'll tell them
to stop it."

Then she called from the window:

"Boys! Eric! Alec! Stop that! You'll disturb mother! Can't you get some books or something and keep quiet for a little while?"

"Okay!" said Eric with a frown. "Can't we go down by the pond? All the kids are down there!"

Then she heard another voice, low-modulated, calling:

"Hey, boys! How about coming over and helping me mark the tennis court? Then we'll have a game or two before night."

The boys turned, entranced, and looking down Maris saw Lane Maitland standing on the other side of the hedge that separated the property next door, vacant just now. Why, did the Maitlands still own that place? How nice that was of Lane to help her out! He must have heard her call the boys.

As if he knew her thoughts he lifted his eyes to the window:

"How about that, Maris? Is that all right? I'll keep them the rest of the afternoon if you don't mind."

"Oh, that's kind of you!" she breathed with a relieved smile. "Gwyneth has gone on an errand for the nurse, and Sally has her hands full. I'm afraid I've got a case of measles up here."

"Say, that's tough luck. Have the boys had it?"

Maris shook her head.

"Well, you can count on me for anything you need. I'll handle the boys as long as you say. We might make a quarantine camp of our house if you find it really is measles. Go on back to your hospital and I'll start a detention camp."

He grinned pleasantly and walked off with the two delighted boys. Maris settled down to a few minutes' rest, her mind a tumult of troublesome questions.

But it was not for long. The doctor arrived and things

began to happen. Yes, decidedly, Alexa had the measles, and they were not behaving well either. He took Maris into the playroom at the end of the back hall and told her how serious measles might become if they were not looked after most carefully. He gave most detailed directions, and asked if she wanted him to get another nurse.

"No! Oh, no!" she said, appalled at the thought of the expense that would be to her already over-burdened father. "I want to take care of her myself. She is going to miss mother so. Mother always takes care of her."

The doctor grunted his approbation. This was a girl after his own heart. He had been afraid that she had been spoiled by her rich lover and his family, but she was running true to Mayberry tradition. She was loyal to her family.

"Well, we'd better get the playroom fixed up for her," he said, considering the possibilities. "It's a little farther from your mother's room, and that will give you a comfortable place for yourself. This door opening into the playroom from your room makes it just ideal. And of course you'll have the nurse to consult with in case you have any questions. You couldn't have a better one than Bonny. She's had a lot of experience. Now, don't you worry. We'll pull this little girl through in great shape. It won't be long before we get this rash out. Hard lines, Maris, but you always were a brave little soldier, even the time you had to have that cut on your chin sewed up when you were a kid!"

It was a relief of course to know that Alexa was not in such a serious condition as she had feared, but the immediate future loomed dismal and perplexing before her.

Maris summoned Merrick who had just come in, and stealthily they moved Alexa's little white bed into the playroom tiptoeing as silently up and down the hall as if they had been ghosts, till all was made comfortable for the little invalid. And then the nurse came and helped to get the child into the other bed, warming it carefully with hot blankets and water bottles, and little Alexa opened her heavy eyes and smiled at Maris.

"This is funny, Maris. Sleeping in the playroom!" she said in a weak little voice.

"Yes, isn't it, darling, and you can lie here and look right over to my bed in my room and wave at me in the morning. Won't that be nice?"

"Wes."

"Now, you're going to have some nice hot milk and then you're going to go to sleep again and get well as quickly as you can."

"Are you going to take care of mees, Maris?" she asked anxiously.

"Yes. Won't that be fun, dear? We'll have some lovely times together when you get all better. Paper dollies and stories."

"Wes. I wouldn't want a weal nurse. She's too gwowed-up and starchy. I want you for my nurse, Maris."

"All right, if you'll be a good girl. You must do just what I say, and you mustn't make a noise to make mother worse."

"Okay!" she said sleepily, meekly swallowing the spoonfuls of hot milk and closing her eyes.

Maris tiptoed into her own room to make up her bed afresh, and then dropped down to rest a moment. But Gwyneth opened the door softly and peeked in, and Maris went out to speak with her.

"What am I going to do about school, Maris?" asked the little girl. "Is it really measles?"

"Yes, but you've had them, dear."

"Doesn't make any difference," said Gwyneth sadly, "they won't let me keep on coming to school if I'm living in the house with it. I just telephoned over to Miss Price, and she said, no, I'd have to stay somewhere else if I wanted to keep on coming. And Maris, it's exams in three weeks now, and I'd hate awfully to get left behind and not make my grade."

Maris drew her brows in perplexity. How many problems there were that mother usually settled.

"But where could you stay, dear? You know mother would be terribly worried to have you away from home alone. If only we had a relative near by. But there isn't a soul."

"Couldn't I stay with Erminie Powers? She's only half a block away, and I could telephone every day. You know mother lets me stay all night with Erminie sometimes, and Mrs. Powers is just as particular as mother is."

"Well, but Gwyneth, that's a great deal to ask of anybody, to take in a boarder for two or three weeks."

"I won't have to ask her, she's already asked me," said Gwyneth. "She suggested it just as soon as she heard Lexie had the measles."

"You mean Erminie suggested it. But that's not her mother."

"Oh, but her mother came out to the door just now as I was passing by and said she would love to have me come. She said she counted our mother her very dearest friend, and she would so love to do something to help while mother is sick. She said to tell you she understood just how mother felt and she would take just as good care of me as she did of Erminie."

"Why, that is lovely, Gwynnie. Yes, I guess that would be the best thing for you. I didn't know but you might be needed to run errands here, but you'd be near enough for us to phone you if we needed you. Yes, I guess you'd better plan to do that. Go pack a suitcase, dear, the things you'll need for school, and church, and a couple of pretty dresses for dinner at night. Can you do it yourself, or do you want me to do it?"

"Oh, I'd love to do it," said Gwyneth. "But—Maris,

are you *sure* I wouldn't be needed? I wouldn't like to be away if mother got worse, not even if I failed in my exams."

"Of course not!" said Maris briskly. "We're not going to need you at all, I'm sure. Errands can be done after school, but there ought not to be many of those. And as for mother, of course if mother got worse I'd send for you at once. You don't need to worry about that, dear."

"You think mother is going to get well, don't you, sister?"

"Oh, I think so. I hope so. I'm sure the doctor feels she is getting along—that is, she hasn't had any more bad symptoms for the last three hours."

"Where is daddy?"

"He's in mother's room close by her bed, fast asleep in the big old rocking chair, with her hand in his," said Maris with a tender inflection in her tone, and a sweet look in her eyes.

"Isn't he *dear,* Maris?" said the younger sister. "If I ever get married I'm going to marry a man just like father! I like him a great deal better than these fancy handsome men that are selfish and think their wives have got to do as they say in everything. Daddy always acts as if mother were the most precious thing in the world to him. I never heard him cross with her, or fault-finding!"

There was a conscious little flush on Maris' cheeks, and her eyes were bright with unshed tears as she answered quickly:

"That's right, dear. Father and mother are wonderful with each other."

"Well, there aren't so many," said Gwyneth in a wise tone out of her fourteen years of experience. "I wish you'd see Elizabeth Randall's folks! My! Her father frightens me the way he talks to Elizabeth's mother. That's why I never like to go there when he's home. He always acts as if any of us girls were spiders, or thousand-leggers or something when he finds us there when he comes home. I never go there any more if I can help it, though I love Elizabeth. But she hasn't got a happy home like ours. Her mother always looks awfully sad. I think folks ought to be awfully careful who they marry for the sake of their children, don't you, Maris?"

"I certainly do!" said Maris, her cheeks flaming now, as she stooped and kissed her young sister to hide her own confusion. She wondered as Gwyneth tiptoed off happily to pack for her visit, whether Gwyneth had overheard any of Tilford's lofty rebukes and advice. And it came to her with a pang that there were some serious questions for herself to consider that she hadn't yet thought of in connection with this business of getting married. One couldn't just consider one's own part. There was the future and children to think of. It made life a very grave matter. As soon as mother was out of danger and Lexie on the way to recovery she must take time off and seriously consider her own future and whether she was absolutely *sure*—! But of course it was rather late for that! She glanced down at the blazing diamond on her finger and remembered what Tilford had said it represented.

Of course Tilford was a bit angry. He hadn't really meant that. But yet, there had been a note of seriousness in his voice as if back of all the love and tenderness he was supposed to have for her, the engagement did signify a sort of a business contract, in which he had all the rights, and she would have to submit. Every time she thought of it it troubled her. She must really have a plain tender talk with him and let him know how he had hurt her. He probably had no idea how he had made her feel, or even though he was disappointed and annoyed, he never could have gone quite so far.

Maris looked in on Lexie. She was sleeping nicely, and her head was not quite so hot, perhaps. It almost seemed as if the little hands were more moist. If only that rash would come out fully, and do its work instead of hanging back with that menacing reluctance what a relief it would be!

Maris slipped downstairs and found Sally in her element, preparing an appetizing supper, and making delicacies for the sick that the present state of the invalids would never allow them to eat. Sally would carry on below stairs and there was no need to worry about things there.

Merrick had gone to his father's office on an errand for him, and then to see a man whom he hoped would give him a job for the summer. Merrick would be through with his college freshman year in another two weeks. What a blessing he didn't have to go away anywhere to college, but had chosen one where he could live at home! What would she do without Merrick?

Somehow since morning it seemed as if the whole face of life had been changed for Maris. The family seemed brought back to their close relationships once more, and things were settling into their true values. Was that just since morning? It seemed several weeks as she reviewed the experiences through which she had passed, and today was as far removed from yesterday in all its plans and activities as it could possibly be. Yesterday seemed but a passing dream, and only today was real. Even Tilford and his self-important family did not loom so large. Why had she been so worried about what they thought? She would just go upstairs and lie down a few minutes and put them all out of her thoughts. Then her mind would be clear to know how to solve all her problems.

But just then the buzzer of the telephone, which had been substituted for the bell, burred out and startled her. She answered it, with sudden apprehension in her heart.

"Is that you, Maris?" The voice was a well-modulated one, smooth as butter and honey-sweet, with a neat little tang of authority beneath its honey-flow.

"Yes?" said Maris apprehensively.

"You poor child!" said the voice caressingly. "You certainly are having a terrific time! We have felt it for you all day, and have been talking over ways and means. By the way, I hope your mother is much better by this time, and your mind is relieved?"

"No, Mrs. Thorpe. She isn't any better," said Maris sorrowfully. "I'm afraid the doctor doesn't expect her to be really better very soon. She just isn't any worse this afternoon, and that is an encouragement, of course. It is very kind of you to inquire."

"Oh, not at all. Of course we were much disturbed by the news this morning, but I do trust that your doctor is wrong and she will soon be better. But you have a competent nurse, haven't you?"

"Yes, we have a good nurse," said Maris perfunctorily, wishing this homily would draw to a finish and she could go and rest.

"Well, that's half the battle, of course," said Mrs. Thorpe. "And your little sister? Is it really measles? What a pity! She will be so disappointed not to be in the wedding procession. But a child soon forgets, and I am sure my little granddaughter will be delighted to take her place, so you don't need to worry about that. And now, my dear, Tilford was obliged to go unexpectedly over to the clubhouse to meet a man on business and he asked me to call you up and remind you that you and he had an engagement this evening. I told him I didn't think it would be necessary, you are always so punctilious about your engagements, but I promised I would call. I suppose you remember Tilford's sister Irma is expecting you for dinner this evening at eight, don't you?"

Maris paused aghast! Did they actually expect her to attend another ghastly family dinner when she was in the midst of anxiety and sickness?

Maris took a deep breath and waited a second to steady her voice.

"Yes, I knew we had the engagement," she said slowly,

choosing her words, "but I supposed of course Tilford would make my apologies. I should have called up myself, but every minute has been filled with such anxiety and hard work that it hadn't occurred to me I should have let Irma know. I'm sorry. I hope she'll forgive me, and I'm sure she'll understand. I'll 'phone right away and ask her forgiveness. It was terrible, but of course if she knew the circumstances she wouldn't expect me to come."

"But my dear! You can't get out of a dinner engagement like that! You know that is one thing one has to do if one is alive, to keep a dinner engagement! No, Irma does not know anything about the series of upsets you have been having today. I purposely didn't tell her because I was sure you would see your duty and not cause her embarrassment. Besides, my dear, Tilford and I have arranged everything for you. We have secured a charming young nurse who is a specialist with children, and she will be at your house at five o'clock and take full charge of the little sister until she is well again. And at six o'clock Tilford will be there with the car to bring you and your suitcases, for my child, you are to stay with us until the wedding! We felt that it was imperative that you have your rest beforehand. We don't want a washed-out looking bride. Of course you can run down and see your mother every day or two if you feel that is necessary, and for the rest I shall take charge of you, and see that you live a normal unhurried care-free life. Besides, my dear, you must realize that there are a number of showers and parties that you are expected to attend during the next three weeks, affairs that are made for *you,* and are dependent on your presence for their success. Your friends and Tilford's have gone to a great deal of trouble and expense to show you their love and appreciation, and it would be the rudest thing possible for you to utterly spoil their parties now when it is too late to recall them. Besides, it can't possibly do your mother any good for you to mope in the house until she is well.

I'm sure that if she is not utterly selfish and were consulted she would say that I am entirely right.

"So we are arranging for you to be here during the next strenuous weeks until the wedding is over, and then your coming and going need not affect the patients in the house. So, my dear, run along and get packed, for the nurse will be there soon, and Tilford doesn't want to be kept waiting tonight, he says."

Maris was so still for a long moment that Mrs. Thorpe thought she must have hung up, or that something was wrong with the instrument. She began to jiggle the receiver up and down. Maris was so angry she could hardly trust herself to speak. She shut her eyes and leaned her head against the telephone. This was a crucial moment, and she dare not trust her overwrought feelings. Then she spoke:

"I suppose that you are trying to be kind to me, Mrs. Thorpe, and I should perhaps thank you for thinking of me, but what you have suggested is quite out of the question. We do not want another nurse, and if she comes I shall only have to send her away, so if she has not already started kindly tell her not to come. And as for your other suggestion, that I come to your house and stay, even for only the evening, it is quite impossible. Unfortunately for your plans I love my mother, and my little sister, and I would not be willing to be away from them in this time of trouble and anxiety. I could not, even for the sake of social etiquette, be willing to attend a party of any kind when my mother is lying at the point of death, and my whole family need me as they have never needed me before. I should think that anyone with any heart at all would know this and understand perfectly. My friends all would, and would not expect me to come. But if there are any who do not, I do not care. I shall go out no more till my mother is better, and I am not needed here. I will immediately call up the people who have invited me and inform them of the situation. And please do not trouble any further to make plans for me. You apparently do not understand my situation in the least."

"Oh, *really?*" said Mrs. Thorpe. "I should say you were an ungrateful girl. A headstrong little spitfire! Well, I have done my best to help you through a trying situation. I told Tilford he would better tell you himself, but he seemed to think I could handle the situation more delicately. I see he was wrong. Well, he will probably be around to explain himself how hard we have tried to fix things for you. Good afternoon!" and Mrs. Thorpe hung up.

When Maris turned away from the telephone she was trembling with indignation. The idea of expecting her to go out to dinner when her mother was so sick! Well, of course she should have remembered to telephone Irma. She would do it at once.

So she looked up the number and fortunately got her future haughty sister-in-law without trouble. She explained!

"I'm just as sorry as I can be that I didn't call you sooner, Irma, to let you know that I can't come to your dinner tonight," she said humbly, "but I supposed of course Tilford would tell you all about our trouble here. And to tell you the truth I have been so frightened all day, and so hurried and burdened that everything else was driven out of my head. I do hope you will forgive me for not sending you word at once. My mother is at the point of death and I cannot be away from the house."

"Oh, *really?*" said Irma coldly. "And what am *I* supposed to do? I invite my friends to meet my future sister-in-law and she stays away! Surely you won't put me in that position. You certainly can get away for a few hours, can't you? Aren't there enough in your family to look out for your mother? And there are such things as doctors and nurses. Surely her life is not dependent upon you. And nobody who will be here knows your mother, anyway."

"Oh, Irma!" said Maris aghast at such a cold-blooded attitude. "Would you go out to a dinner party when your mother might be dying?"

"I'm sure I hope I'd do my duty!"

It was very still on the line. If anybody was listening in they certainly didn't dare to breathe. Then Maris said quite calmly:

"Well, I'm doing my duty, and I'll *not* be at the dinner. I'm sorry!" And she hung up.

As Maris turned away again from the telephone there were angry tears in her eyes. She felt outraged that Tilford's relatives were insisting upon her attendance upon all festivities when she was in great anxiety. It seemed fairly inhuman. Just to save themselves embarrassment!

Suddenly she saw it all. They were ashamed of an alliance with plain people like the Mayberrys who didn't live on the Hill, nor own an estate, nor ride in a limousine. They didn't want to explain who was the mother of their son's fiancée. They wouldn't own that they felt that way of course, for they knew the Mayberrys were an old fine family, even if they hadn't much money. But it became just as plain as day to her that they intended, just as soon as the wedding was over, to separate her from her own people, and ignore those people entirely. They meant she should be absorbed into their family, and become a Thorpe!

All at once a great wave of hate for them all came over her so that she was quite startled and amazed at herself. She had never knowingly hated anybody in her life before. Tears of helpless rage poured into her eyes and down her face.

The telephone was in a little hall closet which Merrick had fitted up with a light overhead, a shelf for the instrument and a single pane of glass in the panel of the door.

As Maris came out she was aware of a shadow falling

across the hall floor from outside the door, and as she brushed the tears away from her eyes the shadow moved and became a man standing at the front door just outside the screen.

He was tapping gently on the door with the tips of his fingers. It was Lane Maitland.

"I didn't want to ring the bell lest I would disturb the invalids," he explained in a very low tone. "I just stepped over to say that the detention camp is in full action and the crew seem very well pleased with arrangements. They are scrubbing up for supper now, and sent me over to say that they will stay there till further orders from you. I'm detailed to tell Merrick to bring over a duffel bag with night things and tooth brushes and so on. Will the arrangement please your honor?"

He was smiling and utterly ignoring the tears on her face which she knew he could not help but see, and in spite of herself she smiled back.

"Don't tell me those boys thought of tooth brushes themselves!" she said with a hysterical giggle, openly digging her knuckles into her eyes to stop the flow of tears.

"Well, perhaps they didn't just go into the details," grinned Maitland, and suddenly became grave.

"The patients aren't any worse, are they?" he asked anxiously, taking obvious notice of her weeping now, which his kind tone only seemed to make uncontrollable.

"No," she said shaking her head and flipping away those unmanageable tears with the tips of her fingers, "not that I know of. It's not any worse than it was, I guess. But—well—I guess I'm just plain mad!" She gave a little hurt laugh. "I've been talking with some people who don't understand! Who *won't* understand! Who only think of themselves!"

"There are lots like that, aren't there?" he agreed. "And it's maddening. But when I get like that I like to remember what my mother used to say, that she was so glad God had said vengeance was *His* and *He* would repay where it was needed, and we didn't have to do a thing about it! '*Therefore,* if thine enemy hunger, feed him.'"

She looked at him for a minute and her face changed.

"I never thought of it like that," she said humbly. "I never realized that God would care about what people did to me. I thought I was all alone in it. But it would help a lot to realize He does, and He'll do the getting even if there's any getting even to be done."

A light came into Maitland's eyes, a light of satisfaction, as if she had measured up to what he had hoped.

"Yes, it takes the responsibility off us, doesn't it? I kind of hoped you'd feel that way. And now, is there anything I could do?"

"You've done a lot," she said earnestly. "You don't know how you've helped me. It's wonderful to know the boys are safe, and there's a chance they may not get the measles. But I'm afraid they'll be an awful nuisance to you."

"Not a bit of it. We're getting along fine. They're great kids and I like 'em. We're going to have the time of our lives. And now, I've had the telephone put in and you can call me any time you like, day or night. I've nothing else to do for the next few days but hang around here, and I'm glad to have such congenial company."

"I can't thank you enough!" said Maris earnestly, and impulsively she put out her hand. He took it in a quick hearty grasp, smiling, and was gone.

Maris started upstairs suddenly comforted. After all, if things went wrong, God could somehow set them right. She couldn't, not even with all the apologies in the universe. Then she bethought herself of several invitations for the near future that ought to be cancelled at once, and turning back went again to the telephone. She called up several numbers, telling her friends that her mother had been taken very ill and she would have to cancel all engagements for the present. Some of them were kindly and filled with dismay, and some of them were not at home and she had to leave a message with a servant, but she felt relieved when it was done.

Upstairs in her room at last she heard Lexie moaning and went to see if she could do anything to help her.

Then the clock downstairs struck six in soft silvery chimes, and almost on the dot Maris heard Tilford's car drive up and stop before the house. *Now what?* Her heart gave a frightened beat, and then she remembered.

"Oh, God, you're going to take charge!" she breathed as she heard Sally coming to her door.

5

AS Maris passed by her mirror she saw that her hair was all awry, and there were dark circles under her eyes in a white, white face. Tilford would tell her about it at once probably, but it didn't matter.

Out in the hall she met the nurse with a hot water bottle in her hand.

"Your father's feet are so cold," she explained in a whisper. "I'm afraid he's getting a nervous chill. You know he didn't eat anything at lunch time. I've tried to persuade him to go in another room and lie down, but he won't. I wonder if you could ask the maid to bring him up a cup of coffee. I want to get him warmed up. He oughtn't to be chilly this way."

"I will," said Maris. "Is mother—all right?"

"Well, she's not all right by any means, but she hasn't had any more of those sinking spells since the doctor was here."

With a heavy heart Maris went on her way down the back stairs to give the order to Sally, and then into the living room where a frowning lover waited.

"You're not ready!" he announced in displeasure as she came in wearily trying to smile at him.

"Why, didn't your mother tell you I couldn't possibly come with you?"

"I haven't seen mother since I left the house just after lunch. I told her to remind you of our engagement and to say that you must be ready when I came for you. How long will it take you? Is your suitcase packed? I can wait exactly five minutes and no more. A man is calling me on long distance from Chicago and I must be at home when the call comes in."

"Well, you needn't wait, Tilford. I can't possibly come. I have called your sister and explained."

"That is unpardonable!" he said looking at her with a glitter of scorn in his eyes. "I'm afraid I shall have to insist. I shall have to exercise my authority. This isn't an ordinary dinner engagement. This is my sister's dinner to introduce you to our friends. It is very important. I cannot allow you to disregard it."

"Authority? Allow?" said Maris lifting puzzled eyes to his stony offended countenance.

"You are wearing my ring," he said significantly. "I told you this morning what I felt that means. Your mother has lasted all day. She will doubtless last a few hours longer without your help. I cannot allow you to confuse our wedding preparations this way for mere sentiment. I thought you had more strength of character than that!"

Maris stared at him for an instant longer and then she looked down at her ring as if she had never been acquainted with it before.

Slowly she put up her other hand and took the ring off holding it out to him.

"You had better take it back then. I could not wear a ring under those conditions." Her voice was very firm and very sad.

But he did not take the ring.

"You are beside yourself!" he said in tones like icicles. "You do not know what you are doing. I did not know you had such a temper. Put on that ring and stop acting like a child! You said you were never going to take it off when I put it on, and now look! Put it on quickly or you will drop it on the floor. It is too valuable a stone to be play-acting with. Don't for heaven's sake try to get your own way by being dramatic. It won't go down with me!"

Maris suddenly reached out and pushed the ring within his clasp and turning fairly flew up the stairs. Her face was ghastly white and her head was whirling, but she did not forget to go softly, and to the listening angry man below it seemed almost as if she had melted into mist, so silently she disappeared.

He stood for a minute looking down at the great lovely stone in its perfect setting, catching the evening sunlight that fell through the door, reflecting sharp bright lights in a prism of color. Then his anger rose still hotter. To think she would dare play with as costly a stone as that! To expect she could conquer him, Tilford Thorpe, when he had once given forth his mandate! And he had thought her so gentle! So pliable! So easy to mold!

Almost he started up the stairs after her! Then he thought better of that! That was doubtless what she wanted. She was likely in hysterics now, expecting him to find his way to her and yield to her wishes. But that was not the way to begin with her. Let her see what she had done! Let her go through the night without that wonderful ring! Let her know humiliation and shame and understand what a dreadful thing it was to stand out against him!

So he tucked the ring into his pocket and whirled on his heel, going out the screen door, which would have slammed if Maitland hadn't taken care that very noon to put a tiny pad of cotton in the spot where it would have slammed. He went out to his car and started it with far more noise than he needed. Let her hear that she had sent him away from her! Let her understand how final had been her act! Let her have time to fully realize what an awful, what an irreparable thing she had done in offending the whole mighty Thorpe connection! Let her think that it was all over forever between them. It would do her good. He wouldn't be in a hurry to make it up either. She would have to come crawling after him, and ask forgiveness, too. It wasn't for him to yield. He drove furiously away from her thinking his mad thoughts.

And up in her own room Maris knelt by the window over in the corner where Lexie couldn't see her from the bed, where no one would see her if they opened the door to call her; where only God could see her. And she said quietly in words that only God could hear: "Dear God, were You taking charge? Was that what You wanted me to do?"

And then quite simply she clasped her hands that were empty of her lovely ring and felt entirely naked and helpless, and was suddenly conscious of a great peace. God was taking charge, and it must have been what He willed, for there had been nothing else to do. She could not go away and make merry and leave her dear ones who needed her. And she could not wear Tilford's ring under those conditions!

Then she heard Merrick's hushed footsteps coming to her door and she arose quite calmly to meet him, stepping out in the hall and talking in low tones. Her brother's eyes searched her face.

"You all right, Maris?" he asked with an unwonted tenderness in his tone.

"All right, brother!"

"Where's Gwyn? I can't find her anywhere."

"I let her go over to Erminie's to stay a few days. You know they won't let her come back to school if she stays here, even though she has had the measles. Don't you think that was all right? She oughtn't to stay out of school. She'll only be worrying if she stays here."

"Sure that was all right. But what about the boys? They'll get it, I suppose."

"Maybe not. Lane Maitland has taken them over to his house to stay awhile. They're charmed. You're to take over a bag with some things for them. I was going to suggest that you stay there too, but I guess maybe we might need you here if anything happens in the night. Father isn't so well. The nurse said he was having a nervous chill."

"Say, that's awful!" said Merrick. "No, I'll stay here. Maybe I'd better go look at dad. Where is he?"

"Close by mother. The nurse says he won't leave her."

They went softly to the door, and looked in. It was very quiet in the shadowed room. The nurse was running the water in the bathroom. Their mother lay as quiet as she had been all day, and sometimes it seemed as if she were scarcely breathing. Her eyes were closed. The children's hearts contracted, and Maris could hardly keep from crying out in her agony as she recalled her brother's words that morning: "It's that fool wedding!" Was she the cause of her mother's sudden illness? Oh, she was, she knew she must be! Could she ever, ever forgive herself? If mother should die how could they ever go on living?

Merrick went softly over by his father and laid his hand on his head, startled to feel it hot and feverish.

His father looked up and tried to smile sadly.

Merrick stopped and whispered in his ear:

"It's all right, dad. Mr. Matthews says he'll extend the note. You needn't worry!"

A look of relief passed over the drawn worn features of the father and he drew a deep breath of a sigh.

Merrick slipped out softly and came back presently with a folding cot, and then again with a soft mattress.

The nurse came in with sheets and pillows.

"Now, Mr. Mayberry, you're going to lie down on this cot, close by your wife and then you'll be able to hear her if she stirs and wants anything," she whispered to him.

Maris saw Merrick bring their father's bathrobe and help him off with his coat, and then make him lie down, with another great sigh of relief. Then she hurried back to her own patient. Poor father! He had been worrying about something. A note that had to be extended? What was that? Had father been so hard put to it that he had had to borrow money to pay for her wedding? Oh, how had she been so blind? And she had been so thrilled and so involved in all the intriguing gaiety that Tilford had produced from day to day that she had not noticed! Was it possible that God had to send all these startling anxieties to bring her to her senses?

It was not quite time for Lexie's medicine yet. She seemed to be still sleeping. Maris dropped down on her bed for a moment and let these enlightening facts roll over her tired soul in a great condemning flood.

Then she began to go back and think it out. What a dear family she had always had! How they had always done everything together, and enjoyed it. Even being poor together! There was the year when father had thought that he was going to lose the house because he had had to let the interest on the mortgage lapse. How desperately they had all saved and planned, and tried to make a bit of money here and there to help. Even the children. She recalled Gwyneth at five years going into the woods with some children and bringing home quantities of spring beauties and hepaticas which she had tied in funny little bunches and taken out on the street and actually sold, for a penny a bunch! She could see their father's face now, when she had brought her entire fortune of eleven cents to him radiantly, and told him it was to pay the mortgage off. Such tears and tenderness and love! How their interests had all been one, and how the disasters and troubles had only served to make them love one another more! And now, somehow, she seemed to have drifted away from them all. It was as if she were an alien among them, going her own way, or rather Tilford's way, and having all her interests and pleasures in another world, a world they did not know. Why, she seldom had time to tell any of them any more what she was doing.

She recalled how she used always to come in no matter how late it was, when she had been out for the evening and tell her mother everything she had been doing. And always the whole family took such an interest in her comings and goings. But of late there had seemed to be almost a spirit of resentment whenever she spoke of where she had been or what she had been doing. Was it always like that when children got married? Did all the rest resent it? Did they lose each other forever and ever? A sudden great sob swelled in her throat and threatened to overwhelm her. Was this what being married to Tilford would mean? That she would no more belong to her precious family? That they would have no right to know of her affairs? Oh, she couldn't stand that! It wasn't right. It surely couldn't be the way God had planned life for a universe, to have those who married suddenly cut off entirely from everything that had always been precious. Why, her parents didn't know right now what she had been going through with the Thorpes. She didn't want them to know. It would hurt them terribly.

Or did they know? Was it possible that mother and father with their fine intuitions had sensed it? And could that be part of what had made mother sick? Dear sensitive mother! Oh, what was she going to do about it? And the wedding was only a few days off!

And then as if inanimate objects had become alive they trooped into her room and formed a procession in the darkness, stopping one after another for her consideration.

First came those wedding invitations, as if they had somehow escaped their wrapping in the attic and slid out of their white boxes and filed down two abreast to stand before her, condemning her. The very date of the wedding stood out in flaming letters across her vision, as if they would say: "We are now a day late! And tomorrow will be another day later! And the Thorpes are going to be horrified! What are you going to do about it? Are you going to let us be disgraced forever? Are we to be even more disgraced than we are already?"

Well, and what was she going to do? She had no one to ask. Her mother had passed beyond the consideration of any earthly trouble for the present. Her father was too worried and too much on the verge of illness himself to be consulted. If she dared to speak to Merrick about it his wrath would rise to unspeakable heights. There was no one but God to talk to about it. It must be decided tonight. She had to think it through somehow.

She drew a deep breath of protest and waved the invitations aside for the moment. She had to get Lexie settled for the night first before she took that up. But as she turned to meet the next perplexity in the procession she had the consciousness of those invitations standing just at her right hand sternly awaiting her first moment of leisure.

And next there floated softly up her lovely filmy wedding dress that mother had made, and looked at her with reproachful eyes, sadly, as if it had been set aside. As if it would say, "What are you going to do about me? Those Thorpes will despise me and scorn me if you insist on wearing me! Do you want to subject me to their criticism? You know they won't own I am lovely. They likely haven't the fineness to appreciate why I am better for your purpose."

And behind in the shadows, came a stiff white satin frock rustling arrogantly up beside the other. Though Maris had never seen it, nor even heard its description, she recognized it as the Thorpe dress from the exclusive shop, and it stood there beside her mother's charming creation of loveliness, and claimed precedence.

Just behind the two she sighted a host of dinners and showers and theater parties, and other affairs that she knew were booked for the coming days, and now were standing a-tiptoe for her attention.

And over it all she seemed to see her mother's troubled eyes looking at her. Oh, what was she to do, and however did she get involved in all this trouble?

And then she heard a tap at the door and rose to answer it, quick apprehension in her breast. Oh, was mother worse? Oh, mother mustn't die now, not before she had a chance to tell her how sorry she was that she had been so indifferent, and selfish. Oh, not before she had a chance to undo the hurts and get the troubles straightened out.

She opened the door and there stood Merrick, his eyes standing out in his white face startlingly, his lips quivering with angry excitement, and by his side Gwyneth, softly sobbing into the skirt of her little pink dimity that was all crumpled and pitiful and showed her brief petticoat, making her look such a child.

Merrick was grasping her shoulder furiously, clutching it as if he had a prisoner who must be put in chains at once, a gang leader at least.

"Where do you think I found this kid!" said Merrick excitedly. "Just guess where! This child not yet out of grammar school? Down at the drugstore, sitting at a little round table eating ice cream with one of the worst young bums this town affords!"

He gave Gwyneth's small shoulder another fierce shake, and she began to sob louder.

"Hush!" said Maris quickly. "You'll disturb mother! You'll wake Lexie. Come down in the living room where no one can hear you. You mustn't make a noise up here! You'll frighten mother. You might kill her!"

There came an instant's hush in the hostilities as the dire possibilities confronted the brother and sister, and the three of them trooped silently down the stairs to the far end of the living room, where Gwyneth curled herself into the corner of the big sofa with her head in a pillow and sobbed silently.

"Now," said Maris turning to her brother, "what do you mean, Merrick? Where did you find Gwynnie? I let her go over to Erminie's for the night, you know."

"Well, but she wasn't over at Erminie's. Erminie was there too, with another boy. They were out with the boys, if you please, as if they'd been grown up! And the worst young bums you can find anywhere. Rance Mosher! What do you think of that? His father had to bail him out of jail last week. He was arrested for running over a woman when he was drunk! Only seventeen, but he's got his name up in connection with several terrible affairs up at the 'Dark of the Moon' road house. And he was treating our sister to ice cream, sitting shoulder to shoulder with her down at the drugstore, trying to kiss her and hold her hand! My little sister, out in the public eye that way! The worst bum in the town!"

"He's just Erminie's cousin!" wailed Gwyneth, "and Erminie's mother said we might go with him and Harlan Wescott and get some ice cream! And he wasn't kissing me. He was only kidding!"

"I guess I can tell when a fella is trying to kiss a girl. I guess I could see what he had in his mind. Right out in a public place bringing my sister into disgrace! She's nothing but a child, Maris, and Harlan Wescott and Rance Mosher are a long way on in what our father and mother would call crime, and I'm not kidding! I know what I'm talking about! The nurse sent me after a prescription and while I was waiting for it, I turned around and saw my sister—!"

"Not so loud, Merrick, please," said Maris looking at him with troubled eyes.

"Well, it's a serious matter!" said the boy angrily.

"Yes, I know, but we mustn't let mother hear. Now, Gwyneth, tell me all about it. How did you happen to be there? You told me that Mrs. Howard never let Erminie go out evenings. That was why I was willing for you to stay over there. You knew mother wouldn't want you to be going out with big boys in the evening."

"Well, but Maris, it was just to the drugstore and it was only Erminie's cousin and his friend. And there wasn't any dessert for dinner, cause the maid was out, and we were hot and thirsty and—"

"Do you mean that Mrs. Howard *told* you to go? Did she say it to you, Gwyneth?"

"Why, no, it was Erminie who went upstairs and asked her."

"Did you hear her ask her?"

"No, I was downstairs talking to the boys, but she came down and said her mother said it was all right to go anywhere the boys wanted to take us, and they were going to take us afterwards to the movies. They said it was a swell picture, and we ought to see it!" Gwyneth burst into tears again at thought of her humiliation and loss.

"Well, I wouldn't be so sure Mrs. Howard knows anything about it, Gwyneth. I never did trust Erminie. But whether she said so or not, I'm sure mother wouldn't approve. And as for going to the movies with boys, you know she wouldn't like that. I think if Merrick will run over to Howards' and get your suitcase we'll just bring this visit to a close."

"Sure I will," said Merrick.

"Oh, *Maris!*" Gwyneth began to cry again, with heart-rending sobs. "Then I can't go to school, and I'll not get promoted!"

Maris sat down beside her on the sofa and gathered her resisting young form into her arms.

"Listen, little sister, you mustn't cry so loud. You don't want to kill dear mother, do you? And we'll talk about the school afterwards. It is more important to take good care of you than to have you pass your examinations."

"But I was being taken perfectly good care of," she argued. "I wasn't really sure I was going to the movies, only they told me it would be something I ought to see. And Rance Mosher is a perfectly nice boy. He was awfully polite to me. He said I had nice eyes and he liked me, and he treated me just as if I'd been a lady. Merrick just doesn't like him, that's all. He was always fighting him when they were in school. Erminie says it's because Merrick stole Rance's girl once—"

"Look here, Gwynnie, you're talking about something you don't understand in the least," said Merrick severely. "I never stole Rance's girl. I didn't like her and didn't want her. But the girl came and asked me to take her home from the senior party because Rance was so drunk she was afraid of him, if you want to know the truth! And I know a lot of things about Rance that I'd be ashamed to tell you. If you knew all I know about him, all I've *seen,* myself, you would run from him worse than you would from a rattle-snake."

Gwyneth went into another fit of sobbing then, and Maris signed to Merrick to go after the suitcase and explain to Mrs. Howard that they needed Gwyneth at home.

"But I'm the head of my class, Maris! I'll l-l-lose my s-s-standing in s-s-school!" wailed the little girl.

"It's a great deal better to lose your standing in school than to lose your standing at home, and in the town, and—" she hesitated at the word that came to her lips, and then finished, almost in awe at herself—"and before *God!*"

The child lifted her wet eyes wonderingly.

"What do you mean, Maris? How could I lose my

standing at home or in the town, or even before God by eating ice cream in the drug store?"

"You could lose your standing at home by not keeping your word about staying in the house when you knew what mother and father would feel about your running around the streets at night after dark with older boys, even if they were Erminie's cousins! You could lose your standing in the town by letting yourself be associated even for a little while with boys who do not have a good reputation. You can lose a reputation very easily, but it's not so easy to get it back again. And then, Gwynnie, there are other things. I would rather mother told you about them, as she once told me when I was a little older than you, but it is never good for little girls to run around with boys much older than they are. It isn't natural, unless they belong to you. Lots of harmful things grow out of such friendships. I haven't time to tell you about them tonight. I'm very tired and so are you. But it's better for you to stay at home. I've been needing you ever since you went away."

"But—my s-school!" began Gwyneth again.

"We'll talk about the school tomorrow and see if anything can be done about it. In the meantime go to bed, and let's wait till another day."

But it was some time before she got the child quieted down and in bed, and even after she was asleep from sheer exhaustion, Maris found her catching her breath now and then in another sob.

The plot thickened. Problems on every hand. Gwyneth was another! And little Lexie, tossing and turning and crying out in delirium was the next one. Would the doctor never come?

Very late that night after the doctor's visit, when she had made the little girl as comfortable as possible, and stood watching the nurse and the doctor in a grave talk down the hall, of which she could make nothing, she crept to her bed, too weary to try to think. As she sank away into a restless sleep it seemed to her that all about her room were standing those problems. The wedding invitations slithering across the floor in a white heap as if they had done their best to attract her attention, the two dresses like ghosts of enemies in opposite corners, the shadowy parties grouped here and there about the room, and in the midst of them all, stalking in as she dropped from consciousness, stood Tilford and his mother watching her with angry questioning eyes.

6

OVER at the old Maitland place matters were moving along at a very satisfactory pace for the little boys who were temporarily parked there.

"Well, boys, we've received our orders from headquarters and now we've got to get to work," said Lane Maitland as he came back from his brief interview with Maris. "There are two more beds to be put in shape before dark, and the commissary department has got to rustle some food for supper. Tomorrow our old cook and her husband are arriving and we'll have more leisure then for amusement, but tonight we've got to get busy. How about jumping in the car and going down to the store with me? I need to lay in a supply of good things. What do you like best to eat?"

"Ice cream!" said Alec promptly.

"Aw, shucks! You can eat ice cream any time if you get a nickel. How about hot dogs and cook 'em out doors? That's more like camping."

"Well, how about both?" said Lane.

"Okay!" shouted both boys at once.

"Or how about strawberries? Does anybody like strawberries?"

"We sure do!" shouted Alec.

"Well, there used to be strawberries down in the garden. Let's go see if they have been choked out by weeds. There might be a few, you know, and then we could save the ice cream till tomorrow."

So they tramped down to the old overgrown garden and discovered a few late berries here and there, tasting more like wild ones than the old rare varieties that used to be cultivated in the years when the Maitlands were living there. The host went into the house and brought out a dish, and eager young fingers managed to fill a bowl in spite of the many surreptitious journeys they made to eager young mouths.

"Pretty nice work, old man," said Maitland when Alec brought him the bowl. "All right, now we have our dessert, we'll go down to the store and get our supplies. We'll need soap, and bread, and marshmallows to toast, and bacon for breakfast, and eggs. You like bacon and eggs, don't you, boys? And cream on your strawberries?"

"Oh, sure!"

"And toasted marshmallows?"

"I should say! Oh boy! This is going to be great!"

"Sure! We're going to have the time of our life!"

"We sure are!" said Eric.

"Oh, boy, don't I wish our new brother-in-law was going to be like you!" said Alec wistfully. "Then I wouldn't mind Maris getting married so much."

"Oh, do you mind her getting married?" asked the young man busying himself about putting the strawberries in the window where they would be cool.

"Why, sure we mind. Wouldn't you?" said Eric with a frown. "Wouldn't you mind having your best sister taken away from you entirely?"

"Oh, maybe it won't be like that," said Maitland, trying

to be matter-of-fact. "Maybe your new brother-in-law will be great. Perhaps you don't know him. Wait till you know him," he added hopefully.

"Who, Tilford? Not he!" sighed Eric hopelessly. "He's a snob. He's some swell! He can't take a joke, nor see one. He hates boys, and anyway we never would get to know him. He doesn't like us. He always acts as if we didn't exist."

"Well, let's forget it for tonight and have a good time, what do you say?"

"Okay!" said the boys, and they climbed eagerly into the car and were off to the store. And how they did enjoy going around the store picking out things they thought might be needed.

They made a fire out in the back yard, and cooked their sausages, made some cocoa there too, and when they had eaten their strawberries with plenty of cream and sugar they were really too full to hold another crumb of anything.

"And now," said Maitland cheerfully, "we'll wash up the dishes and go up and get our beds in order. After that it will be time to turn in."

"So soon?" said the boys who hated to lose a minute of this grand picnic.

"Oh, people always go to bed early when they are at camp. It's one of the rules, you know."

So they submitted and hurried back and forth to the house, bringing supplies and dishes and washing up.

Merrick came over with a suitcase of garments while they were making their beds, and grinned as they both tried to talk at once telling him about their supper out of doors.

"That's all right, kids, but if I hear of you making any trouble over here I'll come over and lam you one you won't forget, and I don't mean maybe."

They promised good behavior and dived into the suitcase arraying themselves for the night.

Merrick reported that there was little or no change in the sick ones, and looked gravely troubled as he said it, and when he was gone Maitland ordered lights out and everybody kneeling for prayers. He suggested that they pray for their mother and little sister. And the suddenly serious boys knelt and were very quiet for a long minute, beside their cots, till Maitland's voice broke in upon their devotions:

"Dear Lord, we want to thank You for being with us all day, and keeping guard over us and those we love. Keep guard over us during the night, both here and at the home house, and especially be with the sick ones. If it's Your will make them better in the morning. And help these boys to be strong and courageous, and to conquer themselves so that they will be ready to help in this time of stress. Teach them to trust themselves to Thee. We ask it in Christ's name."

Subdued and quiet they got into bed, and it was all still about them. They lay for awhile thinking of their mother, and the terrible possibilities that life held, life that had been so bright and engaging before this. They realized that God had bent down and was taking account of them, that they were, perhaps, in His eye more than they had thought. It was barely possible that He expected something of even them—just boys. They hadn't thought of that before.

But long after they fell asleep Lane Maitland lay across the room from them and thought of the girl in the next house who was bearing so many burdens just now. The girl he used to know so well, and who had grown even more lovely than she had been when they were in school together!

He thought of what the little boys had said about her fiancé. Was that just children's chatter? Was the man her equal? Was he worthy of so lovely a girl? He sighed as he thought about it. Well, it was not for him to think about. He would like to help her somehow, but that was not his job of course. Only it would be nice to know that someone was taking it over and doing it well. She needed comforting, he was sure, for she had looked terribly troubled that afternoon, and she had been grateful that he was looking after the boys. Well, he could at least do that. They were lively youngsters, and there was no place for such eager thoughtless vitality around sick people. Now, he must just stop thinking about that girl. She belonged to another man.

But it was not easy to turn his thoughts away from the affairs of these dear old friends of his boyhood days. The more perhaps because he had so recently lost his parents, and was practically alone in the world. For hours he lay thinking and finally got up to look out of the window toward the house next door and observe the lighted windows. They were not getting much rest over there, he was sure, for he could see shadows of moving forms now and again. He longed to know how the battle with death in one room, and with disease in another, was going. How would the others stand up under this hard time?

And while all this was going on, up in the Thorpe mansion on the side of the town always designated as "The Hill," the family were having a counsel of war.

Tilford had not gone to his sister's dinner. Since his fiancée for whom the dinner was given could not be there it would certainly look better for him to stay away too. So he stayed at home with his father and mother in a gloomy silence, and ate in an offended way through an excellent dinner.

"Well, really, Tilford, what happy circumstance has made you a guest in your home after your many and continued absences?" the father asked facetiously, as Tilford walked into the dining room and took his seat.

"Don't try to be funny, dad!" said Tilford heavily. "It's anything but a happy circumstance. I'm on the verge of insanity with all that has happened, and it seems impossible to work anything out that will better matters."

"Ah! Indeed! I hadn't heard of an impending disaster. Am I to be favored with a recital, or would you prefer to suffer in secret?"

"You're so trifling, dad, no wonder you don't hear the news. But of course you'll have to know," sighed Tilford heavily. "The whole trouble is with Maris' family. They have seen fit to throw a panic into the camp. I haven't been able as yet to ascertain whether it is something they planned in order to annoy us and assert their own importance, or whether it is just upset nerves, or what. But the long and the short of it is that Maris' mother had some sort of a nervous upset this morning, fainted away or something, and they are making a mountain out of it. Maris declares she can't go to Irma's dinner, given tonight wholly to introduce Maris to our friends. She has got hystericky and declares her mother is at the point of death and she can't leave her. I have tried my best to reason with her, but all to no avail, and then as if that wasn't enough, her baby sister comes home from kindergarten with the measles! Imagine it! Such a plebian common little childish ailment! And Maris insists she has to care for her. And she wouldn't be moved even when I secured a special child's nurse, and offered to pay her myself."

The father watched his son seriously.

"Well, now, that's too bad. Her mother sick! That's hard on a girl, I imagine. I don't see that that's anything to be so disturbed about, her not going to a dinner. Anybody would understand that. I thought she was a very nice sweet little girl myself when she was here last night. I thought you had made a very wise choice, and we are going to like her a lot. She'll fit right in with our family beautifully. Didn't you think so, mamma?"

"You don't understand, Mr. Thorpe," said his wife. She always called him Mr. Thorpe before the servants. "It's just her family trying to get in the public eye. They are very plain people and not in our class at all, and they're taking this opportunity, just at the most inconvenient time, to try to force themselves into the foreground. That mother has kept up all through the weeks perfectly well. She has seemed pleased enough at the way things were going, and she hasn't broken down. People don't break down all at once like that. If she has kept up so long and been perfectly healthy why should she suddenly start up and faint away? And what's a little faint anyway? I've had more than one myself, but I never let it interfere with my social duties, nor embarrass my family. But she, just the very day those invitations should have gone out, she chooses to collapse and scare the bride out of her wits. I say it's premeditated. She's just trying to force us to recognize her and show how important she is by putting a stop to all the festivities. Imagine daring to do that to Tilford's family, after all we've done for her."

"Why, now, mamma! What have we done for her?" Mr. Thorpe looked over his glasses and regarded his wife leniently.

"Done for her! Do you have to ask? Haven't we taken her up and made much of her, put her right on a pedestal, just as if she belonged in our set, and got her all these invitations among our social equals?"

"Social equals? Why mamma, what kind of an idea have you got of the Mayberrys? Don't you know I looked them up and they really belong to one of the fine old families?"

"Well, that may all be very well, Mr. Thorpe. Old families, yes. But old families without money degenerate. They live on the lower side of town, don't they? They live in an old rackabones of a house that needs painting terribly, and they go to a queer little church without a particle of style to it, and then insist on having the wedding, *our* wedding, in their own church, when I had gone to the trouble of asking our rector if they might have the use of our great beautiful church edifice, with its stately arches, and lovely chancel. It lends itself so gracefully to a formal wedding. I even offered to superintend the decorations myself. But no, they had to have their own ugly little church, and minister. I declare it's too vexing. And then, she insists she is going to wear some little frowsy dress that *her mother has made,* instead of a perfectly exquisite imported one that I suggested. She is certainly being too trying for anything. Do you know, Mr. Thorpe, that those wedding invitations haven't gone out yet? And this is the day they should have been mailed! Of course she is utterly ignorant of all social customs. But Tilford has exerted his utmost influence, and can't make her give them to him. She declares her mother is at the point of death and she can't send them out at present. And here are we all *disgraced* by having the invitations go out a day late."

"What difference does it make when the invitations go out?" asked Mr. Thorpe amusedly.

"There! That's just like you, Mr. Thorpe! As if you didn't know manners and customs, and understand that we'll be the laughing stock of all people who know what is the right thing to do."

· "Well, I think you're all wrong, mamma. I think you ought to let that little girl manage her own affairs, at least until she's married to Tilford."

"Oh, you would, of course," sighed Tilford's mother. "I ought to have known better than to mention it before you. I wish you wouldn't say any more about it. My nerves are simply at the limit. I'm going down there tomorrow morning the first thing and have some words with that hystericky mother, and make her understand that she can't upset all our plans by a little gesture of illness! Tilford if you will come up to my room after you have finished your coffee, I'll be glad to discuss this matter with you and see what we can work out together about those invitations, but I simply can't stand your father's stupid remarks any longer. He knows better but he likes to annoy me. You'll have to excuse me!" and Mrs. Thorpe swept from the room.

Later Tilford went to his mother's boudoir and they continued their discussion.

"Listen, Tilford," said his mother as they settled down to talk, "has that child really got measles, or did it turn out to be scarlet fever?"

"I'm sure I don't remember," said Tilford gloomily. "What difference does it make?"

"Well, one is supposed to be a little more deadly than the other, that's all," said his mother frigidly. "And I've been thinking back. It wasn't real measles you had when you were a child, it was German measles, and it seems to me that I've heard that you can have all three. The other is French, isn't it? I can't remember. But if it's regular measles you'd better stay away from that house. *You* might get them, you know, and it seems to me I've heard it goes very hard with grown people when they get them. It's either measles or mumps. I'm not sure which. But you'd better be on the safe side and stay away. It would be simply dreadful if you should get the measles. It certainly would bring that family into the limelight with a vengeance. It would make you ridiculous, Tilford. People would never forget it that you couldn't get married because you had the measles!"

"For heaven's sake, mother! Haven't I trouble enough now without your bringing up an idea like that! You can't get measles unless you come into contact with the patient, and you can make sure I'll never do that."

"No, but seriously, Tilford, you'll just have to tell Maris that she can come here if she wants to see you, but that we don't approve of your running into danger! You'll simply have to make that girl give up her headstrong notions and let her precious family look out for themselves or *give you up!* I fancy that will bring her to her senses!" The mother finished with a triumphant gleam in her eyes, but

Tilford continued to march gloomily back and forth across the room.

"You don't know Maris," he said bitterly. "It wouldn't faze her in the least. When she gets started on something she has to finish it, no matter what she upsets."

"Well, but I thought you said she was so pliable, so easy to mold, so ready to yield to whatever you wanted. Those are your very words, my son."

"Yes, I know. I thought so. But I've found out it isn't so. She's got to have her own way if the heavens fall!"

"But can't you appeal to her love for you?"

"I don't know whether she has any. I thought she was crazy about me, but now she is simply blind. She's mad to have her own way and sacrifice herself for her poor ailing family."

"But Tilford! She must realize what a different station in life you are giving her. She must understand the enormous value of being your wife, and having everything that money can buy. She cannot look at that gorgeous diamond you gave her without realizing that. You can't tell me she'd give all that up just for sentiment."

"Wouldn't she? What would you say if I told you that she gave me back my ring tonight. Look at there!" and Tilford paused beside his mother and held out the flashing stone in the palm of his hand.

"Tilford!" His mother stared at the ring, hardly able to believe her eyes. "You don't mean you've quarrelled!"

"Call it what you please. There's the ring!" said the young man in a hard tone.

"The little ingrate!" said his mother indignantly. "And after all we've done for her! And just now at the last minute when the eyes of the whole town are upon us, and the wedding almost at the door! It would certainly serve her right if you were to take her at her word and let that end it. You know I always told you that you were in too great haste, especially when she was not in your social set. I told you no good would come of this engagement, and you would find it out after it was too late. But I certainly didn't expect it to end at this stage of the game. Have those invitations gone out yet? Perhaps it's just as well."

"Don't be a fool!" Tilford flung out at her. "You don't suppose I'm going to let her make a laughing stock of me after things have gone this far, do you? No! Certainly not. Rather than that I'll marry her and divorce her! Let her see that I'm her master! No girl can make a fool of me like that!"

"Well, that's true too, of course," sighed the mother. "Well, I suppose we've got to work out some plan. I think I'll appeal to the mother. That's a good line, you know. Tell the mother how she is spoiling her daughter's life and clouding it forever."

"I doubt if they'll let you see her," gloomed the son. "They've got her entirely surrounded by a nurse."

"You leave it to me!" said Mrs. Thorpe capably. "I'll soon quell the nurse. I never saw the nurse I couldn't command. Nor the mother I couldn't reach by some kind of an appeal. I wonder what time of day I'd better go? Doctors usually receive their patients in their offices in the morning, don't they? I'd better go before the doctor gets around. You'd better not appear in this at all. I'll speak as woman to woman, mother to mother, and all that, you know. It's probably the only way Maris can be managed, to get her mother roused up to the situation so that she'll tell her to snap out of this idea that she's got to be a sacrifice to them all. You leave it to me, Tillie dear. I'll bring it all out right. And about those invitations, if we can get them off in the morning I'm sure I can get the postmaster to fix the date on the postmark. That's a little thing to do, and nobody will be the wiser. People will just think their invitations were delayed on the way. Now Tilford, I'll tell you what you do! You run over to your sister's. They're about through with dinner now. You needn't stay long. Just look very serious and say that Maris is so disappointed, but you felt she ought to stay by her mother tonight, but that you're quite sure she will be all right in a day or two. Don't say anything about the measles. That's too grotesque. A bride having to stay away from a dinner especially made for her because her baby sister has the measles. Now, Tilford, cheer up, and take this thing sensibly. Don't give way to the idea that Maris is going to get away with a thing like this, or you'll have it to deal with all your life, and you'd better just take it in hand at the start and get it over with. You must be master of your own house, master of this situation. She's probably just trying to see how much she can get away with. But mother will stand by her boy, and we'll bring things into shape tomorrow all right. Only I do wish you had heeded my warnings and got to know Ethel Framer well. She is so smart, and so correct, and has so much money. You would never have caught her giving back a magnificent ring like that even in a joke."

"There, mother, don't begin on that. I'm fed up on that line. I may have made a mistake in choosing Maris but I don't intend to let anybody know it, and I certainly don't regret Ethel Framer. I had all I wanted of her the winter you tried to stuff her down my throat."

"Well, Tilford, I suppose you'll have to learn your lessons by experience just as we all do."

"Don't tell me *you* ever learned one that way, mother," sneered the spoiled youth. "If you had you wouldn't spend your time trying to force things upon me."

"Now, Tilford! What do you mean? Haven't I just offered to go and appeal to this girl's mother and straighten everything out for you, when you know she wasn't my choice in the first place?" The mother spoke in a high aggrieved tone.

"I wasn't referring to that, mother. I was thinking of that impossible Ethel person that you tried your best to make me marry. And you knew I never could bear a person with that kind of hay-colored hair and light lashes."

Mrs. Thorpe retired behind an expensive handkerchief and wiped a sketchy tear or two.

"Well, I'm sure I don't want to go and invade this impossible person's home and try to teach her her duty to her child," she complained pensively. "If you don't want me to do it, just say so."

"Oh, it won't do any harm to try it," said Tilford loftily. "Personally I don't think you'll get anywhere with it. She's a small woman but she's very much set in her way, and she doesn't like people to tell her what her duty is any better than you do, mother."

"Well, she shall hear it from me for once, anyway, whether she likes it or not," said Tilford's mother firmly. "Now, darling, go to Irma's first, and then why don't you run over to your club for a little while. You are looking awfully haggard and it really isn't good for you to dwell on your disappointments. You trust me! I'll work this thing all out for you. And Tilford, dear, just to be on the safe side, better talk to Maris over the phone instead of going to the house. I wouldn't run any risks at all of getting measles at your age!"

"Nonsense!" said Tilford sharply as he took himself out of his mother's room and shut the door firmly.

"Tilford," called his father, as he passed the library door on his way out, "how about a little game of chess with your old dad? We haven't played in a long time."

"Nothing doing!" drawled Tilford disrespectfully. "I'm going over to the club and play pool! I've got too much on my mind to play chess. Besides, that's an old man's game!" and Tilford went out the front door and gave it a decided slam.

The father sighed and went back to his paper. He did not really want to play chess. But it seemed to him that it was a very long time since Tilford had been a little boy.

7

IT had been a very hard night at the Mayberry house. The mother had had another sinking spell. Not so terrifying as the others, but enough to make them send for the doctor, and look at each other with frightened eyes.

The spell had not lasted so long as the others, and she had responded more quickly to the medicine. But when it was all over and her tired heart was going steadily on again in almost a normal way, Father Mayberry had a shaking chill and had to be put to bed himself, though he protested most earnestly. Merrick had established himself as night nurse to watch over his father, and had come in once or twice when he heard Maris in Lexie's room. His eyes were large and worried, and he seemed to have matured during the night. He proved himself most efficient, administering his father's medicine on the hour, helping Maris to smooth the bedding and lift the little restless patient into a more comfortable position. Maris thought of it gratefully as she lay down again after the child was quieted. And then he came tapping at the door again with a glass of milk for Maris. His thoughtfulness was unprecedented.

"You've gotta keep your strength up, you know. What

would we do if you got sick?" he said earnestly. And Maris was so tired and anxious that she almost wept on his shoulder, though she managed a smile and a thank you.

The doctor came in about five o'clock and went the rounds of the patients. He looked relieved, but said he would run in again during the morning. He gave special directions that the mother was not on any account to be disturbed. Her hope depended upon utmost quiet and freedom from excitement. So far she had not seemed conscious of what was going on about her, but he warned them that she might come out of this state of utter collapse and even ask questions, and that they must maintain the utmost serenity and calm, and smile, and tell her to go to sleep, that all was well.

Then he went away and quiet settled down again. The nurse even caught a few winks of sleep, and hope seemed to have descended upon the house, with a certain degree of peace.

When Maris awoke from the longest nap she had had that night she found the bright sunshine streaming into her window, and the song of thrushes in the tall old tree around the house thrilling in the clear crystal air. A soft breeze was blowing the curtain. Oh, what would this day bring forth? Was the brightness of the morning a good omen?

As she washed her face, brushed her hair, and put on a fresh little cotton dress, she took up one by one the burdens that she knew would confront her, but somehow she couldn't seem to fit them on her back yet. She would have to go slowly. There was Gwyneth and her school to be dealt with the first thing. How good that the little boys were safe for a while at least. Of course they must not presume upon Lane Maitland's kindness, but he had seemed so genuine in his friendship that it was a relief to rely upon him for a few days anyway, till some other haven was offered.

Then she heard Lexie stirring and went to her at once. The problem would be more than ever how to keep noise from mother. Lexie must not be allowed to cry, poor little soul, miserable as she was. She must make her understand that mother had to be considered first. So, with a weary heart she marched into a new day.

Mrs. Thorpe usually took time by the forelock in anything she had to do, especially if it was something she did not anticipate with pleasure. It was a little after half past ten when her car drew up in front of the Mayberry residence, and she got out, pausing to lift her lorgnette to her eyes and take a long critical survey of the house before she walked up to the front door and applied for entrance.

She was smartly attired in a spring morning costume of black and white, designed to impress the family with her importance.

She was annoyed by the faint buzz of the doorbell after her vigorous attack upon it, and followed it up by a smart rapping with her immaculate white-gloved knuckles. But Sally came striding.

"Don't do that!" she whispered. "You'll wake the lady, and she's had a bad night!" She glared at the caller ominously.

"Oh, really? Well, I'll be the judge of what I'll do, and I'm in a hurry. Your bell didn't ring adequately. Where is Miss Mayberry? I want to see her at once."

"Ye can come and set. I'll tell her. She's gettin' her little sister ready for the doctor. She mebbee can't come right aways," said Sally grudgingly.

"Well, you can tell her I have no time to wait. I want to see her at once. Tell her it's Mr. Tilford Thorpe's mother."

"It wouldn't make no difference who it was," said Sally scathingly. "She can't come till she can," and Sally moved heavily away toward the stairs.

Mrs. Thorpe was not good at waiting. The house seemed deathly still to her. Nobody stirred to meet her.

She decided to take matters in her own hands. She arose and glanced about the room appraisingly, then she sailed into the hall and listened a moment. She heard a door open almost noiselessly, but no one was coming toward the stairs. With quick resolve she mounted the stairs, determination in her face. She had come to do something and it was best to get it over with as soon as possible. It was certainly fortunate that nobody was around to stop her. She didn't know the way to the sick room of course, but it would be easy to find. She would beard the lion in his den as it were before any keepers found out what she was going to do.

So with strong step she mounted the stairs, gave a swift glance about, decided on the door that probably opened into the master bedroom, and made for it with long easy steps.

She loomed in the doorway for an instant, a smart, well-upholstered figure, took in every detail with a glance, then marched over and stood at the foot of the bed, looking down on the white-faced woman who lay there with closed eyes, utterly limp.

The nurse had stepped across to the bathroom to fix fresh medicine, and had not seen her come. She was running the water, and had not heard her. No one else was about at the moment.

Mrs. Thorpe cleared her throat and began in a cheerful resonant voice.

"Good morning!" she said briskly. "I've come to have a little heart to heart talk with you, Mrs. Mayberry. I've come to beg you for the sake of your daughter and her future happiness, to rouse yourself and put off this desire to give in. Just rise up and conquer your natural feelings. You must know that every mother of a daughter has to face the matter of losing her some time or other, and it isn't worth while to make her and her bridegroom unhappy and spoil all their plans just for a little sentiment. Of course

I know how you feel. I'm having the same thing to bear, you remember. But I don't give way, and I felt sure if you realized how you are hurting Maris and Tilford you would just shake off this illness and let them go on with their plans. I—"

Suddenly a voice spoke in her ear, low but dominant:

"Stop! Get out of here!" and a large firm hand went over her mouth that was open to go on. It held there so firmly that the woman was almost choked. Then another hand went around her ample waist and gripped her arm in an iron clutch, the firm fingers digging into her flabby flesh painfully. And when she tried to cry out and struggle she only found herself more firmly held and unable to make a sound, as she was ignominiously propelled from the room and the door closed in her face.

She had caught a fleeting vision of great dark green eyes with fear in them, in the white face on the pillow, and a nurse hurrying in with a glass in her hand. Then the door closed and she was outside on the stair landing, suddenly confronting the doctor. And it wasn't any little cheap doctor as she had supposed, either. She recognized him as Doctor MacPherson, a man very high in his profession, and much sought after among her own social set.

She tried to speak but she found herself propelled at a breathless pace down the stairs, held by that vice-like grip, and actually a man's handkerchief stuffed in her mouth as any common gangster might have done. She had to clutch the stair rail with her own free hand lest she would fall headlong, but as soon as she arrived at the foot of the stairs and her feet felt solid floor beneath them, she wrenched the handkerchief angrily out of her mouth and flung it on the floor.

"Really!" she puffed. "What do you think you are doing, Doctor MacPherson?"

"I think I am getting you out of this house as rapidly as I know how!" said the eminent physician sternly. "Did you know what you were doing? Did you know you were talking to a woman at death's door, and you are very likely to have killed her? We've worked all night to keep her alive, and you come here and harangue her like that! Get out of this house as fast as you can, and don't you dare come here again until the family are able to look after themselves."

He opened the screen door and almost flung her—if one could be said to fling anything as substantial as Mrs. Thorpe—from the house.

"I guess you don't know who I am!" blustered Mrs. Thorpe breathlessly, as she drew herself up and tried to look dignified.

"I don't know who you are, and I don't want to know. I know you're a fool and a criminal. That's enough for me!"

"I am Mrs. Henry Watterson Thorpe of Heathcote on the Hill."

"I don't care a copper who you are! Get out quick!"

"You are most insulting! I shall certainly have you arrested!"

"If that woman upstairs dies I shall certainly have you indicted for murder! Now scram!" said the doctor.

Mrs. Thorpe scrammed with as much dignity as she could muster, and got into her car while her chauffeur held open the door for her and pretended not to see how upset she was. When they were started on their way toward home Mrs. Henry Watterson Thorpe of Heathcote on the Hill found that she was weeping. She hadn't been so shaken since she thought once during the depression that Henry had lost all his money. Somehow her ego was shaken. She was going home in disgrace, having failed in her mission. Like a warlord who instead of wearing a wreath of laurel in token of his victory, is brought home wounded lying on his shield.

But back in the old Mayberry house they were giving

little heed to how the intruder was feeling. They were doing all in their power to avert calamity.

They were all there, Maris her eyes wide with horror, and even her lips drained of every particle of color; Merrick just wakened from a bit of a morning nap he had snatched, trying to understand what had happened; even the father in a hastily donned dressing gown, his hand gripping the door frame, his lips trembling as he tottered over to the bed where his wife lay looking wildly from him to the nurse. For even though the doctor had been most miraculously quiet in his treatment of the intruder, the whole household was aroused. Gwyneth came rushing upstairs, with Sally just behind her trying to hush her, and from the farthest end of the back hall, where the playroom door had swung ajar, came Lexie's frightened wail; "Maris, vat's the matter? I vant my muvver!"

It was incredible how soon the doctor got back into the house and upstairs, after having expressed himself to the unwelcome visitor. And with what patience and tenderness he worked! Maris as she watched him turned away feeling that if any human doctor could save her mother he would.

He shut them all out of the room but the nurse and gave his orders in quick low tones.

The mother was still wide-eyed and apparently conscious for the first time of all that was going on about her, suffering acutely, too, for her hand would go to her heart feebly, and she would moan, and cry out sharply.

"There, there, sister! That was just a bad dream you had. Forget it! You're all right. We're going to have you all right in a little while."

The troubled eyes searched his face.

"That woman—?" she faltered.

"She's gone!"

"Why—did—she—come?"

"Oh, she just made a mistake and got the wrong house.

Don't think any more about her. Nurse, bring me those drops."

"Maris—?" the tired lips formed.

"Yes, Maris is right here," said the doctor, and at a sign Maris came in and stood by her mother.

"Show her how you can smile this morning," ordered the doctor as he carefully measured out the drops. "You're happy, aren't you, Maris?"

"Oh, yes, mother, I'm happy. You're—looking—so much—better!" The girl's voice faltered. She was wondering if she were saying the right thing, struggling with the tears that wanted to flow.

"Father—?" the word was so weak it could hardly be heard.

"Oh, he's right here too!" said the doctor breezily. "It's early though, Mrs. Mayberry. He isn't exactly dressed yet, but we don't mind. Now, you drink this and then take a little nap and you'll be all right."

The troubled eyes rested on Mr. Mayberry as he came in from across the hall where he had stood grayly by the door listening. He tried to smile as if there was nothing the matter. He took his wife's hand in his tenderly, and almost the flitting shadow of a smile came to her lips. Then the terror went out of her eyes, and she swallowed the medicine the doctor held and sighed gently like a tired child.

"The—children—?" The words were scarcely audible.

"All here and happy as clams, but you've had enough excitement for one morning. The children will come in later."

The doctor's voice was very low and gentle, but had that quality of authority that his patients always recognized. Mrs. Mayberry had another fleeting ghost of a smile in her eyes as she closed them. Suddenly Maris felt as if her mother was dying, and was trying to bid them all good-bye. Oh, was that it? She turned her head away to hide the quick tears that came. Oh, if mother died it would be herself who had killed her! Her wedding, just as Merrick had said! How could she ever go on living knowing that all her life?

"Now, all of you go away a little while, for mother wants to sleep," said the doctor in that cheerful tone of his that seemed to quell all fears and drive away fantastic shadows as if they were but smoke. "Mother's going to feel much better when she wakes up. Oh, much, *much* better!"

He waved them all out of the room, paused to give a direction to the nurse, then he came out to them where they were herded together, a frightened little group, around their father, Maris with slow tears running down her cheeks of which she was not aware.

"Well," said the doctor coming up to them with his grave tender smile, "that was a bolt out of a clear sky! But I think she has a chance even yet. She reacted better than I could have hoped. Who was that old horned toad, anyway, and how ever did she happen to barge in here?"

He looked from the one to the other of them, and suddenly Maris' white face flushed crimson, and then the color receded and left her whiter than before. It seemed almost as if she were swaying and about to fall.

"Oh, I see," said the doctor, "one of those things! Well, we won't say any more about it. But I certainly would like to get her up a tree and keep her there for awhile. I'd like to tell her a few more things that I didn't have time for at the moment."

The nurse came softly out of the room and caught the last few words. The semblance of a grin adorned her plain features for an instant.

"If you ask me," she said grimly, "I should say you said plenty. The last glimpse I had of the party as I passed the window showed her withering like Jonah's gourd."

"I'm not aware that I asked you, nurse," said the doctor with a twinkle. "Now, nurse, we want to keep that pulse going steadily without a lost beat. See what you can do, and telephone me at the slightest change. We're running no risks. Scatter, folks, and get some rest and some food. Wash your faces and comb your hairs. We aren't conquered yet. We may have to get another nurse for a night or two to relieve Miss Bonner till she takes a nap or two, but aside from that I believe we're going to win."

"You'll get no night nurse for me," said the nurse irately. "I'm good for another couple of nights if need be, and I want no other nurse messing in on my case, not when I've come this far."

"All right with me!" said the doctor with satisfaction. "I'd rather have you exclusively than any other two nurses I know. Now! Where's that little measle girl? How is she getting on?"

Maris led the way, brushing off the tears and trying to get a cheerful face before her little sister saw her. She paused in the hall with her hand on the doorknob.

"Doctor," she breathed softly, "please tell me! If—my mother dies—will you think—it was that woman's coming?"

The doctor looked her straight in the eye.

"Well, of course I wouldn't recommend performances like that as a general rule in treating a patient with a heart condition like your mother's, but, at the same time, I'm relying on your mother's rare sense of humor, Miss Maris. I think that was perhaps the best comedy ever put on in a sick room. It was so well enunciated that I heard every word of it as I was coming up the walk from my car. I didn't miss a thing. I thought at first it was some radio artist and the neighbors were indulging in an early morning broadcast. At the same time, of course you understand that I should leave no stone unturned to prevent a recurrence of the performance. Have you an idea that it is likely to happen again?"

Maris' eyes were darkly blue and inscrutable, and her lips trembled a little as she answered:

"I shall certainly do everything in my power to prevent it. No, I don't think anyone would dare do a thing like that twice. Not after what you said to her. Thank you, Doctor MacPherson."

Then they went into the room to see the little girl who was lying there crying softly into her pillow lest she would disturb her mother. The doctor called her "a brave boy" for being so thoughtful, and made her giggle in the midst of her tears.

She was a very miserable and uncomfortable little girl that morning for the measles were beginning to come out in flocks and she didn't like them. But the doctor was pleased with the way they were doing.

As he went out he looked sympathetically at Maris:

"You're having your hands full," he said, "but I'm not sure but it's just as well. You won't have so much time to worry about your mother. And you know it's going to be quite a time before she gets back to her former self. She'll need great care and rest, but I think she has a wonderful constitution, and there is good reason to hope she will get well. You can keep that in the back of your mind when you get discouraged. Of course I'm not promising anything, but that's what I really hope for. I'll do the best I can, and then it is all in God's hands."

A great relief flooded Maris' soul. She had been so sure that her mother was going, that she scarcely dared believe even now that the doctor still had hope.

"Oh, God!" she said in her heart, "I thank You! I thank You!"

Then she turned to her duties with a little lighter heart.

But when all was said it was not an easy day that was before her. A little girl who was not used to discomfort and pain, and not old enough to be philosophical about it, at least not for long periods at a time, who had to be entertained and kept from crying, both for her own physical good, and also for her mother's. Maris' strength and ability were to be taxed to the utmost. But the problems of yesterday had taken a back seat. The wedding invitations and twin wedding dresses might still be lurking in the shadows of her bedroom this morning, but she had no time to go there herself, and so she need not consider them. How trifling and unimportant any of them seemed in the light of this new day with its anxieties and duties.

Gwyneth came up to the door with a tray that Sally had sent. Orange juice for Lexie and a nice breakfast for Maris who hadn't eaten a mouthful yet since she got up.

Gwyneth's face was long and dreary.

"Sister, what am I going to do about school?" she asked in a desolate whisper, with a fearsome glance toward the far door of her mother's room.

"Oh, yes," said Maris cheerfully. "I've been thinking. You go to the telephone—perhaps you better wait til recess time, or noon, whichever you think is best—and call up your teacher. Or perhaps the principal would be better, whoever has the say about you. Tell her that mother is very sick and that your little sister has the measles. That you have had them and we do not think it likely you will take them again, but that you cannot be spared to go away from home at present as you are needed here to help. Ask if it is possible for you to have your lessons assigned each day, and you to take your examinations with the rest when you are able to return. If she doesn't seem willing call me and I will talk to her."

"But Maris, suppose I didn't understand something. Who would I ask?"

"I'm quite sure I would be able to help you. Or you could telephone to your teacher."

Slowly, reluctantly, the little girl went down to her task. She didn't like the thought of asking, and she would have felt so much more important and on-her-own to have stayed with Erminie. There was a lot more freedom of one kind and another at Erminie's house than either Gwyneth's mother or Erminie's knew about.

But a half hour later Gwyneth came back to Maris' door and announced happily that it was all fixed. The principal was to send her advance lessons each week, and she was to do her homework, and then when she went back there would be tests and all would be explained if she hadn't understood something. She seemed quite interested in apportioning her time for study, and keeping up with her classmates. It was a kind of game, and she was satisfied. After all there were only two more weeks to go.

Maris was downstairs later in the morning hunting a certain pair of scissors she needed for cutting out endless strings of paper dollies who could dance about upon Lexie's bed and be blown away with a breath to make a laugh for the restless little invalid. The telephone rang.

Maris started and looked troubled. This would likely be Tilford. There would be more discussion, and what could she say more than she had already said? Reluctantly she went to answer it. Would his mother have talked with him yet? If she had he would be very angry of course. It hadn't occurred to her before that *they* would be aggrieved at what the doctor had said, but of course they would.

But strangely the whole thing did not seem her burden any more. She was in a hard trying place, and it might be days before she got out of it, but God was going to lead her out some day, and she did not have to depend upon herself to get out. She had asked God to help and she believed He was going to do it. Anyway she hadn't any strength or wisdom of her own for this complicated situation. It was in the strength of this trust that she went to the telephone.

And then it wasn't Tilford at all. It was Lane Maitland. She almost laughed aloud with relief as she recognized his voice.

"This is Broadcasting Station Number Two," he said

solemnly, "reporting on Maitland Detention Camp. Twelve o'clock, noon, daylight saving time. The entire force of cadets slept well through the night, save for an hour when they were called out to engage in combat with a bat who had stolen into the barracks. Nevertheless, they arose on time, made their beds, took a swim in the creek, ate a hearty breakfast, had devotions, went through setting up exercises. Then an hour of study personally conducted by the scout master, played two sets of tennis, and now are about to indulge in a noonday repast. They will then put up a lunch and start on a hike to Conner's woods where they will hunt for wild flowers and lichens for tomorrow's natural science study, eat their lunch and return to camp about sundown. Communication may be had with them by telephoning to Conner's, Severn—1188, who will at once advise the scout master. In case cadets may be needed, they will return by bus which passes Conner's every fifteen minutes. If these arrangements are not agreeable, kindly advise at once. Lane Maitland speaking."

Maris gave a pleasant little giggle, and the heavy burden she had anticipated rolled away out of sight for the moment. It was like stooping to pick up a great iron weight and finding it only a bundle of feathers.

"Delightful!" she said. "Won't that be grand for the boys! I know they will love it. I approve most heartily. I only hope you won't be worn out. I don't see how I can ever thank you for what you are doing."

There came a tremble in her voice, and an answering sympathy in his as he replied:

"I'm having the time of my life, myself. But how about you? Did you have a hard night?"

"A busy one. Not so hard perhaps as it might have been. We were all up most of the night. Dad wasn't so well, and Lexie was restless, but we're all very thankful it was no worse. Mother seems to be resting all right just now."

Her voice trailed off sadly, and the listener thought he discerned anxiety returning to it.

"You are sure it's all right to take the boys away even as far as Conner's? I can keep them happy here at home if you prefer."

"No, I think it's all right. The doctor seems to think mother has a good chance, though of course he doesn't promise anything."

There was a catch in her voice, and the young man was quick to understand.

"Yes, I know," he said gently. "We've been praying, the boys and I," he added half shyly. "That helps!"

"Oh, thank you!" said Maris fervently. "That does help."

"Well, I won't keep you longer now. I'll report again this evening."

Maris turned from the telephone strangely comforted. What was there about that simple little conversation that had taken the tiredness away from her heart?

What a blessing that Lane Maitland had come home just at this time.

And then it suddenly came to her mind to wish vaguely that Tilford were something like Lane Maitland.

How Tilford would have loved that!

8

AS the day wore on toward sunset Maris had need of all the comfort there was to be had. It was not that any fresh calamity occurred, it was just that it was not easy to go on making endless strings of paper dollies, reading stories with eyes that were heavy for sleep, and a voice that lagged from very weariness. To be patient hour after hour with the poor petulant baby who couldn't understand why she felt so hot and miserable, who wanted things until they came and then snarled at them.

By this time, too, old friends and neighbors were getting to know that Mrs. Mayberry was very ill, and they kept coming to the door and asking for Maris, or calling up on the telephone and demanding to speak to her. Even the sign of quarantine on the door did not deter them. And every time she was called to the telephone or the front door she went with a tremor lest it would be some of the Thorpes. And yet she would not let herself think about that possibility. She could not prepare to deal with them, because it would surely be the unexpected with which she would have to deal. So she fell into the habit unconsciously of letting her heart cry out for help to God, as she went downstairs.

But the day wore on and still there was no word from the Thorpes, and now as she went to lie down and rest a little during an interval after supper, it began to seem ominous, this silence. What did it mean?

True, she had given Tilford back his ring and left him. But she could not think that he would take a repulse like that without an argument, or some kind of retaliation. A word was never final to him unless he were the one to speak it.

It suddenly came to her as she lay thinking this over, that she was falling more and more into the attitude of criticizing Tilford, comparing him with others, fearing his decisions. What was the matter with her? Didn't she love him the way a girl should love the man she was to marry?

It wasn't thinkable that Tilford was letting another day go by without making some move about those wedding invitations, either. And now it was definite in her mind that there was nothing she could do about them for the present. Her mother's condition all day had been unchanged. So far as she herself could judge her mother seemed to be sinking hour by hour. Each time she went to the room and cast a glance toward the bed, her mother's frail sweet face looked more delicate and ethereal, as if a great change was coming over her. And yet the doctor and the nurse did not seem to be particularly troubled. But to her inexperienced eyes there seemed no hope at all that she would rally. Obviously, under such conditions one could not send out wedding invitations.

And if mother should die?

Oh, she couldn't go into that thought, not so long as there was a breath of hope. But if mother should die what heart could she or anyone have for weddings?

And if mother didn't die, was the prospect of a wedding any more likely?

Even if she got well it would be a long time before she would be able to take up life again and look after her family!

The darkness had settled down about Maris and she had not turned on her light. Lexie was asleep, and there was no need to disturb her with a light. Besides it was pleasanter here on the bed looking out into the soft night. She could even see a few stars twinkling between the tree branches, and there was a soft radiance in the east where sometime soon the moon was about to rise. There was a soft little stir of a breeze that rustled the leaves of the big beech tree outside her window. She was so tired, that she longed to drift off and forget all her perplexities, yet her thoughts would not let go while those troublous questions were in her mind.

Suddenly she heard voices, just the other side of the hedge in the Maitland place, under the hemlock trees. It was Merrick and Lane. They had come to the old rustic seats to talk, in order not to disturb the boys, very likely. It was Merrick who was speaking. By the sound Maris judged he had stretched his length on the rickety old seat, and Lane was hanging up the hammock between the trees. She could hear the grating of the rings as they slipped into the hooks. The old hammock they used all to use so freely, the old hooks! Wouldn't they be rusty and unsafe?

But when Merrick spoke it seemed as if there must have been some thought-transference between him and herself, for he was voicing some of the very questions that had been in her mind.

"Well, I'm sure I don't know what's coming to us all," Merrick was saying in gloomy voice. "Even if mother gets well, it'll be a long time. The doctor owned that to me. A long time before she's able to be about among us again, looking after everything, you know."

Lane's voice was quiet but had a clear ring to it as he said:

"Well, you know that nothing can come to you except with God's permission."

"You think that?" Merrick's voice was almost bitter as he asked the question.

"I know that."

"Doesn't look that way to me," said the younger fellow. "Looks more like some of them came from the devil."

"Well, the devil may have had something to do with them, but for some good wise reason of His own God permits them."

"I can't see that," said Merrick, and Maris, listening, could almost see the narrowing of Merrick's eyes and the wry twist of his lips. "I'm beginning to think God doesn't have anything to do with things. Look at marriage now. They say that marriages were made in Heaven. But most of 'em are a mess! I hope I never fall in love. If I do I'll go and drown myself or something. Marriage makes a lot of trouble for everybody."

"Look here now, brother! I object to a man that has as wonderful a father and mother as you have saying a thing like that!"

"Oh, yes, dad and mother, of course that's different. There aren't many like them. Why I believe if anything was to happen to mother, dad would just wilt away and die himself, he's so bound up in her."

"Well, I had a mother and father like that too, so I'm not listening to any tirades like that on marriage."

"Oh, well, I mean modern marriage. Of course, people used to be all right when dad and mother were young. But you take today. Take my sister. Here she's all wrapped up in that poor fish she's going to marry, and what's going to become of us when she's gone? Mother down sick for at least a year, dad hardly able to hold up his head till mother gets well, and there'll be only me to bring up the family. Nice hand I'll make bringing 'em up. I might make a stab at looking after the boys, but what am I going to do with

Gwyneth and Lexie? Where do you think I found Gwyn last night, after we'd sent her over to Howard's to stay all night and study? Down at the drugstore eating ice cream with Rance Mosher, the little rat! Maybe you don't know what he is, but I do, plenty!"

Merrick lowered his voice and talked earnestly. Maris couldn't hear what he said, but she knew he was telling Lane about something dreadful Rance had done, for Lane's low earnest tones showed that he fully agreed with Merrick in his judgment that Rance was no fit companion for Gwyneth.

"But look here, Merrick," said Lane, and now his voice was louder again so that she distinctly heard the words, "you don't need to worry about that. There'll be some way provided to take care of the family if such a situation arises. Maris and her husband would probably arrange to come and live with you, and she would take charge."

"Not she! She wouldn't be allowed to! You don't know Tilford. He's the most selfish brute that ever walked the earth!"

"Oh, but surely in circumstances like that! No decent man could refuse."

"Couldn't he? Well, maybe he isn't decent then. But even if he would we wouldn't want him. He thinks we're the scum of the earth and he's the top layer in paradise. Gosh! I couldn't ask any worse fate than to have to have him come and stay in the house awhile. He makes me so mad the way he bosses my sister around and makes her like it, that I can't see straight. It's partly what's killing mother, too. Maybe it's even that altogether. That and the fact that she's pretty sure that when Maris is married to him that's the end of her so far as we're concerned. And Gosh, mother's all bound up in Maris! That's what I mean. If God lets that thing happen to us all I can't see that He can care for any of us!"

"Well, even at that, God might have some great good wrapped up in it for you," said Lane Maitland's slow earnest voice, thoughtfully.

"I can't see it!"

"It might be there, even if you couldn't see it."

"Well, have it your own way, parson, but I tell you it's a pretty tough thing to swallow, having Maris marry that pill. He's all kinds of rich of course, and is taking her around the world or something like that for a honeymoon, but she might as well be going to Heaven as far as we are concerned, and I don't hope to ever see much of her again. Of course she doesn't see it. She thinks he's all right. But I'd rather see her marry a day laborer that was a good honest man than this poor fish, even though he did give her a diamond as big as a hen's egg."

It was all very still for a minute and then Maris heard Lane say slowly:

"She's a wonderful girl! It seems as though she ought to rate a man who was exceptionally fine!"

"Yes, that's what I'm saying," broke in Merrick. "She's a wonderful sister! She's always been wonderful, and fine and unselfish, and when I think of her tied to that bird, and having to put up with him all her life, and run around and pretend she likes it, it makes me see red! I don't see why God lets it happen. That's why I say marriage is a mess and I hope I never fall in love."

"Say, you know marriage wasn't meant to be a mess, and God planned the first marriage to be helpful to both the man and the woman. It wasn't till the man and woman tried to be independent of God that sin came into the world, and happiness was spoiled. It's somebody's fault when marriages go wrong."

"Oh, is it! And whose fault would it be?"

"Well, people ought to be careful who they pick to fall in love with in the first place. You don't *have* to fall in love with everybody you admire. You have to watch yourself.

You have to choose the right one. You have to get the one God planned for you."

"Oh, *yeah?* And how would you know who that was? Now I know a girl I like real well, but how do I know but she'd turn out to be some poor lily like all the ones that run down to Reno today to get disengaged? How you going to tell, I say?"

"Well, I don't know just whether my rule would apply to you or not, but in the first place, if I found I was getting really interested in a girl I'd find out whether she was a real sincere Christian or not. If she wasn't, and wouldn't take Christ as her Saviour and Lord, I'd quit right then and there. That would be my first step in deciding."

There was a sudden prolonged silence out under the trees. Merrick had been listening to a new idea. At last he said embarrassedly:

"Well, that's a new one on me. I'm afraid if I found a girl was all that I'd know I wouldn't qualify with her."

"Yes? Well, that would be something to think about, too," said Lane quietly. "In a true marriage both parties would have to qualify, wouldn't they? It's only as two people are dominated by the same Spirit, and are surrendered to the same Lord, that they can live together in harmony, isn't it?"

"I guess you're getting rather too deep for me, but you may be right," mused Merrick. "My sister is as good a Christian as there is, at least she was till she took to going around with this worldly guy, but I don't believe she's ever tried your system for I'm sure her precious Tilford is no Christian! She does a lot of things now that she didn't used to do, things she wasn't brought up to do. Oh, not bad things, you know, just worldly. She didn't used to think they were in her line. I don't believe she knows how she's changed."

"Yes, I feel sure your sister accepted Christ as her Saviour some years ago," said Lane almost reverently. "I remember when we were kids she told me about it. Her testimony was one of the things that made me want to know the Lord myself."

"I remember," said Merrick thoughtfully. "There was a Bible class started about that time, too. I went once or twice myself. It was real interesting. But the teacher got married and moved away. That's what I say, marrying is a mess. It's always breaking up things. I'm never going to fall in love."

"Well, at least wait till you find the right girl," said Lane, amusedly. "You know, really, Merrick, you're young yet! So am I for the matter of that, and we don't need to get so excited about it. For after all, the world has been going on this way for some time, marrying and giving in marriage, and where would we be if our parents had never married?"

"That's different," growled Merrick illogically.

"Just how?"

"Well, it's different from Maris marrying that poor fish, I tell you. I guess you never met him, did you? He's just too good-looking for any use, and he knows it, too."

"No, I never met him, but I sincerely hope your sister will be happy!" Lane's tone was suddenly very grave and sweet, and there was a tenderness in it that thrilled Maris and soothed her tired soul. There at least was one person who wasn't criticising her!

But Maris, as she lay there thinking for some time after the boys had said good night and gone away, felt as if somehow their conversation had thrown open a door which hitherto had been closed and locked. A number of things were disclosed to her startled view that she had never dreamed before.

There for instance was her family! She had not known that they felt unhappy about her marriage. Did they really, or was that just a figment of Merrick's imagination? Merrick, jealous that his sister should be going away with any-body else?

New insight seemed to come to her as she stared at the dark wall ahead of her and began to remember little things that had been said, little actions, withdrawings, that she had not noticed at the time, but that now stood out sharply. Her father, sighing heavily without explanation, only a sad smile when she questioned him. Her mother wiping away a tear and pretending it was only perspiration. Little things that in her hurry had passed without her taking much account of them. If she had stopped to consider she might have only laid them down to the natural premonition of the coming separation while she was on her wedding trip. But now she saw that it had been more than that. A stolid indifference on the part of her father and the children to anything that was said about Tilford. Mother always asked after him, and spoke brightly of him, but especially of late her father had been silent where he was concerned. Had they all taken a dislike to him? Did the rest feel as Merrick did? Of course she had known for some time that Merrick and Tilford did not hit it off very well, but she had laid it to the fact that Tilford was a little older. She had reasoned that when they were really related and got to know one another better, all that would pass away and they would all be fond of him and enjoy the good things of life together.

Now she suddenly saw what a fool she had been to imagine any such thing. And then once more came that shocking question, as it had the morning before when she awoke, was she *sure* that she was altogether satisfied with her choice of a life companion?

And was Tilford satisfied with her?

He had made it quite apparent that he was, until just recently, and perhaps his entire taking over of her affairs and ordering them had flattered her so that she did not see everything clearly. For certainly he had not been very comfortable to get along with the last day and a half. She had never imagined he could be as disagreeable as he had proved himself to be ever since her mother was taken sick. And that was just the time when one would have expected sympathy and devotion more than any other. It was the time when she had needed someone to lean upon. Her mother too ill to know what was going on, her father incapacitated by his love and anxiety, and Tilford only concerned about wedding invitations!

But towering head and shoulders above that thought there was another consideration, that made even the choice of a life companion take second place, and that was the dire straits of her beloved family, and their immediate need of herself.

It suddenly became very plain to her that the machinery of her pleasant days had been stopped short and utterly changed, and that she could not possibly go on with what she had planned. For even if her mother should rally soon and get back to a semblance of her former self, they could not get along without her. She was needed right here. Mother would not be fit for a long time to take over the reins of the household, and there was just nobody else in the world to do it. It was obviously her job.

Perhaps she hadn't recognized it before she heard Lane Maitland's clear-cut statement of what he seemed so sure she would do. Perhaps she hadn't even thought ahead so far. Her heart had just stood still and gasped at the great calamity that had come to pass. The future was nothing in her mind until she should know whether mother would live and be with them again, or would go away forever from this life. That was the one and only question in her mind. All the other matters, caring for the little sick sister, decisions about Gwyneth, ordering the household matters, and placating her angry lover, she had performed as in a dream, by a sort of automatic action of her brain. Her heart had been in attendance upon her mother, her dear, dear mother.

But now it was clear to her that even if mother got well sooner than she could possibly hope, that she would not feel free to get married and go away to the other side of the world seeking pleasure. Her place was here, at least for the present. And somehow she had to make that plain to her irate bridegroom.

Instinctively she knew it was going to be a battle, and while the contemplation of it wearied her inexpressibly, yet she was surprised to find that it was not the blasting disappointment that it might have been a few weeks before. The trip to Europe had lost its glamour in the light of immediate events. Being a grand lady in a new apartment of her own, furnished in the taste of her new mother-in-law, no longer loomed large on her horizon. All those things had faded and become unreal before the glaring light of real trouble. And somehow she was too tired to think what she ought to do about it. Had God sent all this distress down upon her to give her pause to think what she had been about to do?

Just what she would have thought if she could have known that Mrs. Thorpe, when she found out that the wedding dress had been rejected, had sent down her check to the Archer Shop and ordered the dress sent up to herself, it is hard to speculate. Fortunately she was spared that knowledge.

But Maris did not have a night of ease. Her rest was broken by a wailing voice:

"Sister I vant a dwink of vater!" and from that time on the night was disturbed. Lexie was restless and uncomfortable, and cried for this and that. Once at almost two o'clock the doctor came slipping in quietly, and Maris stole out to watch and listen at her mother's door, her hungry eyes searching his face as he went away, but his only answer to her unspoken appeal was a kindly smile.

As she stole back to Lexie again, Maris felt as if her heart would burst with the very uncertainty of it all.

For three days the strain went on, the doctor coming and going frequently, but saying little. And during those three days Lexie also was very sick indeed. Maris had little time to consider herself, nor even to realize that Tilford had not been near her in all that time, nor sent her any word. And when at last it did come to her mind, it was only with a sigh of relief that she had not had that to deal with also.

But the third night, during a respite, when Lexie seemed to be definitely better, and was sleeping quietly, and their mother was at least still with them, it did occur to her that perhaps Tilford had called and Sally had said she was busy. That would be like Sally. Sally was not given to graciousness. And after all, Tilford had his rights.

Or did he? Had he perhaps taken his ring with all it stood for and was counting himself free? Well, if he was like that she couldn't help it, and it was better to find it out now rather than when she was married to him. But she was too tired to think about it and dropped into a deep sleep.

The doctor came earlier than usual the next morning. He put them all out and stayed in their mother's room a long time. When he came out he called them into the living room and his manner was graver than usual.

"I want to tell you all the whole situation," he said looking straight into the anxious eyes of Mr. Mayberry. "I haven't told you much before because I wanted to be entirely sure and I didn't want to give you hope if there wasn't any. But I'm telling you now, Mrs. Mayberry has a clot of blood in one of the valves of the heart. It is a very serious condition, and one which may take her away in a moment's time. But at the same time if she can be kept alive, and kept absolutely still, I mean *still,* without moving hand or foot, for six weeks, it is possible that the condition may clear up and she may get well. I must tell you frankly that there isn't much hope for that, but there is a little hope, and you as a family can do a great deal to help this hope become a reality."

There was a tenseness in the room during this quiet speech that was fairly electric. Gwyneth in a frightened huddle by the piano gave a little gasp and put down her young head on her folded arms on the closed lid, but no one else stirred. Maris could not have got whiter than she already was, but her eyes seemed to grow wider and darker as she faced the doctor, and Merrick stood with folded arms just inside the door, his young face stern with purpose.

It was the father who lifted his bowed head with a sudden light in his eyes and spoke in a husky voice, but vibrant with a new hope:

"I need not tell you, Doctor," he said, "that we will everyone do all that is in our power to keep our dear one with us!"

Even in this darkest trouble there was something about their father's voice that the children would never forget. Gwyneth lifted her pretty little sorrowful face streaming with tears and looked at him, sighing as it were her own small name to his promise. Merrick murmured hoarsely:

"We sure will!" and turned away toward the window to hide his emotion. And Maris, wide-eyed, white-lipped, recognized that God had accepted her sacrifice and was putting her to the test, but her voice was clear and resolute as she said:

"Of course," without any reservations.

"Well, now, of course I knew you would feel that way, and I'm glad to have been able to give you even an atom of hope. But you'll have to know all that this entails. It will mean, first of all, a quiet house. It will probably mean another nurse so that the one you already have shall not give out before we are done, for Mrs. Mayberry must be watched every minute and run no risks of any interruption to her literally immovable condition. It is a state of things that could better be carried out to the letter in a hospital, but I do not dare risk transferring her to a hospital in her present state, therefore we'll have to bend conditions to meet the necessity, and make a hospital out of this house, and to that end *everything* else must have second place. She must have nothing to frighten or startle her, nothing *whatever* to worry her."

The eyes of the family assented to all he said and pledged their all to carry out his instructions.

"If, at the end of six weeks, I find Mrs. Mayberry's condition such as I hope, then as soon as she is able to be moved she should be taken to a quiet restful place that I have in mind where I am hoping she will in a few months regain her normal health."

He gave them a swift anxious glance and then went on:

"Now I realize that even with the slight hope I have been able to give you, these conditions will be hard for you all to bear, and will very much upset your life as a family, yet I am relying on you all. With your help much can be done!"

He finished with a grave sweet smile that endeared him to them all as they realized that he had at least taken away their utter hopelessness and given them a chance to do something for the beloved mother.

Then came the father's voice:

"Nothing will be too hard for us to bear if we may have our dear one back among us again!" and Maris and Merrick looked at the sudden new light that was growing in their father's eyes. Yes, their father was wonderful. They left the room with a kind of triumphal awe in their hearts that they had such a father and mother.

Half an hour later Tilford's car drew up in front of the house and Maris, looking out of the window just in time to see him coming up the walk, realized that her time of testing had arrived.

9

MERRICK had lingered in the hall until his father came out with the doctor, lingered as they stood at the door talking for a minute, and then, as the doctor left, he put his hand on his father's arm and spoke earnestly:

"Dad," he said, "You can count on me for every ounce that's in me. I got a job last night driving a bus on the Pike. I begin as soon as exams are over. The pay isn't great, but every cent of it's yours, and at least it'll help out for the extra nurse, and maybe a little over for what I eat. And when I get something better I'll lift all the burden I can from you!"

The father looked up and could not conquer the feeling in his voice:

"Son!" he said. "*Dear* son! Thank God for such a son!" and then he went upstairs wiping his eyes.

Merrick, his heart full of love and anxiety for the father who had seemed so stricken, and was struggling so bravely to have courage to go on, looked after him until he heard him go into the mother's room and softly close the door, and then Merrick went out the door and through the hedge to the Maitland house to tell his new friend what the doctor had said.

He found Lane out in the back yard superintending a painting job. He traced him by the sound of eager young voices, punctuated now and then by an older voice of instruction.

Lane gave one glance at Merrick's face and knew he had news.

"I've engaged some painters," he explained with a wink at the brother. "I'm glad you sent over those overalls. They just came in handy. This house has needed painting for some time, so the boys are going to try their hand at doing the back kitchen for a start. We have a good strong ladder, and it isn't far to the roof, even if they do take a drop now and then."

He grinned at Merrick.

"But they don't know how to paint," said Merrick. "They'll make a mess of it!"

The two little boys cast anxious eyes at their brother. Was he going to spoil everything for them now, just when they were having the time of their life? They looked fearsomely toward their host. But he only smiled and shook his head.

"You're mistaken," he said. "They are doing admirably. I gave them a lesson on painting just now. Not that I know so much myself about it, you know, but they are following my instructions to the letter. Let's you and I go over there under the trees and sit down a bit and talk. That's right, boys, long smooth strokes and not too much paint on the brush."

"Say, you're some friend!" said Merrick in admiration. "I don't think we're ever going to be able to thank you for what you're doing for these kids."

"Don't try," said Lane dryly. "I'm just having a chance to get a little back for what your mother did for me when I had typhoid fever. And incidentally these fellows are helping me through a very hard time. You know it hasn't been an easy thing for me to come back all alone to this house where I was so happy. I knew things here had to be looked after or they would go to wrack and ruin. So I came on to put the house in shape to sell. Then I was going to get away as quickly as I could. But these fellows have just helped me over the hard part and made me feel I love the old place almost too much to leave it. Here, get into that hammock, boy! You look as if you hadn't had a wink of sleep all night. Now, get on with your story. The boys won't hear, they're too intent on seeing how much paint they can slap on a single board. How are things over at the house? Any worse?"

"No! No worse than they have been, I guess, only the doc decided to tell us what was going on, that's all."

He told briefly what the doctor had said.

"Well, say, that's good, old fellow! I know it's serious, but it's good, too, to know there is *some* hope. I've been afraid all along there wasn't. But I knew a man who had that same trouble and he got over it. He was one of the professors at our college. Everybody thought he was going to die of course, but he came through in fine shape. But he had to lie absolutely still for several weeks. Now, what can we plan that will help things? Why couldn't you all come over here and live till the stress is over? There's plenty of room for everybody, and I could get out if that would make things any easier. Or couldn't you all be spared?"

"Say, you're great! But I don't think anybody could be spared just at present. Lexie's still in bed, and Gwynnie has to be watched over. She's like a ship without a rudder, that kid, without mother. But it's great of you to think about it. It's been enough for you to keep those noisy boys. I don't know what we would have done with them over there! They can't keep still a second. Oh, we'll have to talk it over. I don't just know what's coming. The doctor wants mother to go away when she's able, if she gets well enough, and then I don't know what'll become of everybody."

"What about that wedding? Will Maris really be going away?"

"Oh, I suppose so! I haven't asked. I don't know as she's even thought of it yet. But she'll have plenty of thinks coming pretty soon, I reckon. I thought I saw Tilford's car coming down the street as I started over here. He's the limit. It's lucky he's too refined to talk loud or we might have another catastrophe. If mother should happen to hear him talk she might not want to live."

"Well, look here, Merrick. You quit worrying! There'll be a way. Even if Maris goes off to Europe next week, or is it the week after?—we'll plan a way. You'll have to consider me a real brother and let me in on this thing. Maybe we can work something out. Anyway it isn't necessary to cross all the bridges on the highway before we come to them. We may find a detour or two and eliminate some of them. But you know I've got another house down in Virginia. Inherited it from an old aunt who just died, and that can come into the picture too, if it's necessary. There's a sweet old Scotch lady staying in it now. My aunt left provision in her will for her, and I just asked her to stay on for awhile. She used to be my aunt's companion, just an old friend of hers, but a real gentlewoman. We might work her in somehow if we need a woman to look out for the girls. Anyhow, don't you worry!"

"Thanks awfully, Lane! You're great! But whenever I think of the necessity I'm so mad I can't see. Any other decent man would be willing to put off his wedding awhile, or at least suggest they—well—we wouldn't *want* him to come here and live with us—that would be the limit. But he won't let Maris off, I know. I've overheard some of the things he's said to her, and he's impossible!"

Lane Maitland drew his brows down and set his lips

firmly for a minute as he stared at Merrick thoughtfully.

"Of course Maris ought to be strong enough to resist him," went on Merrick in a discouraged voice, "but I suppose that's a good deal to expect of a girl when her wedding invitations are all out and her man isn't willing."

"Are they out yet? I wondered."

"Why, I s'pose they're out. I haven't asked. I know they were all addressed, and I heard him roaring up the stairs at her about them. Everything has to toe the mark to live with him, but I s'pose she'll knuckle down and do just what he wants and then everything'll be lovely. My sister really has a nice disposition. That is, she did before that bird came around and spoiled everything."

Meantime Tilford Thorpe had arrived, and Maris answered Sally's tap on the door, lingered an instant to brush her disordered hair, and then with sudden impulse knelt beside her bed.

"Oh, Lord," she prayed earnestly, "help me, please. Show me just what to say. Show me definitely about this whole matter."

Then with a calmer heart than she had had since her mother had been taken sick she went quietly down the stairs.

It was like Tilford to act as if nothing had happened. To start right in on the thing in hand and ignore what had passed till he got ready to bring it up again and utterly demolish it.

He was standing out on the doorstep impatiently looking down the street, as if he had no part nor lot in this house and couldn't bear even to come into it. As if he resented that it had any right in Maris.

He turned, hat in hand, as she arrived in the hall like a shadow of her former self, so white and tired-looking, yet somehow more assured and at her ease.

"Good morning, Maris," he said formally. "Suppose you come outside in the sunshine. It isn't worth while for me to run any risks of contagion so near the wedding time now. Mother seems to think I may not have had measles. I just ran down to ask if you had mailed those invitations yet. Because it really is necessary to do so at once. I cannot allow this foolishness to go on any longer. As it is we shall have to do a lot of explaining. If you will get them for me at once before there can be any further interruption, then my mind will be at ease and we can talk about several other important things that must be settled this morning. Bring the list, too, and I will take them right to my secretary down at the office and that will be off my mind—that is, if you haven't sent them. Have you?"

Maris looked at his cold handsome face and wondered how she had ever thought him lovable. He suddenly seemed so hard and self-centered. Why hadn't she felt this before? Why hadn't she known he would be like this in a time of stress? He hadn't even asked after the sick ones. Just plunged right into the one thing that he was so determined about. But perhaps it was as well. She could more easily say what she had to say if he was this way than if he had been gentle and kind. She studied him for a second before she answered, trying to imagine what it would be like if he should ask her pardon for the way he had talked to her the last time he came; trying to think how it would be if he should draw her into his arms and kiss her tenderly and say how sorry he was that she looked tired, and he wished there was some way he could help her.

But the imagining did not get very far with a screen door between them, and Maris somehow felt a repugnance toward going out on the front porch to talk. Tilford was holding the door open for her now however, and rather than make a scene she came out.

"Have you sent them?" he reiterated as she stepped out into the sunshine. He could not help but see the ravages of anxiety and loss of sleep now. "Heavens!" he added as he glanced at her. "What a sight you are! You had no right to do this so near to the wedding! You will look so old and worn I shall be ashamed of you. When did you send the invitations, Maris?"

"The invitations have not gone," said Maris quietly. "I did not send them because I am not going to be married on the thirtieth of June. There would be no point in sending invitations if there was to be no wedding."

"What do you mean, Maris? You can't possibly change the date! I have all my arrangements made, and have gone to a great deal of trouble to get those particular reservations. You can't do that to me."

"I'm sorry," said Maris calmly. "I did not plan this. I could not help it."

"Oh, really! Who did plan it? Your family? And just what date are they arranging for the wedding then? I should have supposed since they are so careful about expense they would have remembered that it would cost a lot more to get the invitations engraved all over again. But perhaps they are figuring to get the town crier to go out and publish the banns or something of that sort."

Tilford was very angry. There was a bright red spot on each cheek. His handsome eyes had sparks of wrath in them. He was forgetting himself and being unforgivably and quite plebeianly rude. He seldom allowed himself to overstep a formal address at least, no matter how angry he was.

Maris' face was desperately white, and her chin was lifted just the least bit.

"My family had nothing whatever to do with it," she said steadily. "They do not even know about it. They have not had time to think about weddings. We have been living in the midst of desperate sorrow here, Tilford. You do not seem to understand."

"Oh, pardon me! Did your mother die, Maris? Was it as bad as that? I should have supposed you would let me know if that happened. But I don't see why that should delay the wedding. I am sorry for you of course, but your mother is better off, and she wouldn't want you to change your plans. People don't stop for such things nowadays, you know, and since we are going abroad everybody will understand why we went ahead. Besides, if the funeral is soon, there will be really quite a decent interval between. Since it had to happen, I'm glad it happened now instead of next week. People will understand why we were late in sending invitations."

Maris looked at him aghast. Had he been drinking? He did drink sometimes at parties and big dinners, but not usually at other times. Not in the morning.

She was so still that he stopped talking and looked at her puzzled. There were tears in her eyes but she had that aloof look to which he was not accustomed in her.

"What's the matter? Why are you looking at me that way? I'm only being perfectly sensible. It's all out of date to be sentimental about the inevitable."

"Stop!" said Maris suddenly. "My mother is not dead!"

"Oh!" He looked at her as if she were somehow to blame. "Really, Maris, I don't see why you tried to give me that impression then. What is it you're trying to do? Just have an argument? Because I haven't time. Won't you get those invitations for me at once, and let us have done with this foolish argument!"

"Listen, Tilford," she said, trying to control her voice and speak quietly, although the thing she wanted to do most of all was to scream and burst into tears and run away from him. "Listen! I'm not going to get those invitations now or any other time because there can't be any wedding on June thirtieth! My mother is very sick. Far worse than we dreamed. She has a clot of blood in the heart, and while the doctor says there is a possibility that she may get well, it is just as possible that she may die at any minute. Under those circumstances you certainly know that I could not think of leaving home. Even if my mother should get well it would be at least a year before she would be able to take up her life again and look after her home and her children."

"A year!" said Tilford coldly. "Are you expecting me to put off my marriage for a year?"

"No," said Maris haughtily. "I did not suppose that you had anything to say about it. In fact I supposed that since I gave you back your ring you understood that that ended all between us. You made no protest and you did not come back to talk it over. But since you have insisted on having the invitations I am only making it plain to you that I cannot marry you. At least not for a very long time. And I'm not sure, since all this has happened, that I would want to, even then. I am just telling you that everything is over between us."

He looked at her with vexation and a kind of wonder in his eyes.

"Look here, Maris, of course I'm not going to allow you to carry out this ridiculous idea. In fact I'm sure you didn't expect me to. You think that you will gain a little time, and get me to coax you up and pet you and all that. I didn't come back with your ring because I thought you were in no mood to take care of it just then and I had better keep it until you came out of that silly mood. Just heroics, that's all it was when you thrust that ring into my hand. Of course I knew you were all worn out with the demands of your ridiculous family. But I knew if I gave in to you then you would only think you could go farther. I thought it would do you good just to go without your ring for a few days and see how it feels to have a ring like that and then have it gone. But you needn't think you can keep this up. I shall exercise my authority and demand that you come away from this house and take a good rest, and then we'll go on with the wedding as quietly as it can be done, and get away on the ocean to different scenes and get you all over this nonsense."

"Authority?" said Maris. "You have no authority over

me now. I gave you back your ring which you said was the sign of your authority. And I have no idea of leaving this house or family. They are my family and this is my home, and I would not go away from them now for all the rings in the universe. I love them, and they are in trouble, and that means that I am in trouble too. They belong to me, are a part of me. I owe them all the love and care I have."

"That's all nonsense, Maris. That's a fallacy of the dark ages. We don't owe our parents a thing in the world. That's an exploded theory invented by parents to keep their children cowed. We're done with all that now. Each one of us has to live his own life as he pleases. The modern generation has shifted all that nonsense and are proving that life is a free adventure each works out for himself. We—"

"Stop!" said Maris. "I don't want to hear another word of that kind of stuff. I thought you were a Christian—at least I supposed you thought you were."

"A Christian?" laughed Tilford disagreeably. "Well, why should you question that? I often go to church, don't I? I give to the Red Cross work, and the Welfare, I'm always generous! I was confirmed ten years ago. I've told you that, I'm sure—"

"None of those things make a Christian," said Maris. "I don't know much about it myself and I realize I haven't been a very wonderful Christian and have no right to criticize, but in these long nights of anxiety I've had time to think, and I've seen myself as God must see me, and I'm ashamed."

"Oh, for heaven's sake, Maris, don't go religious on me! I can't endure ranting women. Maris, think of all our plans! Think how much I've done to make you happy on this trip. Think of your love for me. You're angry now, but you do love me. You did love me when I gave you your ring, didn't you, Maris?"

Maris lifted clear honest eyes:

"I thought I did, but—I wonder—if I ever did? Perhaps I was carried away with the glamour of having you compliment me and take me around in a beautiful car."

"That is ridiculous, Maris. You are just overwrought. You loved me of course. I've seen it in your eyes. Here, let's go somewhere out of this awful glare of the sun and talk this thing out. I can't think what has got into you. Just because your mother is a little sick and you've sat up a few nights—You've made a mountain of a molehill. Come, get into the car and we'll take a little ride. It will freshen you up. No matter if you aren't dressed, we'll drive out into the country where nobody will see you."

"No!" said Maris firmly. "I can't go, and I can't stay to talk any more. There isn't anything to say, anyway. My mother is very low, and must be absolutely quiet for six weeks at least, not even moving her arms or hands. And if she lives to get better she will have to go away for several months for absolute rest. My sisters and brothers have no one but me to keep things together."

"Nonsense! Let your father get a housekeeper. Other men have to do things like that."

"A housekeeper could not look after the children. Lexie is only a baby yet, and the boys are very young."

"Oh, that's easy. The children can be sent away to good schools. They have schools for very young children conducted by the very newest methods, which would doubtless be far better for them than to be coddled the way your mother has been doing. For the matter of that if the children went away to school your father and brother could board. There are cheap boarding houses. They could let the house furnished and take a room somewhere near their business and take meals at a restaurant. I understand that is a cheap way to live."

They had been sitting down in the porch rockers as they talked, but suddenly Maris arose, drew herself up to her full height and spoke sharply:

"That is all I want to hear about that!" she said, her voice like icicles. "Even if I were sure that I loved you as I thought I did awhile ago, even if you had not done and said all the unpleasant, unloving things that you have done the past week when I was in trouble, I would never want to go away with you and leave my family in distress. I *know* I love my family, but I'm not at all sure that I *ever* loved you! Goodbye!"

And before Tilford's astonished eyes Maris turned and walked into the house and up the stairs.

Tilford sat there in the chair a long time expecting her to come back and ask to be forgiven, but she did not come. He was shocked at her stubbornness.

Now, what was his mother going to say? And after she had bought that wedding dress, too!

10

MARIS shut herself into her room and faced herself in her mirror. It was as if she felt the need of telling herself what had just happened. Lexie was comfortable for the moment and the mirror was out of her range. She stood and looked into her own eyes facing facts. She was not going to be married in a few days! She was not going to marry Tilford *ever!* That was as clear as if a voice had spoken and told her so. She realized now that she ought to have known that long ago. She was not going to Europe on her wedding trip! She was just a girl in her father's home, with a great many things to regret, and a great many to undo, and suddenly heavy burdens upon her unaccustomed shoulders.

So now, what was she going to do about it?

It was imperative for her soul's sake that she do something at once. She could not just stand and face this thing supinely. She had to go vigorously at something to right matters, now that she saw her mistakes. She must burn her bridges behind her.

Strange, she had no compunctions. No fears that perhaps she was going too fast. That perhaps Tilford would be back and change the whole thing, ask her to forgive him, show his real repentance for his hardness, tell her it was his mistake, that he truly loved her family and wanted to be a real son to them, that he loved her with all his heart and could not think of going on through life without her by his side. No possibility of that sort even crossed her imagination. If it had she would have known at once it could never happen. She had seen Tilford under the merciless light of testing and she could never again have illusions about him. Moreover she had seen her own heart in the light of this testing, and she knew that she too had been wanting in a number of things that a true heart union should have. She had looked upon her erstwhile engagement and forthcoming marriage as a beautiful gesture that would interfere not at all with the roots of her life, but would keep a continual round of pleasures always in the offing. And that wasn't what marriage should mean. That wasn't what it had meant to father and mother. For instance, she couldn't imagine herself lying on a sick bed as mother was at this moment and Tilford giving up everything to sit beside her and hold her hand. She couldn't even imagine herself getting much comfort out of it if he did.

Phrases of his with regard to her mother's possible death came floating sharply to her memory, and a wave of anger crimsoned her face, and receded leaving it deadly white again. If she had needed anything else to open her eyes after the way he had acted during the past few days that one thing was enough to have killed any love she might have had for him. No, it was better not to think of him at all. He was out of her life forever now, and it was best to be actively at work clearing away the debris from her little dead romance, if it could rightly be called a romance when it had not been built upon true love in the first place.

Well, what should she do first? Something decisive. Those wedding invitations! Those should be destroyed at once!

With a glance into Lexie's room to see that all was well

with her, she opened her own door softly and slipped out into the hall. As she did so she saw her father coming out of the room where he had been sleeping, dressed as if he were going to town. With troubled eyes she watched him go slowly downstairs, holding to the handrail like an old man, though he had never seemed old to her before. She followed him down, watching him wistfully. Wasn't there something she could do to relieve his worries? That note! She wondered if Merrick knew how much it was.

Her father had taken his hat from the rack in the hall closet and was going out the door! He ought not to go out! He wasn't strong enough. Where was Merrick? Perhaps he could go with him, or go for him.

Then Merrick appeared at the door and put out his hand to stop his father.

"Now, dad, where are you going?"

The father looked annoyed as if he had been caught playing hookey.

"Why, I just have to run out on an errand for a few minutes," he said apologetically. "I'll be right back."

"Now, dad, you're going down to the bank, you know you are, and you mustn't, see? We can't have you dropping down the way mother did. You've got to stay in and rest a bit. If somebody has to go down I'll go for you."

"You can't sign a note for me, son. I want to get that off my mind. If anything should happen to me I want that note signed."

"Look here, dad. Mr. Matthews said you needn't hurry. He said it was all right any time this week. He said for you not to come till mother was better. He said if you wanted him to he would send you up a note to sign."

"Well, I'd rather go myself. I want to talk it over with him. I may need a little more money than I had expected, with mother sick, you know. I've got to talk it over with him and get it off my mind. It will be better for me to go, son, and get this done."

"Not today, dad. You mustn't, really. If mother should have another turn like the other day you wouldn't want to be away. Suppose you just jot down on a paper how much more you want and I'll go down and talk to him myself. I'm a man and I think I can put it over. Mr. Matthews is a prince. He was great yesterday. You trust me, dad. If you don't I'll call up the doctor and raise the riot act, for you're not going out in this hot sun this morning!"

"Look here, son, it's only two blocks to the trolley, and it won't hurt me in the least. I tell you I've got to get this thing off my mind and it's a great deal worse for me to sit still and think about it than it is for me to go down town for a couple of hours and get things fixed up. And I must run down to the office, you know, for a few minutes. I haven't been there for three days."

"That's all right, dad. The office won't run away. You trust Mr. Temple, don't you?"

"Perfectly. But there are things that he can't decide. I must go and see about some orders that ought to have come in. They're important."

"Yes, dad, all right, you write down just what it is you want me to ask about and I'll bring the letters up. I'll talk it over with Mr. Temple and get him to send up any letters you ought to see."

"Son, you really can't interfere with me this way!" Mr. Mayberry tried to speak sternly, but his voice was shaken, and Merrick's heart was wrung. Poor dad! He was carrying a heavy burden! If he'd only had his eyes open before, and not let his father slave to keep him in college. He ought to be at work earning money to help in this time of need. But dad shouldn't go out today, weak as he was! Not if he had to tie him to keep him at home.

"See here, dad! Nothing doing!" Merrick put his strong young arms about his father, and turned him around by force. Loving force it was, else his father would have struggled with him and got free. But he walked with him the few steps back to the door, earnestly arguing.

"Son, it's very kind of you to take such care of me, but you don't quite understand. This note has got to be renewed today, and I must go down and attend to it myself. There are things that you wouldn't understand."

Suddenly Maris opened the screen door and stepped out beside them, laying her hand on her father's arm.

"Father," she said quietly, just as if she were going to ask him to buy her a dozen oranges at the store, "I heard you talking about a note. How much is it? Why don't we pay it off and get it out of the way?"

The father looked at her with a shamed, hurt look, as if she had discovered his inmost secret, and he had no more courage to face the world.

"My dear—!" he said and his voice trailed off uncertainly, "you wouldn't understand. It's just a little matter of business I must attend to at once."

"Why, of course I'll understand," said Maris smiling. "I know what a note is and I want to know how much it is."

"It's only a small matter," evaded her father, "but it's necessary to be businesslike even in small matters."

"Yes, I understand, father, but why don't we pay it off? You have to pay interest on notes, don't you, unless you pay them off? Isn't it better to get them paid and be done with it? Doesn't it save money to do that?"

"Yes, my dear," said her father with a sad little smile, "but you see I don't happen to have the money in hand just now, and there's likely to be more need very immediately. I must be prepared. I haven't the money—" he passed his hand over his forehead with a kind of desperate motion and sighed heavily.

"Yes, but I have it," said Maris briskly. "Have you forgotten that three thousand dollar legacy grandmother left me?"

"But that is yours, my dear! That is in the nature of a dowry. I have been so glad that you had a little something of your own, that you do not have to leave your father's house absolutely penniless. No, Maris, my dear, I couldn't possibly use your money."

"You certainly could, and you certainly will," said Maris briskly. "Come over here, father, out of the sun, and let me tell you about it. That's my money, you said, and I have a right to use it as I choose, don't I? And I choose to use it this way."

"Yes, but my dear, though I know and love you for your loving generous heart I could never use that money. What would your—what would Tilford say if he knew I took your money to pay my debts!"

"Tilford has nothing whatever to do with it!" said Tilford's erstwhile fiancée with a wave of her hand. "Tilford does not even know I have any money. I never told him and I never mean to. I'm going to use this money to lift the burdens off of us as a family. That is, as far as it will go. Perhaps it won't go very far. You haven't told me yet how much that note is. If I haven't got enough we'll raise the rest some other way, but we'll pay off as much as we can right now and have that out of the way. Is it more than three thousand dollars, father?"

"Oh, no," her father laughed. "It's only eight hundred and fifty. But you see I was going to get a couple of hundred more if I could, just to ease things up a little here, keep us going from day to day, you know, and pay a few of the smaller bills. I was hoping things would look up at the office in a month or so, and then everything would be all right again. You know there have been a number of necessary expenses—" He paused in dismay and Maris took up his words almost gaily, briskly, as if she had her hand on the helm of their little lifeboat now, and was steering straight for shore.

"Yes, I know, father, a lot of *un*necessary expenses, if you ask me, and all connected with getting me married off. But you see I've come to my senses at last, and I'm taking over as many bills as I can and helping you to get clear of all this that has rested so heavily on you. Now, Merrick, if you'll just get the data from father I'll run up and get a check. Merrick, don't dare let father go down town today, I'll be right back!" and Maris was off on light feet speeding up to her desk.

"Oh, but I can't let her do that!" said the father looking dazedly at his son. "It was to have been her dowry. Mother and I were so glad she had it. And Tilford! What will he think of me?"

"Tilford be hanged! What's he got to do with it? She'll never tell him. She *wants* to do it, dad. She's a peach, and you mustn't make her feel bad by refusing it. She's been worried about you, I could see. You've got to take it, dad. Haven't you been giving, giving, giving ever since we were born? And we've just taken and never helped a cent's worth!"

"It is the parent's place to give."

"Well, not forever. It's our place now. I only wish I had a legacy and I'd turn it all over to you. But I'll find a way to help too, you'll see."

Suddenly the father's head went down on his lifted hand, and Merrick could see that he was deeply stirred.

"Listen, dad," said Merrick trying to clear the huskiness from his throat, "that's no way to take it. It's no humiliation. Why can't we all be glad one of us has got it to clear the rest? Why aren't you pleased Maris isn't selfish? Why aren't you glad this note can be paid and you won't have to worry about it any longer?"

"I am. I will be!" said the father lifting his head with a sudden smile.

"That's the talk. Here comes Maris. Now, smile again. Turn on the works, quick!"

Mr. Mayberry met his daughter with a smile that was almost blinding, as she came down with a check in her hand.

"I'm just so happy I had it, father," she whispered as she put her arms around his neck and kissed him, and he held her close for a moment.

"You precious child!" he said. "It is wonderful of you to do this. Of course I didn't mean anybody to find out I was in a tight place, but this has lifted a great burden from me. Wait till I tell your mother about it. Just as soon as she is able to hear it."

"Don't be in too big a hurry, daddy," warned Maris. "Let her forget for a while that there are burdens. But we're going to make it our business to see that the burdens don't get heavy again, father. Now, if you want to do something for us you'll go in and drink that nice cold milk and egg that Sally has just made for you, and then you'll go and lie down and sleep a little while before lunch."

When father had obediently gone smiling in to follow her orders Maris turned to Merrick.

"Merrick, will you have time to step down to the stationer's and pay that bill before father sees it? Here's a blank check and you can fill it in. Here's what I think it is, but there may be something extra I've forgotten. I'd like to get that bill paid before father ever sees it."

Merrick flashed her a look.

"I certainly am proud of my sister!" he said. "It's the greatest thing I ever knew a girl to do, right on the edge of her wedding day, too!"

A startled look came over Maris' face and she almost opened her lips to explain, and then she closed them again. Somehow she felt as if she mustn't tell yet that there was to be no wedding. It seemed as if she must tell this first to her mother and father before she broadcasted it to the family. She struggled with a sudden desire to hug her brother who all at once seemed so grown up and dependable, but she knew it would embarrass him so she only smiled.

"It's only what you would have done yourself, you old fraud," she said tenderly.

"Never having been a girl before her wedding I don't know, but I'm sure I'd like to have the money to try," he said. "Wait till I get to working! You'll see!"

"Of course I will. Now, get away to the city and get that note paid. Have you got father's bank book and all the data? And say, Merrick, do you think there are any other notes or things?"

"No, I guess not, but I'll find out. He told me there would be a big caterer's bill and a florist bill, and cars for the wedding and—"

"Yes? Well, we won't worry about those just now," said Maris, "but if there's anything else he ought to pay please let me know."

"I should say it was my job if there's anything else."

"Well, you haven't got a legacy just now, Merrick."

"No, but I've got an expensive set of golf clubs, two tennis rackets and a canoe up at college I think I could sell. Watch me! I'll go my share, too. So long! I'll be back in time for dinner. Tell dad not to worry if I'm late," and Merrick hurried away in the sunshine.

Maris watched him a minute, her heart lighter than it had been for several days. What a dear boy he was anyway! What a precious family she had, and suddenly her heart thrilled with gladness that it was her right and privilege to watch over them and help them now without anyone to hinder nor say her nay.

She would have to explain Tilford's absence pretty soon of course, but not until she had got used to things herself and adjusted her life to its new order.

Then she turned and sped upstairs to her patient who about this time would be demanding some amusement.

But the wedding invitations were still hidden in the attic.

THE rest of that day was very full. It seemed there was no time to do the things she wanted very much to do at once. Lexie was hard to please. She was hot and restless and wanted her mother. She wanted to have the window shades up and be given a picture book, both of which were against the doctor's orders, for her eyes must be guarded carefully.

Maris did her best to make the child happy, meantime letting her own thoughts run ahead with plans. But it was not until almost eight o'clock in the evening that the little patient was finally asleep and Maris free to do what she would.

She slipped into her mother's room for a minute, and saw her father lying on the cot sleeping with a look of real rest on his face, and her heart was glad that she had been able to relieve him from at least one of his heavy burdens.

Quietly she slipped up to the attic and brought out the wedding invitations. She had a feeling somehow that she was committing burglary.

She had planned to burn them out in the incinerator, but when she touched their smooth thick surfaces, the double envelopes making such bulky firm white slabs, she realized that things like that wouldn't burn very easily. She would have to pull them out of their envelopes and burn them one by one. It wouldn't do to leave any traces of them about for Sally to wonder over and perhaps gossip about in the village.

Looking about her she saw a large box of excelsior that had come around the only wedding present she had as yet received. It was a great ugly old-fashioned lamp sent her by an old friend of the family, now in her nineties, who had moved out west some twenty years ago, when Maris was a baby. It was a hideous thing. The old lady had written that she had heard the Mayberry's oldest girl was going to be married pretty soon, so she thought she would send her a present. It was a lamp that had been given herself as a wedding present, and she thought Maris might like to have it because it was so old.

It was an oil lamp with a terrible glass shade on which a floral decoration had been poorly painted. Maris had looked at it in despair, and written a nice little note of thanks, and then hastily gathered up its parts and dumped the whole thing in the attic out of the way, for it came to her that it would never do to let Tilford see that lamp!

So here it was beside her as she turned to go down with her boxes of invitations, an ugly old lamp lying in a great lot of excelsior. Just the thing to start the thick envelopes burning.

Quickly she removed the lamp and took the box down with her. Soon those carefully addressed invitations were roaring up in smoke into the summer night, licked by crackling flames. The notable names of the town's four hundred stood out boldly in Maris' clear handwriting for an instant, and then were crumbled into black parchment.

Maris stood there and watched them burn, fascinated by the thought that her hopes of yesterday, and all she had built up for what she had thought would be happiness, were so quickly destroyed. An expensive little fire, but how much it meant! How quickly God had showed her when He got ready to act. It filled her with a kind of awe. Was God watching all her acts and plans that way? Did He watch everybody so, and take account of what was best for them? Was God as personal as that?

She lifted her eyes to the clear sky above, set with many stars. God taking account of her. God arranging things to make her see her mistakes before it was too late!

But yet, she had had her own free choice. Suppose she had yielded to Tilford and gone on? Would God have let her have her way and bear the consequences? That was something to think about when she had time. She gave a little shiver there in the darkness when she remembered Tilford's face as he talked to her that morning. What would it be to be under authority to a man who did not care for her dear ones? From whom even death could bring no sympathetic word?

She was poking among the ashes, lifting an envelope here and there that was sliding out of the way of the flame and keeping its identity in spite of the fire, when she heard Gwyneth coming through the kitchen. She had left Gwyneth studying hard in the library. Why didn't she stay there? She didn't want Gwyneth to see her holocaust. Gwyneth wouldn't understand, and might be horrified. She didn't want to have to explain, not yet. Not while trouble was in the house. Not while mother lay so ill.

She turned swiftly and met Gwyneth as she opened the kitchen door.

"Oh, here you are!" said the little girl. "Someone wants you on the phone. I think it's the doctor, but I'm not sure."

With sudden fear clutching at her heart Maris left her fire and hurried in, yet even as she went, reason returned. If it was the doctor it would only be some direction about her nursing. Nothing terrible could come from the doctor when he wasn't at the house. So, more composedly she went to answer the call. And then it was only an agent for a remedy for seasickness. He said he had heard she was going to take a sea trip for her honeymoon and he wanted to recommend this marvelous remedy. Might he call and tell her more about it. He had a list of notable people who had used it with great success.

Maris cut him off abruptly with the information that she had no need for any such remedy, and half vexed with a world that was continually meddling in other people's business, went back to her burning.

The fire had died down, and all the white corners seemed to be gone. Just to be sure, however, she put in the last of the excelsior with the box that had contained it, and the flames leaped up again in great shape and took every vestige of telltale white paper with them. Maris turned away with a sigh of relief. Those invitations could no more make trouble. They did not exist. It had all been a bad dream, those last days of frantically making out lists and addressing envelopes, of having Tilford telephone that some mistakes had been made in addresses, and he had another list, of having her father hover near worrying lest some old friend was being left out, or lest the plain little church they attended would not hold all these high and mighty guests. That was over. Purged by fire!

She turned a last look at the now dying fire, and cast upon it in her thoughts, the memory of that pretty wedding procession, the white trailing veil, the rainbow tinted bridesmaids, her two little sisters, Lexie as flower girl, and Gwyneth in her first long dress as maid of honor. All that pretty dream was gone now. She probably would never marry. Though if she did the dress that mother made would of course be used, no matter if she married a royal throne—which of course she wouldn't—having just turned down the nearest approach to anything like wealth and influence that would likely ever cross her path.

Nevertheless it was with a light heart that she locked the kitchen door and went upstairs. She felt easier in her mind than she had since she had caught that glimpse of the dear shabby old house and sensed the contemptuous scorn in Tilford's tone as he voiced the sentiment that he was not expecting her to have any further connection with it after she was married.

There was one more thing she meant to do tonight before she slept. She must make one more visit to the attic. She wanted to put that precious wedding dress away out of sight, where nothing could happen to it, and where no alien eyes could possibly search it out and bring it into criticism. If anything happened to mother—or if it didn't —that dress would always be her most prized possession.

There was a great white pasteboard box lined with satin paper. It had held a pair of lovely white pure wool blankets, the softest, finest blankets that could be found, with wide satin bindings. They were the last things that mother had bought for her, and she treasured them greatly. They were over mother now, tucked softly about her quiet form, covered scrupulously with an enshrouding sheet by the careful nurse so that no soil could possibly come to them. Maris was so glad that mother had them about her. It comforted her to have them there. The dear blankets that mother had bought. Precious mother who so seldom bought anything pretty or fine for herself.

And now that beautiful, strong box would be the very thing in which to put away her wedding dress.

She carried the dress to her own room and closing the door between it and the playroom where Lexie was, she folded the exquisite dress, breadth by breadth, with its perfect needlework and beautiful lace puffed out by tissue paper till not a fold nor crease was possible.

She looked at it there in the box as it lay, with a little spray of orange blossoms they had bought that last day of shopping together, nestled at the throat. It looked so like a lovely personality that had been sinned against, that dress. As if it were glad to be folded away and rest.

A bright tear sprang into Maris' eye and she closed the box quietly and tied it up. There must be no tears shed on that dress. Only smiles should greet it if it ever came out again.

She stood on a chair and put the box on the highest shelf of her roomy closet, far back where no one would ever be likely to notice it.

Then Maris went with swift soft tread back and forth a few times to bring the lovely dresses that had been prepared for her trousseau. There were not a great many of them, but each one was charming of its kind, and Maris had been pleased with them. But now they must go into seclusion. No one wanted to see the trousseau of a poor dead wedding hanging around. Besides, another nurse was coming now in a few minutes, a night nurse to relieve the first nurse, so that mother would not be alone a minute. She must hurry and make room for more stiff uniforms. There were a few things still hanging in the other guest room where father was sleeping at night now. She must get those out of the way before the nurse roused him and sent him to bed in earnest.

So, almost ruthlessly, those garments that had been bought so carefully, one at a time, and admired as each a prize in itself, were gathered into a heap on her arm and dumped unceremoniously on her bed to get the other closets empty before anyone discovered what she was doing. She locked her door while she was hurtling them into her own closet which suddenly seemed to lose its spaciousness as the grand garments were ushered in.

But at last they were all hung up, with a garment bag

guarding the entrance. In the morning she would find time to slip them into bags, or under covers, and then later if mother got well, and everything was all right and normal again she would bring them forth casually one by one as if she had always worn them, and nobody would remember that they had been wedding clothes.

Just then she heard Merrick drive up in Lane Maitland's car. The new nurse had arrived and she must go down and meet her.

But while Maris was showing the new nurse her way about, and helping to get her father settled for the night, Gwyneth had hopped into the car beside Merrick and was riding around to the Maitland garage with him.

"I gotta go with you because I gotta ask you something," she declared when he protested that she ought to be in bed.

"Listen, Merrick, isn't our Maris going to get married after all? Because the telephone rang and someone wanted her, and I smelled paper burning, so I went out into the kitchen and she was outside at the incinerator burning a whole lot of things, a big bonfire, and it flickered down and almost went out just as I got there. And so I went out to see if it was all safe while she went to the telephone, and I found down in the corner against the stone, just beginning to scorch around the edge, one of her wedding invitations! It was addressed to Tilford's aunt up at Coral Crest, so I knew it was an invitation, and anyway I pulled it out and took out the invitation and saw what it was."

"Oh, that was likely some that got spoiled in addressing," said the brother lightly. "You've just got one of your spells of romancing. You ought to be in bed."

"No, but truly, Merrick, it was. And there were a lot more little black squares down in the incinerator. I lighted a match and looked."

"All right, have it your own way. You'd better get a

detective and find out. I don't know anything about it," said Merrick crossly.

"Oh, but don't you wish it was true, Merrie? Don't you wish she wouldn't get married?"

"Oh, sure! Anything you want. I wish the sky would rain roses and the grass would grow gold dollars. Now, scram and get to bed before I spank you!"

12

TILFORD Thorpe went home to his mother and told her he was done with women. He didn't intend to marry ever, and he wanted it thoroughly understood that she needn't fling any of her stupid million-heiresses at him. He told her Maris was a liar, she had broken her word, and she had been stubborn and mulish about foolish things. And in the same breath he informed her that it was all her fault. That she had tried to force a silly dress on a girl who had too much pride to take advice, and she had broken his heart, and he would never be happy again. He prattled of suicide, and said it would serve his mother right, that she was always trying to manage his life for him and he hadn't a chance in the world to be himself, and a lot of like phrases, until she wept bitterly and wished she had never been born. And when he had exhausted his hurt pride upon her in invectives, and refused every kind of an offer to help she could think of, telling her if she had kept her everlasting tongue out of the whole matter he would still be happy, and soon married and off to Europe, he told her he was going off and get drunk, and she needn't try to find him either. He was his own master and he wouldn't be bound by her any longer.

When she suggested that he take the ring back to Maris and tell her he would let her put off the wedding till her mother was better, he raved and fairly bit the air, and slammed away to haunts known only to himself and his fellow club members. He remained away for three days, getting drunk. Thoroughly. Playing poker for high stakes and losing heavily.

He arrived home at last having run down an old woman carrying home a basket of groceries, got himself arrested and bailed out again, and came in looking like a wreck.

"Oh, Tillie dear! Where have you been?" wailed his mother as he entered her bedroom where she had been more or less in her bed, except for a social engagement or two, ever since her encounter with Doctor MacPherson.

"Now don't begin that song and dance!" said the youth insolently. "I've been where I've pleased to be. That's where you are too, isn't it? I came up here to see if you had any more light on the matter that concerns me most. Has Maris telephoned? I understood you to say that a little silent treatment might bring her around. Has she come?"

"I haven't seen her," said his mother sadly. "No, she hasn't telephoned. I'm afraid you're going to find that your girl is an utter failure in every way. It is as I told you in the first place, Tillie, it is never wise to go out of your own class when you really settle down seriously to get married. And really, my dear, even if she had come, I should not have received her. Not after the treatment I received in her home. They are an utterly worthless lot, my dear, and you are well rid of her!"

Tilford lit a cigarette and flung himself down in a white brocade chair, his hat slung to the back of his handsome head, his haggard eyes fixed angrily on his mother.

"Can that stuff!" he said fiercely. "You don't think I'm going to give her up after all this, do you? You don't think

I'm going to have the whole town see me trampled under foot and scorned, do you? Not if the whole generation of Mayberrys drive you out of their house. I'm in this thing to win, and I'm not going to be beaten off. After all, you had it coming to you. I told you you wouldn't get anywhere with that stubborn little woman. She's playing to win, but she's going to get the surprise of her life when she sees how things come out. I've got my plans all laid, and *I'm* going to win! Don't ask me anything about it. Just be ready to do whatever I tell you when the time comes. We may not have any wedding on June thirtieth in their little old dinky church, but we'll have a wedding all right, and don't you forget it. And we're sailing as per schedule, too. And when she's married and finds herself out on the ocean I guess she'll sing another tune."

"Now, Tillie!" said his mother with apprehension, "what are you going to do? You mustn't do anything scandalous! You mustn't get us in the papers."

"Oh, no! Don't you worry about that," bragged the young man. "I'll attend to what gets in the papers. I'll send in the write-up myself, just what I want printed. There won't be any scandal except in the eyes of her precious family. I'll fix it so there'll be plenty for them to contemplate."

"Oh, Tilford! You frighten me! You haven't been drinking, have you? You don't sound like yourself!"

"Well, if I have, is it your business?" he asked in a surly tone. "I can look out for myself, can't I? You brought me up to drink like a gentleman."

"Oh, Tilford!" wailed his mother. "You are being rude to me. If I brought you up to anything at all I brought you up to be courteous!"

"Courtesy be hanged! I'm done with the things you brought me up to. I'm going to get my wife the way I please and you can take the consequences."

"Oh, Tillie! You have been drinking. You never spoke

to me like that before! You certainly must be drunk!" wailed his mother looking at his wild eyes in horror.

Suddenly the father's substantial form loomed large and impressive in the doorway.

"Tilford!" his voice thundered. "You're forgetting yourself! Get out of your mother's room at once! Come with me!"

Tilford turned bewildered. His father's voice was reminiscent of his childhood's days when at rare intervals the usually loving indulgent father became a stern parent and administered a long needed chastisement most thoroughly, so that it was not soon forgotten.

Mr. Thorpe's large strong hand laid hold on his son's arm and propelled him out of the room and down the hall to his own room.

"Now!" he said, eyeing the young man with mingled sorrow and disgust. "See if you can get yourself sobered up. You're not fit to be around with decent people. And when you're sober, perfectly sober, I've something to say to you that will be to your advantage!"

"Now look here, dad, you've no right to treat me this way. I'm a man! I have rights!"

"Oh, are you? You don't look one! Look at your clothes. You appear to have been on a brawl for several days! You need a bath and some clean clothes. But even they wouldn't make a man of you, I'm afraid. Take off those clothes! Get under a cold shower and come to your senses. Get in there, I say!" and he took hold of his son's arm and literally shoved him into the luxurious bath room.

"Let me alone! You've no right—!" protested the angry son.

"Oh, haven't I? Well, we'll see!" and the father deliberately took the key out of the door and put it into the other side of the lock.

"Now, stay in here until you've had a bath and are fully sober!" he said. "I'll be back in half an hour and if you have come to yourself I'll let you out." The father shut the door and turned the key in the lock, then strode down the hall again to his own domain called by his wife a "den" and shut himself in.

A moment later, Mrs. Thorpe in an elaborate frilly negligee of grass green, her feet thrust into green satin mules that flapped as she waddled so that she had to change them for bed socks, because they made too much noise, stole cumbersomely down the hall, with furtive backward glances toward the den. She arrived breathlessly at her son's door, tried it, and entered, gave a frightened glance about and immediately located a sound in the bathroom. She hurried to the door and found it locked.

"Tilford!" she whispered softly. "Mother's precious boy!"

"Oh, *shut up!*" roared Tilford angrily. "Will you get out? Can't I take a bath without being trailed?"

Mrs. Thorpe heard the far sound of an opening door up the hall and beat a hasty retreat, making a dive into the sewing room and coming back with a pair of scissors and a thimble in her hand as if she had gone after them, in case she met her husband.

But the door of the den was closed again and she was unmolested. She retired to her bedroom to sob over the sorrows of the woman who had an ungrateful child and couldn't do anything about it.

Exactly half an hour afterward Tilford sat in a big comfortable chair in his own room, clothed, and to a degree in his right mind, sulking.

His father entered the room but he did not look up nor notice him.

His father sat down in a stiff straight chair, clasped his hands firmly together in front of him, leaned forward a little, and gazed steadily at the graceful form of the handsome youth attired in a costly silk dressing gown and expensive slippers. There was something unutterably wistful in the father's expression as he looked at his boy, and saw in retrospect the whole span of his life so far from baby-hood. There was a depth of sadness in his eyes that told how much of a bitter disappointment that young life had been to him, the father.

When Mr. Thorpe broke the silence that was becoming painful to them both, his voice had a business-like crisp-ness that belied his expression.

"Now, Tilford, have you recovered your sanity enough to understand what I am about to say, or shall I have to wait until you have had a sleep?"

"Don't be an ass!" was the boy's disrespectful reply.

"That will do. Don't add to your troubles by being insolent to your father. Are you sober yet?"

Tilford summoned all the dignity belonging to past generations:

"Certainly. I have been sober all the time."

"No, you were not sober. If you had been you should certainly suffer more than I am going to mete out to you at present. But I want you to understand that you cannot speak to your mother in the way I heard you speak. It is inexcusable, and I will not stand for it. If it is ever repeated you will discover that I have power to make you exceed-ingly sorry that you ever did it. Your fortune, you know, is all in my hands, and I shall certainly not leave a cent to a young man who does not treat his mother decently."

"Oh, dad! How tiresome you are! Mother's such a fool! She won't let a fellow alone!"

"Exactly. According to you, your father's an ass and your mother's a fool. Then, may I ask, *what are you?* I think it might be well for you to reflect for awhile over that question, when you have a little leisure from your own important affairs."

The boy flung himself about in his chair, leaning over with his elbows on his knees, his face in his hands, and groaned aloud.

"Oh, why do I have to be tormented this way, when I already have enough trouble to drive a hundred men insane?"

The father's face softened and a tortured look came into his eyes.

"Son, I know you are unhappy, but this is something basic that must be maintained, no matter what you are suffering. You must never lower yourself, no matter what you are going through, to be insolent to your mother, and I demand that before you do anything else you go to your mother and apologize."

"What nonsense!" flung out Tilford. "I'm not a little kid!"

"No!" said the father with a sigh, "I would that you were! I would certainly try to whale some sense into you. But you are supposed to be a gentleman. At least you were born one, and I intend to try and keep you one if I have to fling every cent I might leave to you into the depths of the sea. I may not be very wise about training children and I may not know anything about philosophy or religion, but that is one thing you know I have always insisted upon, that you shall be respectful to your mother. Now, Tilford, before I say anything more to you I want you to go across the hall and beg your mother's pardon."

"Gosh, dad! Of all the silly baby ideas!"

"If you keep on you'll have a few more apologies to make before you get through. I intend to see this through to the end."

There was a long silence, and then Tilford arose haughtily, contemptuously:

"All right! Let's have it over with," he said. "Do I go alone or are you coming along to see whether I do it right?"

"I'm coming along!" said his father with dignity.

Silently they went across the hall, the door opened to the mother's astonished eyes, and the two entered.

Tilford stood like one himself aggrieved, and made a scornful apology.

"Mother, dad seems to think I was rude to you. I sincerely apologize. I have been so much upset the past few days that I scarcely knew what I was doing anyway."

"Yes, of course, my dear!" murmured the mother with a gush of tears. "Don't think any more about it, Tillie dear!"

Then the young man turned away with a look of disgust.

"Is that all, dad? Or is there more to this?"

The father answered sadly:

"If that is the best you can do we will let that go for the present, and you and I will return to my library."

"Heavens and earth!" ejaculated the irascible youth. But he followed his father across the hall and stood at the window scowling, awaiting the next act.

"Sit down, Tilford."

His father's voice was almost tender now.

"Tilford, perhaps you don't know how your father's heart has been yearning over you during these last few days. I couldn't help but see that something was wrong when I got back from Chicago. But your mother was so upset over you that I hardly liked to ask her for particulars. Suppose you try to tell me the details. Is Maris still in trouble? Is her mother no better?"

"Oh, Gosh! Dad! Have I got to go into all that? No, her mother isn't any better, at least they won't admit she is. And Maris hasn't sent out the invitations, and thinks she can't get married on June thirtieth, and that leaves me all up a tree. What am I to do? She's given me back my ring, and lets on it's all over between us."

"Well, but let's understand this, son. What did you do to get her into a state that she wanted to give back your ring? Were you kind and helpful to her in her distress when her mother was sick? Did you offer to do anything you could?"

"I? What could I do? I couldn't get a chance even to talk to her for more than a minute. She comes downstairs with a hot-water bottle, or to get a bowl of ice or something, and has to run right back upstairs before she hardly gets down. She won't send out the invitations, nor let me send them. Helpful? I? Certainly I tried to be. I offered to get those invitations off in plenty of time. But no, she wouldn't even tell me where they were. Said she couldn't send out invitations when her mother was at the point of death. Said her kid sister had measles and she couldn't do anything but hover over her family day and night. She looks like an old crow with black circles under her eyes! Pretty bride she'll be! Helpful and kind? Why, I even got a special child's nurse to go there and tend that hateful little spoiled brat so Maris could go out and keep her engagements with me. Would she go? Not she. Said she'd send the nurse away if I sent her. Said the kid wanted her or her mother."

"Of course. What could you expect?"

"Expect? I'd expect her to take the help I gave and do her duty toward me. Isn't that what being engaged means?"

"No, I wouldn't say so. She can't leave her duty at home when they are in trouble. You ought to have tried to enter into her troubles and sympathize with her. You ought to have tried to find out her burdens and help to lighten them."

"Well, I did. Certainly I did. There was the matter of a suitable wedding dress for the kind of wedding due our family. Mother found a peach of a dress and suggested she go and see it. Would she go? Not one step. I tried to explain that mother had had it reserved for her at a special price, but no, she said her mother had *made* a dress for her! Imagine a mother being able to make a good enough dress for our wedding! And when I tried to exercise my authority, and tell her that she had no right to carry things with such a high hand she gets mad and flings me back my ring."

"Son, look here! I don't know what is the matter with you. You have a wonderful little girl in that Mayberry child, and you don't seem to know it. You shouldn't try to order her ways, you shouldn't tell her what to wear, and you shouldn't expect her to leave a sick mother and sister. There are such things as right and wrong in this world, though the young people of today don't seem to recognize that any more. You've probably hurt that child more than she has hurt you. I don't know whether you've got it in you to love her the way she ought to be loved and guarded or not. And I don't know her well enough to know whether she loves you well enough to stand your doldrums and tantrums or not, but I should say there was just one thing that would set you two right, if you can be set right, and that is for you to get down on your knees and be a little humble. Take your ring back to her and tell her you have seen yourself, and you are ashamed of yourself. Tell her you've been a fool and an ass yourself, and ask her to forgive you. If you do that, and she really loves you, she's bound to forgive you, and you can start all over again. If she doesn't really love you then it's all wrong from the beginning and better broken up.

"But son, you'll have to make concessions! When you ask her to forgive you you've got to tell her that you're willing to put the wedding off till she's ready, and that you'll come and help her nurse her sick ones back to health, and comfort her and sympathize with her. You'll have to tell her that it's grand for her to have a mother who can make a wedding dress for her daughter, and that of course she must wear that dress and no other, whether our world or her world or anybody else's world considers it the latest thing or not. There is something rare in a dress that a mother's love prepares. But my son, I'll miss my guess if you don't find that dress quite the fit thing after all. The mother of that girl wouldn't want her to wear anything that wasn't all right. Don't you know enough to know that? Now go get your evening togs on and run over to her house and say you're sorry, and you'll see how quickly your troubles will smooth out."

The son whirled on his father with a great scorn in his face, a perfect fury of indignation in his voice:

"*Me* go and tell Maris I'm sorry? Not on your life I won't! Do you suppose I'm going to do the little whipped-dog act you've done all your life, giving in to every blessed thing mother has demanded? Not me. I know my way around better than that! I'll get her back, don't you fear, but it won't be that way! Not on my life it won't!" and the son angrily slammed out and down the hall to his own room, and locked himself in.

The father sat stricken in his chair, with his face buried in his hands, and let the whole disappointment of the years roll over him. That was what he was in his family! A little whipped dog! And his son, the hope of his failing years, had told him so! There was nothing he could think of that life had to offer so bitter as that.

13

THE second nurse who had come to relieve Miss Bonner was most kind and helpful. She didn't stay during the daytime usually. Her home was not far away and she went home to her own bed to sleep when her night's work was done. But now and then she would run in an hour or two earlier than she was due to begin work, and suggest that she look after Lexie while Maris ran out to get a breath of air, or do an errand. Lexie had become very fond of her. She was Scotch and had a store of quaint little stories about foxes and birds and "beasties" as she called them. She had a Scotch accent that fascinated the little girl, and a winning way with her, as well as a deep fund of humor. Lexie always hailed her coming with delight.

She came over thus one afternoon when Maris was particularly worn and discouraged, and with a sigh of relief Maris went downstairs, glad to get away for a few minutes from the scene of hard work and anxiety.

Maris went through the downstairs rooms. All was in order. There was nothing here that demanded her attention. She had already gathered all the bills out of mother's desk and attended to them; hunted up estimates from florists and caterers and let them know that the wedding was called off on account of illness in the family; written notes to her bridesmaids and a few intimate friends who knew about the wedding plans. There was absolutely nothing to demand her hands to work or her tired brain to think.

She went out into the kitchen, but Sally had it immaculate. Preparations for the family dinner were in progress as they should be at that hour. The specially prepared dishes and trays that would be needed for the invalids were in the ice box in order, and she could hear Sally stepping around in her own room just off the kitchen, getting into a clean dress to serve the evening meal. There was no reason why she should linger here.

She stepped out of the back door and looked up into the cherry tree, laden with its brilliant fruit, reached up idly and picked a cluster, eating them as she walked on around the back door and into the garden. She had a strangely desolate feeling that she was all alone in the world and there was no one to turn to for a comfort of which she felt in sudden terrible need. She told herself that this was what came of relaxing even for a minute in the midst of hard work and anxiety. It was better to keep right on and not take time off with a beautiful world in June, when all the things that belonged in such a June life were hanging in jeopardy. Here was she who was to have been married in lovely grandeur and off on a dream-trip to foreign lands in just a few days now, suddenly snatched from all this idyl of a luxurious life and plunged into heavy hard work and desperate anxiety, shot through here and there by stinging annoyances from people who ought to have been her strongest/ reliance, and finally separated entirely from them and left to go alone. It was strange! So strange!

And this desolate feeling.

It wasn't just anxiety now. One can get used in a way to

the monotony of a long drawn out anxiety. It wasn't just weariness nor yet a longing for the gaieties of the life she had been living for the last six months since she had been engaged to Tilford. It was this sense of having no one in heaven or earth to depend upon.

Everyone to whom she would naturally turn now to rest her soul had to be carefully guarded for their own sakes. Father, how frail he was! Not so stooped and tortured looking perhaps since he had that note paid, and some bills out of the way that had tormented him, but still it seemed as if a breath might blow him away. He would not get over that, of course, till mother got well.

Merrick mustn't have any more anxieties. He was only a boy anyway. He had finished his last examination and was to start driving his bus route tomorrow morning. She mustn't load her trials on him. He had a responsible job and must keep his mind free from worry. And of course Merrick wouldn't understand all her problems anyway.

But it wasn't just problems, either, this afternoon. It was just a hungry longing for something that satisfies. The feeling was strong that she had given up the life that had stretched out so enticingly before her, and while it was the right thing to do, of course, and she couldn't have done anything else, wouldn't have wanted to, would do over again all that she had done, yet now in the late afternoon waning of the sun, while the shrubbery made long shadows on the grass and the poppies and roses were still and lovely in the garden, and the sky so heavenly blue, the heart of her cried out for some part in the beauty of the world, some real joy that pain and sickness and peril could not take from her.

She paused to watch a big velvet bee roll and tumble and wallow around in the heart of a scarlet poppy with deep black center and ruffle of white. Then he bumbled up and buzzed across the bed, creeping deep into the heart of a purple iris, and dusting his coat with yellow pollen from its sleek purple walls. Was a bee happy, she wondered? Did God think of bees, or were they all just a part of a great creation that He had started and then left to go on its careless way? Oh, she knew better than that, of course. She knew the Bible said that not even a sparrow can fall without Him. But she couldn't get the sense today in her weary lonesome young heart, that God really cared about her and the uphill road she had started to walk.

It had been interesting to ease her father's financial difficulties, to see the furrows of his brow relax, and a look of relief come into his eyes. It had been good to feel that Merrick trusted her again. Although neither Merrick nor any of them knew yet that she had given up Tilford, it had been restful to have some of her troubled doubts settled by her definite stand for her family. But what was life going to be, as it went along, a long lonely stretch, bearing a mother's cares and anxieties, without the help of a strong love in her life?

Well, her heart was still too angry with Tilford to wish him back. He had been too appallingly indifferent to her desires for her to get over it so easily. Yet fragments of her broken dreams came often, floating tantalizingly just above her head, lovely things of gauze and rainbow, making her heart cry out to catch at them and draw them back again into her grasp.

She wandered on past the neat rows of the kitchen garden, where father with sometimes the help of Merrick, and the hindrance of the eager erratic labors of the little boys, had growing things in abundance for his household. Dear hard-working father! They must watch out that he didn't drop some day as mother had done. Working late at the office and then coming home to snatch the very last minute of the daylight to work in his garden!

As she walked around toward the side of the yard next to the Maitland place she thought she heard the echo of the boys' voices in the distance. Were they still painting the house? What a grand friend Lane was, to let them do things like this. The very importance of it, she knew, must greatly intrigue her small brothers.

A little path in the grass led over to the hedge that shut the Maitland property away from the Mayberry place. She followed it to the hedge, lured by the cool quiet under the hemlock trees, and as she paused and looked toward the Maitland house wondering if she could catch a glimpse of her young brothers painting, a voice spoke.

"Hello there, Maris, is that you, really out of doors for a few minutes? That's good. You've been shut in too long without a break. I asked Merrick last night if there wasn't some way we could get you out for a breath of air and a bit of sunshine. But the sun is hot yet, isn't it? How about stepping through the opening here and trying our new garden chairs. I ordered them by telephone and I think they're very comfortable. Come see if you don't think so."

Smiling she stepped through a thin place in the hedge and sat down in the long easy chair he offered her, finding surprising resilience and restfulness in the curious structure of steel that seemed to lend itself to every curve of her tired body.

"It's grand!" she said, putting her head back and relaxing. "Oh, isn't this a lovely place? What deep lovely shadows of almost blueness up there among the feathery hemlocks."

"Yes, I always loved this spot. Mother used to love it so. She used to talk about building an arbor out here so that she might come often and rest. But I'm not sure but I like just the trees above me rather than a roof."

"Oh, so do I!" said Maris taking a deep breath of the resinous pines about them. "How beautiful this is. Somehow I've never had time to stop and look at it. But you're making it look as it used to look when we were children. I remember I always thought your lawn was the loveliest stretch of greenness, with that great flower bed of your mother's, always bright with flowers."

He flashed an appreciative look at her.

"Do you remember mother?" he asked, after a brief moment.

"Oh, yes," she said, "I used to think she was the loveliest woman I knew, next to my own mother. You see in those days I used to think all mothers were like your mother and mine."

A floating shadow of disillusionment crossed her face.

"And you have found out differently?" he asked.

"And *how!*" she said with sudden emphasis.

He waited, but somehow knew that she would not go on. This was something that had to do with a part of her life in which he might not share.

"Your mother is precious!" he said. "My mother used to think she was wonderful."

"She—*is*—!" said Maris, struggling with a sudden unreasoning desire to cry. "You don't know how I miss her, just these few days since she's been sick."

"Don't I?" said Lane Maitland with a tender wistfulness in his voice.

"Oh, of course you do!" said Maris with sudden compunction.

"But it's not as if my mother was lost," went on Maitland. "I'm expecting to go to her some day. We've been wonderfully blest with parents, you and I. Not everybody has that. Both our mothers and fathers know the Lord."

"I suppose that does make a difference," said Maris half shyly. "I never thought of that before."

"Of course it does. It makes a difference to everybody. But I don't know what I should have done if I hadn't had the Lord Jesus Christ, and been conscious of His presence with me all the time. I couldn't have lived through that first loneliness when they were both gone."

There was a long silence and then Maris said wistfully:

"I wish I could realize God. I feel as if I were so alone just now. I've tried several times to pray, and read my Bible, but I don't seem to get anywhere. It's like saying empty words to a brass sky. And the Bible doesn't seem real when I read it."

She paused, half hoping, yet hardly daring to think that this young man, fine though he was, would have any definite help for her hungry heart. Her head was down in her hands and she could not see the gentle yearning look that he turned upon her.

"Perhaps you were asking things that you had no right to ask yet, and expecting light when you hadn't yet met the conditions. You know the condition of having understanding given by the Holy Spirit is that we shall come with a willing heart to believe what we find in the Book, and, too, God has never promised to answer the prayers of any but His own children. But you really did take Jesus Christ as your Saviour that time a few years ago when you united with the church, didn't you, Maris?"

"Oh, yes," she answered in a puzzled tone. "And I believe He is my Saviour of course. It's just that I can't seem to get any joy out of it. I can't seem to meet Him personally the way I'd like to, the way I believe my father and mother do. I used to be quite sure there was something very wonderful, a communion with Him that one could have in this life. I'm not so sure any more that that is for just ordinary people."

"God said 'whosoever *will*' didn't He? I'm quite sure the fellowship with Him is for anyone who wants it."

"Then why don't I have it? When I was saved that time, I thought that everything was going to be wonderful. Do you remember how the evangelist spoke of the joy of Christian living, and painted everything in bright colors? Yet I have never been conscious of that."

"Do you remember," he said, "how visiting speakers in school used to give us lectures on how wonderful it was to have good parents? Yet it was some time after I grew up that I became truly conscious of my father and mother, conscious of loving them and understanding them and wanting to be with them. In fact, it's only since I haven't them that I've learned to long for their companionship."

Maris looked up then as if she were startled.

"Why it's just the same with me," she said. "I think I never was conscious of how I loved my father and mother and wanted to be with them until lately. I've been going my own way. But these last few days I've been seeing how I have failed to appreciate them, and how I have hurt them so many times. Now a few minutes with father means so much. And a word from mother would mean everything, now that I don't have her."

"Yes, I know," he said sadly, "and the Christian life is often like that. Understand, I don't mean it's necessary for a person to live years after he's been saved before he learns to walk with the Lord. It's not normal or right. But if it has been so I think there comes a time when God brings us upstanding, perhaps through trouble, and we realize then that we don't have the fellowship we might have had. We see how we have grieved Him and how we have walked into the world, in ways that He would not go."

Maris nodded sadly. "Yes, I've done that!"

"It is then we wake up to how much we want Him," went on Lane. "And that's what He has been working toward all the time! To draw us after Him! Isn't it gracious of Him to want us?" Lane spoke tenderly, with awe in his voice.

"And then," he went on, "as soon as we find out how much we want Him, He delights to make Himself known to us. At least that is the way it has been with me."

"Does He? I wish I understood. He hasn't done it with me. What do you mean? Do you hear voices, or see visions, or what?"

"Oh, no," smiled Lane. "That is not His way of speaking to us now, because He doesn't need to any more. There is a far more intimate and wonderful relationship now than there ever was when He had to speak to man through the physical senses. Now," he sat up eagerly, "He is *in* us, you know."

Maris looked blank.

"I guess I don't understand," she said mournfully, "or else He isn't in me."

"Yes, He says He lives in everyone who has accepted Him as Saviour. That's why I asked you if you surely had. You see, when you accept Him, you're not just getting a ticket to heaven, you are receiving *His life*. You were dead in sin, now you are born from above. The third person of the Godhead comes into your heart to dwell. Don't ask me how. I only know it's so—because He says so, and also just as you know who is living in your house, even though you don't see them all the time. I found some years ago that the reason I wasn't having real fellowship with the Lord was because I was looking for Him *outside* somewhere. I wanted to talk to someone at a certain distance. I wanted to hear, or *feel* something. When all the time He was living *in* me, quietly waiting for me to recognize Him and yield to Him. It made all the difference in the world.

"And when you get to counting on the fact of His presence within you," went on Lane, as Maris sat listening wide-eyed, "you find that you get to depending on that 'Other' all the time. You are conscious of His personal, intimate love as never before, you're conscious that He is speaking to your inmost soul more clearly than ever you heard a voice, and you are conscious that He is continually pointing out things in His Word that you never saw before when you tried to read it by yourself. And the only thing that can hinder all this is your own will, wanting your own way."

Again Maris was still a long time thinking over the possibilities of such a walk with God.

"And you really think just anybody could have that?—even someone who had—gone—their own way—a long time, and paid no attention to Him?"

"He said so. 'If *any* man hear my voice and open the door I will come in to him and will sup with him, and he with me.' I know that's true," Lane's voice was low and gentle but it rang with glad certainty, "for I've found it so, and there's nothing, not *anything,* that can satisfy your heart like that fellowship with Him."

Just then Maris heard a cautious voice calling, "Maris, Maris." It was Gwyneth sent by Sally to say that dinner was ready.

"Oh, I'm sorry! I'll have to go! I had no idea I had stayed so long. But—I'd like to hear more about this. I'm really interested."

"We'll talk again," said Lane eagerly. "Any time you have a spare minute just give me a call on the phone and I'll meet you here."

"All right, I will!" said Maris happily. "There are a lot of questions I'd like to ask you, things that have come into my mind these last few days. And I do want to know how to understand the Bible."

A great light came into the young man's eyes.

"I'll love to help in any way I can," he said quietly.

Then Maris was gone, and Lane sat there a few minutes in the shadow of the hemlocks thinking, remembering the wistful look in the girl's eyes as he had talked, his heart thrilling that she cared to listen to such things, wondering why he had ever drifted out of touch with a girl like this. Why hadn't he written to her often and kept up their boy and girl friendship? If all that her brother said about her fiancée was true it seemed a terrible thing for a girl like this to be tied for life to a man who was a worldling. Of course it might be that Merrick was prejudiced. But—well—it wasn't his business. Perhaps it was all in God's plan for Maris' life. But oh, he hoped she didn't have to walk a way of sorrow because she had made a wrong choice.

He closed his eyes and could see her sitting there in the opposite chair with the long cool shadows of the branches waving above her softly, and the eagerness in her eyes. He could see the sweet line of cheek and chin, the delicate curving of her lovely lips, the shadows under her tired beautiful eyes, and he wished he could do something to take the weary look from her face.

Then suddenly he flung his hands down from across his eyes and sprang to his feet.

"Look here, Lane Maitland," he said to himself severely, "you'd better snap out of this! This is another man's fiancée you're thinking about! Get busy and think of something else! I wonder what those kids are doing with that paint by this time?" and he turned and hurried away to see.

But the next day, about noon, Gwyneth brought to Maris a little package that she said Lane Maitland had asked her to deliver.

When Maris had time to open it she found it was a beautifully bound Bible, and a note from Lane:

Dear Maris,
I thought perhaps the notes in this special edition might help with some of your perplexities, and I've jotted down a few references you might look up, in line with what we were saying.
The boys send their love,
As ever,
Lane

Maris touched the soft leather cover happily, fluttered the leaves through with pleasant anticipation, noted the neat sheets of paper here and there slipped in, written over with clear characters, in Lane's handwriting, caught a word or two of explanation, and wished she might have time to sit right down and begin her study. It filled her with comfort to have someone interested in her problems and taking all this trouble to answer her vague questions. She laid the Bible on her bedside table and went about her multitudinous duties of the day heartened for her work, and looking forward to a few moments that she would snatch here and there to pursue this new wonderful study.

It was another busy day, and not until late in the evening did Maris have opportunity to get at her new Bible. Her Bible! For she discovered when she opened it with leisure to look it through that Lane had written her name on the flyleaf.

She had a Bible of course, one that she had had since she was quite a young girl, but this one was most intriguing. It had soft dark blue leather covers, and most interesting and enlightening footnotes, and moreover the little loose leaves in Lane's handwriting put her in touch with many verses that seemed to be written just for her own present needs. She pored over it earnestly, and put it down reluctantly when she happened to glance at her watch and found how late it was.

As she lay down to sleep at last it was with the words of Scripture ringing in her heart:

"When thou passest through the waters, I will be with thee; and through the rivers, they shall not overflow thee: when thou walkest through the fire, thou shalt not be burned; neither shall the flame kindle upon thee."

It was a verse she had learned long ago when she was a child but she had not thought of for years. Now from all the verses Lane had marked it seemed to stand out and comfort her. The Lord was in her, Lane had said, and whatever came to her He would not leave her. She fell asleep with the thought in her mind. She was walking through the waters now, but He was here. He had allowed it all to come to her for some wise reason. And the verse said "When thou passest *through*." That meant that it would be over sometime. It was a good thought upon which to go to sleep.

14

FOR the next few days Maris used every leisure moment in studying her new Bible, and following out all the suggestions that Lane had given her in his notes. Now and again questions would come to her mind for which she could not find an answer and she wrote them down in a tiny note book, to ask Lane the next time she saw him.

But there were not many opportunities to talk with Lane, even though he was living just next door. He was much engrossed with his young charges. He had established a private school in the back yard. The two boys were carrying on their studies along the same lines as they would have done in school, only perhaps with a little more individual attention than would have been possible in school. Lane was a fascinating teacher, and the boys adored him. He told them reasons for everything that their young minds questioned, and led them on to wonder over the amazing world in which they lived, giving them now and again a Bible memory verse which clinched the nature study they had been carrying on with birds and squirrels and rabbits and butterflies and flowers as intimate subjects.

Maris, as she heard from time to time a report of their work, realized that her young brothers were enjoying a rare privilege of companionship with this man, the memory of which could not but be of lasting benefit all their lives.

"But how can you spare the time, Lane?" she asked him once in a brief moment when she had speech with him. "Aren't you in some kind of business? I haven't asked Merrick about it, but surely you have interests of your own that must be looked after, and you mustn't let our boys absorb even all your leisure, either."

Lane smiled.

"Don't worry," he said. "They are only helping to fill in an interim. Two positions are open to me in the fall and I'm not sure which I shall decide upon. One will take me to New York. The other is around here. I'll tell you about it sometime when we have more time. But in either case I've got to fix up the house, either to sell, or to live in, and that's going along in fine shape. I have a plumber at work now making alterations, putting in another bathroom or two, a more modern sink, and a new heating plant. I have to more or less supervise those things. And the painters will be here next week to assist the ones who have already started the job on the back kitchen."

He grinned at the boys who were listening wide-eyed, on the other side of the hedge, and they responded with adoring smiles.

"Well, it's just wonderful that you are able to take care of the boys," said their sister gratefully. "I'll never forget it."

"That's nice," said Lane pleasantly. "I like to be remembered." Then he chanted with a merry twinkle in his eye a scrap of the old song:

Thus would we pass from the earth and its toiling,
Only rememberd by what we have done.

Maris gave him a quick keen glance as she smiled. Then after an instant, "It will be more than that, Lane," she said gravely.

He looked at her sharply, quizzically, a great wistfulness in his eyes, and then said:

"Now, just what might you mean by that, kind lady?"

"Why," she laughed half embarrassedly, "I don't just know that I can analyze it, but there'll always be more to your memory than just things you have done, no matter how wonderful they were. Why, you're a very dear old friend, you know," she finished lamely, with a glowing color suddenly stealing over her white cheeks.

He looked at her steadily for an instant, considering that, and a gravity began to dawn in his eyes.

"I see," he said, almost formally. "Well, I mustn't keep you any longer." He went away with the little boys trooping after him, and left her standing there watching him with a vague discomfort in her mind. Had she somehow been rude to him? She hadn't meant to be. She had been trying to make him understand how much she appreciated what he was doing for them, how much he meant to them all as a friend. She might have been blundering and awkward in the way she had put it, but she had meant it all right. Had she hurt him? Just what had she meant anyway when she tried to express herself so awkwardly? And also just what had been the significance of that grave withdrawing look in his eyes when he went away?

But she had no time, of course, to consider these questions. The very air seemed bristling with questions anyway for her weary heart, and there was little time to take them to the Bible for satisfaction, even little time for prayer, when she was not almost too weary to keep awake.

Two days later she found a little resting place in the middle of the afternoon. The night nurse had appeared unexpectedly and sent her out to get some air. She wandered over once more toward the hedge and looked across.

She had somehow felt a reluctance to call Lane on the telephone. He might be busy. Someone might hear her and wonder.

But as she looked across the hedge she heard his heavy voice speaking.

"I wondered if you were never coming again, lady."

"Oh," she said, "you're there! I'm glad. There are some things I have so wanted to ask you. Can you wait a minute till I get my Bible?"

"All the afternoon at your service," he said pleasantly. "The boys are doing the back door and steps. They're stationary for a time at least."

Maris ran into the house and was back quickly with her Bible, and she found when she came through the hedge that Lane had his Bible too, the counterpart of hers, only much worn, and with the bloom of hard usage upon its leather cover.

Maris put her hand out and touched it as it lay on the arm of the lawn chair next her own.

"Beautiful with use!" she said wistfully. "I wonder if mine will ever look like that from the same cause. I'm afraid I don't know enough to use mine as much as you have yours."

"You have the same teacher, the Holy Spirit," he said reverently trying not to show his great gladness in his eyes and voice.

"Oh!" she said with a voice full of awe. "That seems too great to be true, that the Holy Spirit would teach me!"

Their eyes met and something sweet and tender flashed in their glances, something that thrilled even to their spirits.

"You don't know how I prize this Bible," said Maris, struggling to free herself from a sense of confusion that she did not understand. "It was so wonderful of you to give it to me. I shall always count it one of my dearest treasures."

Another sudden glad look passed between them, and

then Lane, unaccountably grave again, said in a quiet voice:

"I wasn't sure whether I might presume to give so intimate a gift, but I thought, since you are to be married soon, you would let me call it a wedding present."

A sudden awful silence fell between them like a pall. Something seemed to clutch at Maris' throat and try to strangle her. Her glance went down and a slow color stole up into her cheeks, and then receded quickly leaving them white again as death. After an instant she spoke and her voice seemed constricted, embarrassed. It sounded very little and far away even to herself:

"But you see, I'm not going to be married soon," she faltered.

He looked up quickly, a sort of breathlessness in his voice.

"You're *not?* Oh, you mean you are putting off the day? You are not going to be married on the thirtieth? I thought you would probably postpone it on your mother's account."

"No," said Maris, and suddenly knew that she wanted to tell him, even though nobody else knew yet. "No, I am not going to be married at all. I have broken my engagement!"

"Oh!"

There was a great deal in that simple utterance. Astonishment, question, almost bewildered delight, and quick caution, ending in tender sympathy.

Maris couldn't seem to think of anything else to say and the pause was long. Then Lane said again, in a more studied tone:

"Oh—!" and then added quickly, "I can't say I'm sorry! I didn't know Mr. Thorpe. But of course I know your family are the gainers by this. Is it—? Did you—?" He paused and wished he had not begun that idea. But she was quick to anticipate his meaning.

"I don't know." She gave a vague little laugh. "I haven't got used to it enough to know whether I should count it a calamity or not. In fact there have been so many calamities that I haven't been able to differentiate them yet from each other. And, yes, I suppose I did it because of my family. That is, of course I couldn't go away now. But it didn't *have* to be for that reason. If things had been right—something could have been arranged."

"I understand," he said gravely, and she knew he did.

"I thought you would," she said, although she had had no idea of saying that. The words just came out of her inner consciousness without her knowledge. "That's why I wanted to tell you. The family don't know it yet."

"Thank you," he said, and then after a pause. "The family will be very happy over it."

"Will they?" asked Maris. "I've been wondering."

"They will!" said Lane with emphasis, as if he were very sure.

"It almost seems," said Maris, hesitating, "as if God, perhaps, sent all these things—just to interrupt—!"

"I'm sure He did!" said Lane with a ring of assurance in his voice. "He does things like that sometimes."

The pause was longer this time, and then Maris said with a light little laugh that covered a great deal of feeling very inadequately:

"Well, then, in that case wedding gifts are usually returned. Do you want me to give this Bible back? Because I don't want to do it. I want to keep it always."

His eyes looked at her very tenderly.

"That's what I want you to do, keep it always," he said. Then in a matter-of-fact tone, as he reached for his own Bible:

"Now, shall we get to those questions before you are called away again? By the way, apropos of what we were talking about the other day, here's a bit of a quotation I found last night:

O Lord, my heart is all a prayer,
But it is silent unto Thee;
I am too tired to look for words,
I rest upon Thy sympathy
To understand when I am dumb;
And well I know Thou hearest me.

I know Thou hearest me because
A quiet peace comes down to me,
And fills the places where before
Weak thoughts were wandering wearily;
And deep within me it is calm,
Though waves are tossing outwardly.

She listened as he read and a great longing came into her heart to have an experience like that. To be able to trust and rest and find such a peace. But she couldn't put what she was feeling into words. It seemed to choke her, and the tears were blocking the way.

"Oh!" was all that she could utter.

"Yes," he said smiling, as if he understood. "It's like that."

"You have experienced that!" she challenged in a kind of wonder.

"Sometimes." He wasn't exactly smiling, but there was a sort of radiance in his face as if he were remembering things too wonderful to tell.

"Oh, I would like to have a trust like that!" she said hungrily.

"You can have if you are willing to go all the way with Him," said Lane gently. "Listen to this one:

But all through life I see a Cross
Where souls of men yield up their breath,
There is no life except by death,
There is no vision but by faith,

Nor justice but by taking blame,
Nor glory but by bearing shame,
And that eternal Passion saith,
Be emptied of glory and right and name.

Maris was very still as he finished the words.

"That's very high ground," she said at last. "It makes one's petty outcries and questions seem very small and shaming. I wish I might have had that outlook on life when I was a child, and grown up with it. It certainly would have saved me a lot of mistakes later." She drew a sad little sigh and gazed across the far stretch of lawn with its border of tall trees. "I wasn't brought up to cry for everything I saw, nor to have everything I wanted, but when they came without the asking I guess I was carried away by them, and forgot real values. I guess I can see why the Lord had to send me a lot of hard things all at once."

Lane smiled understandingly.

"Yes. I went through that too. It took a lot of jolts to make me understand. I read something the other day that seemed to fit my case exactly. It said: 'We can't understand why God doesn't want to do nice things for nice people like ourselves! That is because we have never seen ourselves as we are, as He sees us. When we do, we shall be dumb with wonder that He has had anything to do with us, and His infinite gift of Jesus Christ His Son shall be all to us, filling our whole heart and life.' When I came to the place where I saw myself in that way I was bowed with shame. And then when I reached that in spite of my indifference and foolish lack of understanding, He yet wanted me in close relationship to Himself, I was filled with a great overflowing joy. It's wonderful, Maris, when you get to realize that. There's nothing like it!"

Maris looked at him wistfully.

"I'm so glad you're like this," she said suddenly. "I didn't know there were any men, not any *young* men, anyway, that talked this way, that felt as you do. Tell me, how did you get to know God? You weren't interested in such things when you were in school."

"No," he said sorrowfully, "I was going my own way then, just having a good time, the world all before me and everything lovely. I never thought of God. And then when sudden sorrow came, two sharp blows one after the other, I began to think that God was cruel. That He hated me! I almost doubted what I had been taught, that He so loved the world that He gave His only begotten Son to save us. But one day I heard someone say that it is because people live in the things they possess instead of in their relationship to God that God seems at times to be cruel. And then I began to think. I began to reach out to God. For I had pretty well tried out everything else that appealed to me. They all had turned to dust and ashes, and I felt God calling me. And as soon as I was ready to listen I found Him ready to reveal Himself to me. You see I wouldn't listen to Him as long as I was happy and comfortable and had everything I wanted. So He had to send sorrow to bring me to Himself."

"I wonder," said Maris thoughtfully, "if that isn't just what has been happening to me. Oh, you're helping me a lot to get my feet on solid ground. It seemed to me at first when all these things began to happen at our house, that I was utterly dumbfounded. Everything I had believed in or rested upon had failed me. I wondered if there was a God. And yet I had no other refuge. But you are making me begin to get a little glimmer of light."

"Oh, I'm glad!" said Lane, with a lilt in his voice. "But now let's go to His Word. That's better than any explanation of mine. I've been digging deep in this treasure store of late and God has shown me some wonderful things. Turn to the first chapter of Ephesians and let's see what God says about what we are to Him."

So they sat and studied for an hour and a half. Others

might have discussed a trip to Europe, the best modes of travel, the best places to stop, the best side-trips to take, but they were deep in the Word of God, talking about the things of another world.

If Tilford Thorpe could have looked in upon them from behind the hedge that shut away the street he would have been hard put to it to understand what they were doing. With their two heads bent low over their Bibles, fluttering over the leaves, discovering new thoughts, Lane with his Greek Testament casting new light on old familiar words, talking with wonder in their voices of a spiritual world which was as real to them as if they could see it, shyly comparing similar heart experiences in the Lord's dealing with them. It would have been as inexplicable to Tilford as if they had been discoursing in a foreign language concerning some hitherto undiscovered country that they hoped some day to find and dwell within. He would not have understood it at all.

They talked until the little boys finished the door and the steps and came triumphant and clamoring, daubed with paint from their eyebrows down, and demanding that their idol should come and see if it was all right.

Maris suddenly discovered that it was time her patient had her tray and she must leave at once. But the two separated with one quick glad look into each other's eyes. It was only good night they said as they hurried away, but each realized that it was a good night that they had discovered this great bond of interest in the Word of God.

Maris as she crossed her own lawn marveled at the thrill in her heart as she thought on all she had been hearing and reading. It occurred to her to wonder how different things might have been between herself and Tilford if they could have had such sweet converse on the deeper things of life together. But it was scarcely conceivable. Trying to imagine Tilford studying the Bible with her was perhaps the most enlightening vision that had come to her yet, to make plain to her how far apart she and Tilford were concerning everything of real value. They would never have been one, no matter how hard she tried. They had so few points of contact. It would have been herself that would have had to measure to Tilford's standards, for it wasn't thinkable that he would be willing to measure to hers, nor even to try. He was all for this world, and had apparently no interest in another life.

Was it possible that she could have brought him to know the Lord? She stared at the question in her mind, realizing how far she had been from ever trying to get him to think of another world. Perhaps God had meant her to do that when He let her get to know Tilford. Perhaps she had utterly failed Him. Oh, it was all a terrible maze, and there was just one thing she could do now, and that was to take God at His word and go forward, learning to know and trust Him day by day, feeling her way with her hand in God's, believing that He knew the end from the beginning.

As she entered the house it suddenly came to her that tomorrow was to have been her wedding night and she hadn't once remembered it all day! That in itself was startling enough. If someone had told her three weeks ago that that could happen she would have laughed him to scorn. She would not have thought it possible. And now here she was with the whole thing taken out of the picture, and herself fully established in another kind of life, as if that had been a dream.

She had a passing wonder about Tilford. Where was he? What was he doing? Was he hurt and sorrowful? She couldn't imagine it. Only angry, and still stubborn. Why was it that she could see that trait in him now so clearly, and only a short time before she did not see it at all. She had thought him charming and admirable in every way. Why, oh, why did all that have to happen? Why did God let her go through all that experience only to put it away from her forever? Could it be possible that this wasn't the end after all? Was God perhaps going to send Tilford back to her, and give them a new life and new interests in better things together?

But to her amazement she found a shrinking in her heart. Was she, then, just angry with him for the way he had treated her in her trouble? Was she perhaps not being fair to Tilford? Had she ever tried to put herself in his place and realize what his side might be? Or had she taken it all out in finding fault with him? Instead of talking things over with him and giving him a chance to suggest that of course she must stay in her home now when they were in trouble, she had given her ultimatum and handed back his ring. Was that right and fair toward the man a girl had accepted? Could he help it that he had a disagreeable, managing, meddlesome mother who overinfluenced him? Maybe she should have been more gentle with him, and realized that his upbringing had been quite different from hers. Maybe she should have sent for him again and talked it over with him before turning him down so completely.

Of course he had been unsympathetic, and heartless, but there were influences at home back of that. Maybe she was all wrong. Maybe the new life to which she had just been committing herself as she read the Word of God with enlightenment, would require her to ask Tilford's forgiveness, to go on with her marriage possibly, sometime later when conditions at home would allow her to leave. Could that be what God wanted of her?

All these thoughts followed her like a deadly miasma that arose in her path and seemed to smother her, whenever she gave them space.

All the evening as she read to Lexie, who was growing restless as her normal health returned, as she did the hundred and one little tasks that filled the end of the long wearisome day, these thoughts pursued her. As she went to her room at last to prepare for rest, and tried to read her

Bible and recall some of the precious things that had gripped her heart, even as she knelt to pray with that new sense upon her of knowing her Lord as she had never known Him before, she kept thinking of Tilford. A great depression filled her spirit, like a premonition of some looming trial yet before her. She tried again and again to shake it off. She tried to regain the joy that had filled her while she was studying that afternoon with Lane, in that clean healthy happy atmosphere of sacred things, where Heaven was almost as if she could see it with her natural vision.

At last, unable to banish these things, unable to fix her mind upon her prayer, she cried out in great earnestness:

"Oh Lord! Show me definitely if I am right in what I have done. Show me once for all whether Tilford is a man with whom I could walk through life. Don't let me misjudge him, nor be unfair to him. Show me my own heart. Show me if he really loves me, and whether I could love him. I am all bewildered and I want to do what is right. Should I go back to Tilford some time and try to lead him to know You?"

It was a strange prayer, for somehow it seemed to be going against the promptings of her own heart, but she was so tired, and didn't understand herself. At last she arose with a feeling that she had put everything in God's hands, and could trust and rest.

15

THE sun shone forth gorgeously on June the thirtieth, Maris' wedding morning that was to have been. The fact came to her and challenged her attention the first thing when she woke up. Where was Tilford? Was he feeling dreadfully about it? Ought she to feel sorry for him? Somehow she couldn't summon any sorrow on that score.

There was something however in the atmosphere, or in her own heart, that tinged the day with regret, some pitiful little harking back to the gay things of the world that had occupied so much of her time lately. How she had hoped for a beautiful June day like this for her wedding day! How she had quoted to herself that foolish little saying "Blessings on the bride that the sun shines on!" and hoped it would be hers. Not that she was superstitious, but it was so nice to have all the silly sayings of the world fit in and be propitious.

And now here was the day she had hoped for, a sky without a cloud, a pleasant breeze blowing just a little, the world full of roses and beauty—and no wedding!

A few tears of hurt pride and broken romance stole out to picket the outpost, but were sternly remanded to their own place. Maris meant to have no nonsense today. Not a soul should suspect that she was shaken by the beauty of the day. Indeed she wasn't even sure she was shaken. It was only that it had come to her with such force last night, and again stronger this morning, that perhaps something more was required of her before this matter was buried forever out of sight. And yet what could she do? Her position had been right. She couldn't have a wedding when mother and Lexie were sick. That was settled long ago. Even if they were well by some marvelous miracle, well enough for the wedding to go forward, there was no wedding, for there had been no invitations, and there were therefore no guests!

Over and over these pestering thoughts went rampaging through her mind. She could not understand it. She had been so happy last night out there, turning her thoughts to heavenly things. She had felt that never again would she need to be upset by the things of the world, and now here this morning she was all out of sorts. Not exactly regretting what she had given up, but beset by tormenting thoughts and uncertainties. Tilford would of course have told her that she was worn out nursing her sick sister, and taking unnecessary burdens upon herself. But what would Lane Maitland tell her if he knew? And what would God tell her?

She did not yet know about the besetments of a Christian life, nor realize that Satan immediately attacks the way of any soul who leaves the ranks of his followers. But at last she realized that to trust God fully was all she could do.

As the day grew high the sun rose hotter, and the air was full of bird songs and perfume from flowers, but Maris resolutely put all thoughts of disturbing things out of her mind. The matter was settled. It was in God's hands. It was definitely out of hers. If there was anything wrong with what she had done to Tilford, God would surely show her.

She noticed that her father and Merrick looked at her anxiously when she came down to breakfast. They saw the shadows under her eyes, and wondered if she were sorrowing. They could not help but notice that Tilford had not been there for days.

They were at the table together for a few minutes, and neither Sally nor the nurse were in the room. There was a bit of constraint upon them all, for everybody realized what day this was, and what it was to have meant to them as a family. But it was left to Gwyneth to voice the feeling in all their hearts.

It was just as Sally went out with the empty plate after bringing in more griddle cakes that she mustered courage. That had been Sally's idea of a proper wedding-day breakfast, griddle cakes and sausage. Sally wanted to make the day as pleasant for Maris as possible.

"This would have been an awful pretty day for your wedding, Maris, wouldn't it?" Gwyneth said in a wistful little tone. She had been upstairs the night before trying to find her own maid of honor dress and hadn't been able to locate it.

Maris drew a little quick gasp of a breath and forced a smile.

"Yes, darling, it's a lovely day," she said, trying to pass it off casually.

Merrick looked up with a frown, and kicked his sister Gwyneth under the table.

"Tough luck, Maris!" he said in a tone that tried to sound sympathetic.

Maris looked up with a sudden thrill of pleasure that Merrick who so obviously had disliked Tilford should be offering her sympathy. But before she could answer him her father spoke.

"Maris, I haven't been saying anything. There really wasn't anything to say. But I want you to know that I—that we all—appreciate the beautiful way you have sacrificed yourself, and given up your plans, and gone sweetly about the new order of things without a murmur or a sign that you were terribly disappointed. It is a great grief to me. It will be a great grief to your mother when she gets well enough to realize what has gone on, that you should have had to put off your wedding. It seems as if we could never make it up to you. But I hope and pray that the Lord may somehow in the future years give you good measure of blessing, pressed down and running over, for the hard things you are passing through now."

Her father's eyes were full of love as he looked at her, and suddenly it seemed to Maris that her heart was so full she could not help breaking down and crying. And she mustn't! No, she mustn't. They wouldn't understand. They would think she was suffering terribly about putting off her wedding. And that was not true. It suddenly became plain to her that whatever God was going to show her as her duty for the future, she was not suffering now, except a little in her worldly pride, that she was not marrying Tilford Thorpe today. It was all at once just as plain as day to her that she did not love him. That she never had loved him the way a girl ought to love the man she was to marry.

That might not make any difference with what God would tell her to do in the future. Maybe God would look upon an engagement as too sacred to break, at least at this last minute. But she knew in her heart now that she never should have made it. The thought of marrying Tilford somehow brought a great burden to her.

Oh, if she could go back and do things over again, and walk carefully through her days, waiting on the Lord to send her joy in His own good time, and not go rushing out to seek it!

But she was aware that her father was still speaking to her.

"You know, dear, that just as soon as mother is really

out of danger, and Lexie is well enough to be otherwise looked after, we shall want you to go on with your plans. We realize that this must have been a very unhappy thing for Tilford to put up with, and we shall not want you to feel that you must hold up your plans forever—,"

Maris could stand it no longer.

"Oh, father, dear! Please don't say those things! I ought to have told you all several days ago, only I was so busy, and I sort of wished I could tell mother first. But I am not going to be married at all. I gave Tilford back my ring and broke the engagement several days ago. I wanted you to know it, but somehow there didn't seem to be any right time to tell you."

"But *my dear!*"

The father dropped his knife and fork and looked at her in dismay.

"My dear child! Your mother would not want her illness to have broken up your life, and put a great unhappiness upon you."

"You needn't worry about that, father. I found out I didn't love Tilford the way I ought to if I was going to marry him. I had begun to suspect it before mother was taken sick, but it took her illness to make it really plain to me. So no one need worry about that. I'm not heartbroken nor anything. I'm just glad and thankful I'm here, and can help, and rejoiced that mother's still here too. It would have killed me if I had been married and gone off, and then found mother was sick, and Lexie was sick, and I couldn't get to you!"

There was a dawning joy on the father's face, but he looked at Maris uncertainly.

"But, my dear! Isn't that being very unfair to Tilford? Now at this last minute? What will he say to that? Surely he will not give you up so easily! Does he know yet about your decision?"

Maris lifted her head a little with a proud tilt.

"Tilford has known it for several days. He has had the ring for nearly two weeks, and he hasn't been around here for more than a week. You needn't worry about Tilford. He is angry of course, but I—somehow I don't think Tilford ever really loved me, either, not the way you and mother love each other."

"Oh, my dear!" said Mr. Mayberry, and now his face really glowed with joy. "If that is all true this will be the gladdest house in the universe. You don't know how your mother has worried about you. She felt from the first that Tilford was not the right man for you. But she didn't want to say anything she would have to live down. Oh, my dear! How she will rejoice when she knows it! Oh, I do hope and pray that she may not leave us at least until she knows it."

Suddenly he got up and came around the table, putting his arms gently around his child and stooping down he kissed her softly on the forehead.

"Our little girl!" he said softly. "Our little girl back again. Our *own* again!"

"Great work!" said Merrick huskily getting up and following his father around the table. He stooped over and gave Maris a great bear hug and a resounding smack on her cheek, never knowing that he left a big tear beside the kiss. Merrick was a dear. She never knew before that Merrick cared that much.

"And won't you ever get married, sister? Will you stay with us always?" beamed Gwyneth. "But oh, sister, your *beautiful ring!*"

Suddenly Maris broke down and laughed.

"There are some things better than rings!" she told Gwyneth. "I'd rather be here at home with you all than have all the rings in the universe."

"That isn't the only ring in the world, kid," said Merrick gruffly as he took his cap and prepared to go out to his daily bus route. He alternated, one day early, the next day late. This was his late morning. He wouldn't be home till late in the evening tonight.

Somehow after that talk with her family the doubts and dismay and compunctions of the night before vanished, and Maris was very happy as she got up from the table and kissed her father and brother good bye. Then she stood in the doorway and watched them go away smiling. Father was going down to the office for a few hours. He had been well enough to go every day for the last week.

"Maris," said Gwyneth looking up after they had vanished around the corner, "what I'm worrying about is my maid of honor dress. Do you think I'll have any use for it? It won't stay in fashion long enough till I grow up big enough to wear a long dress, will it? What shall we do with it?"

"Oh, my dear sister. That's nothing to worry about. There are dozens of things to do. We can hem it up and use it for a party dress. It is very simple."

Gwyneth sighed.

"I wouldn't like it to be wasted," she said, "it's so pretty. It's the prettiest dress I ever had!"

"Yes, darling. It is pretty, and you'll wear it and have a lot of enjoyment out of it yet, I'm sure! It's simple enough, hemmed up, to wear to church even." Maris patted her sweet young cheek, and thrilled to think that these dear people all belonged to her. Her precious family!

Then the nurse came downstairs and her eyes seemed to be happier than usual.

"Do you know," she said stepping up to the door and speaking in a jubilant tone, "I believe your mother's pulse is a trifle steadier this morning than it has been at all."

Then all suddenly the morning became brighter than it had seemed before, and Maris' heart grew light as she went upstairs to her duties.

A wedding day! What was a wedding day beside a bit of hope like that. Not a wedding day with Tilford Thorpe, anyway!

The rest of the day went on glad feet. Maris had feared just a little that Tilford might appear on the scene and be disagreeable again, but now it didn't seem to matter. Her dear people were restored to the old-time fellowship that had been broken up ever since she had got to know Tilford Thorpe, and somehow other things grew small beside the joy of the family understanding. If only mother was well enough to know it too! If Tilford came let him come. Somehow that trouble too would dissolve like others.

So the day passed in tender ministrations.

There were duties for the household that she had long put by till a convenient time; they simply could not wait any longer. There were unexpected interruptions of callers, and telephone messages, and the evening came down, without a chance for Maris to go alone and do some Bible study as she had promised herself that morning to do. There was a game to play with Lexie who was allowed to sit up longer now. As she sat there beside the little girl's bed with the bedside table between them holding the Halma board, she could hear the boy's voices over on the Maitland lawn. They were playing ball with Lane! How good he was, caring for those children exactly as if they were his own brothers. Oh, if Tilford had been like that how different things would have been!

The game presently was finished. The boys' voices had trailed off farther, and she knew they were being sent to bed. Lexie would soon be asleep now, and she would have her promised Bible reading. So she sat down at last quietly in her own room, with her new Bible in her hand.

She heard a cab drive down the street and pause somewhere, but she was on the other side of the house from the street, and paid little heed to it. She had given up the thought that Tilford would come. The wedding day was almost over. In a few more hours it would be a thing of the past, a thing that never had been.

The Bible opened to Isaiah, and her eye suddenly fell upon a verse that Lane had marked. She had not seen it before. Such a strange arresting verse, as if it were spoken by the Lord straight to her soul, as if it were a kind of promise for her to take with her into her life:

"No weapon that is formed against thee shall prosper; and every tongue that shall rise against thee in judgment thou shalt condemn. This is the heritage of the servants of the Lord."

She had read so far when the nurse tapped at the door.

"I think there is somebody at the front door," she said, "and I saw Sally go out a few minutes ago. I can't leave your mother just now. Can you go? Your father is asleep."

Maris laid down her Bible and went downstairs, patting her rumpled hair smooth and glancing down at her neat little cotton house dress. Her wedding night and just about the time when she would have been walking down the church aisle to the time of the wedding march!

She went to the door, but at first saw no one, though there was a taxi standing at the curb. Then she discovered a man with a cap drawn low and a rough look about him.

"Are you Maris Mayberry?" he asked in a husky voice that she did not recognize.

"Yes," she answered, her heart beginning to beat excitedly, though she did not exactly know why.

"Well, step out here so your sick folks won't hear. I've got a message from your brother."

Maris with suddenly trembling limbs stepped out.

"Your brother Merrick has been in an accident, and he wants you. Doc MacPherson sent word you were to come with me quick. He may not live but a few minutes. Hurry!"

The man put out a strong hand and seized her wrist as she hurried to the cab.

"Get right in!" he said roughly, pushing her inside as she suddenly drew back and hesitated. "He might die before you get there and he wants to see you quick!"

Maris was pushed off her balance and thrown back into the taxi seat, and before she could get her balance again the man had jumped in beside her and slammed the door shut. She tried to speak, to protest, to ask a question, but the throb of the engine covered her voice and the cab had started on its way. There was a strange acrid smell about, and suddenly a revolting wet cloth was stuffed into her mouth, dripping down her throat in spite of her best efforts not to swallow the liquid. The pungent odor poured over her, filling her nostrils and driving away her senses, till her struggles grew less and less.

"No weapon that is formed against thee shall prosper—" the words floated through her mind like a call as she drifted out of the world she knew. "No weapon . . . this is the heritage of the servants of the Lord—! Oh, God! You are here!"

The light went out and she was away into a dark strange world where there was no longer anything that she could do.

16

THE little boys had lost their ball as darkness came down, over in the corner of the Maitland lot where the rhododendrons grew, close by the street. The boys had gone to bed, and Lane Maitland was out in the corner hunting among the rhododendrons for the ball. It was foolish of course to look for it when it was getting so dark. Better to wait till morning. But the boys had been distressed lest a neighbor's dog might find it and carry it off, so he had promised to hunt for it at once.

But he couldn't find it, of course. How could a dirty ball show up in the leaves among the rhododendrons? He was just about to go over and get a flashlight from his car which was still standing in the driveway not far away when he heard a car stop in front of the Mayberry house. He paused to look out through the shrubbery and see who it was. Could that be Tilford Thorpe? On Maris' wedding night?

Then he saw a man slink out from the car. No, that shabby sedan was not Tilford Thorpe's shining car, and that thickset, slouchy man with a stealthy gait was not Tilford. But who could it be? Perhaps he had the wrong house. Should he go and enlighten him? No, perhaps it was someone to see Sally. He waited a moment and in the silence of the evening heard the buzzer of the bell next door sound softly. If his ears had not been attuned already to everything that went on in that house he might not have recognized it, it had been muffled so effectively.

The Mayberry front door was standing wide, with only the screen door closed, but the man was not standing in the patch of light on the doorstep, he was in the shadow at the side of the door, where Lane could not see him. He could barely discern an indistinct shadow among the other shadows.

Then he heard someone come to the door. A low muttering from the man. "Maris!" He heard that. Too bad the way everybody bothered Maris, making her come down to the door for every little message. Well, perhaps he would run over himself and speak to her after the man was gone. He could just slip through the hedge and catch her before she went upstairs again. There were some verses he wanted to call her attention to. She might like to have them tonight. So he stood still where he was among the shrubbery.

The street was a quiet one, and there was little traffic at this time of night. The air was not stirring much, even the leaves were quiet, and across the space between his standing place and the Mayberry front door the man's words, though guarded, came in detached fragments. Then he saw Maris come out the door and stand in the shadow near the stranger, who edged along nearer to the street, while Maris followed. They were standing more nearly opposite to his position now, and he could hear that low mutter better. He distinctly heard the word "accident" and caught Merrick's name. And was that "MacPherson" he mentioned? Did the man say "Doctor"? Ah! That word was "dying." His heart missed a beat and he stood in consternation. Surely, surely he was mistaken.

And then to his horror he saw the burly fellow grasp Maris' wrist and draw her toward the sedan which was suddenly beginning to throb rapidly, and before he could stir or even cry out he saw Maris thrust into the car, and heard the door shut.

"Maris!" he called. "Maris, I'll take you!" but the car was already off down the street.

Desperately Lane turned and dashed across the lawn to the driveway where his car stood. He had left it there when he came in in the afternoon thinking perhaps Maris would like to take a short drive in the evening.

He swung into the seat and started his engine almost in one motion. Could he catch that car? Where were they going? Was Merrick really desperately hurt? Or had he not heard aright, and just jumped to conclusions? It was so easy to misunderstand someone at a distance. Who was that man who had come after Maris? One of the other bus drivers? Or just a passerby? Had Doctor MacPherson really sent him? Or was Maris simply on some errand, while he was getting all wrought up over nothing from the few indefinite words he had caught?

These questions danced around him as he drove, and taunted him. He couldn't answer them. He couldn't think it out at all. He couldn't be sure that he was even following the right car now. It was far ahead, and in the darkness he could only see a wink of light. The car that had stood in the street but a minute before might have turned down the pike, though he was almost certain that it had gone straight across. If he could only get a little nearer, enough to recognize it.

Lane stepped on his accelerator making his car shoot forward in great leaps. It was fortunate that there happened to be little traffic on this road just now. He was doing sixty, seventy, seventy-five! But the car ahead was speeding too. Would he make it before they reached the highway where he would be sure to lose them? Blindly he shot ahead, straining his eyes, his hair blowing in the breeze.

They were coming to the highway now. The traffic was thick. The other car was slowing down. The distance between them was less. He could almost read the license. He had made note of that while it stood beside the curb. There! It was dashing through traffic! It was gone! Straight across! He was held up by the light but the instant it changed he dashed across, and on the other side he saw again a speck in the distance, a single car. The road was so shadowed with trees just here that it was hard to discern. If it had not been for the little blinking tail light he would not have been sure whether a car was still there. And sometimes even that light disappeared as if it had been turned off for a minute.

They were coming into the wide country. He knew the general direction. There were no towns for some distance now, and there were wide stretches of fields. Was he going on a fool's errand, following some farmer's car perhaps, much like the sedan he had seen at the Mayberry's curb? Or was this really the car he had started out to follow? Perhaps he was wasting valuable time and ought to go back and report to the police. But just the thought that Maris might be in that car in trouble, and that if he abandoned it and went back now he would be losing the last possible clue, kept him rushing on through the night. Thank God there were telephones. If he got too far away from the city and found he was following the wrong scent he could at least telephone to the police and get action at once. So he kept on. He glanced at his gas. He had plenty. He was glad he had had it filled up just before dinner when he and the boys were out for a drive.

On and on they went, turning now and then an obscure corner into a narrow dirt road, just a country road between fields. But he was still so far behind that he could not read the license plate of the sedan. What could they be going away out here for? It was miles from Merrick's bus line. He couldn't be in an accident away out here! There must be something crooked about this, or else he had not heard aright. Perhaps Maris herself was in some kind of danger! "Oh, Father in Heaven," his heart cried out, "help her! Let me save her."

And now as they turned into a narrow lane he grew cautious. If there were crooks ahead, kidnapers perhaps, and they felt they were being followed there was no telling what they would do to throw him off their trail. So he turned out his lights. There was no danger here of meeting other traffic. They hadn't met a car for miles.

And then suddenly the car ahead turned sharply off the road into a field and went lurching and bumping across the rough ground, slowing down now because it was impossible to speed in such going.

Abruptly Lane stopped his car at the side of the narrow road. He was just emerging from a dense wood which ran on each side and he was well hidden. But the sky was luminous overhead, for the stars were thick and there was the brightness of the soon-approaching moon. The landscape ahead of him stretched far to the horizon, with just at that point no intervening towns or woods to hide the vision. He could discern the lurching car easily now. It showed clearly against the light of the sky. And then suddenly he saw what made his heart stand still with fear. There was a small airplane standing out there in the field, and the car was going straight toward it!

Even as he looked the lights of the plane winked on, and there was the subdued sound of its motor warming up. The car he was following signaled with its headlights. This was all prearranged, that was obvious. He was convinced now that Maris was in that car. He remembered how as he had watched it at the curb it seemed as if she had been forcibly pulled into the car.

What were they going to do with her? Kidnap her? But

why would they kidnap the daughter of a plain business man who was known to have little money?

Ah! But it was known that she was to marry the scion of a millionaire! Perhaps that was it! He ought to have stopped to telephone the police before he came off on this wild chase alone, but how could he? There would have been no clue at all then. Nothing for them to follow even if they knew. It would be just one more kidnaping case with a hopeless wait for contacts from gangsters, and maybe an unknown grave at the end. No, he must do this thing alone! It was almost hopeless, but he must try. He must somehow rescue Maris himself, or at least find out whether she was surely in that car. In a moment more it would be too late perhaps. That plane was revving up. He could not follow it into the sky, that was certain.

If he only had a revolver in his car he might try shooting the air out of those tires and stopping the car before it reached the plane. But he had no gun and likely it would not be wise to try if he had. Criminals would have more guns than he had, and be a thousand times more skilled in their use.

If he started his car again they would know they were being watched and followed and would soon put him out of the running. Perhaps it would be better to try reaching the place on foot. Certainly the other car was making slow progress over the rough ground.

Silently he got out of the car and started into the field, trying to keep as much as possible against the background of the woods so that his moving form would not be visible to the enemy. But he had gone but a few steps before a low sharp whistle reached his ears. They must have sighted him and were signaling one another.

The sedan rushed along over the bumps heedlessly now, and quickly covered the remaining space between it and the plane. He could see a figure detach itself from the plane and run toward the car. Maitland started on a run toward them. The back door of the sedan had swung open and the driver reached in and lifted something, someone perhaps, wrapped in a long dark cloth.

"Maris! Maris!" Maitland's voice rang out, but there came no answering voice, only muttered curses from the men. Another man came from the plane and took one end of the burden, while the thickset one ran back and started his car, lurching wildly away over the field.

"Maris! Maris!" cried Maitland in great gasps as he ran, but the inert burden the men carried gave forth no sound, and an instant later a shot rang out and a bullet spattered by his feet, startling him so that he stumbled and fell, which perhaps saved his life, for the next bullet was aimed a little higher.

But as he dropped he saw the men against the sky lifting their burden into the plane, and almost at once it moved off circling the far end of the field and then rose through the night.

Lane Maitland was on his feet again instantly, but the plane was a mere bird against the night. It carried no light to pick it out among the stars. His heart was heavy with fear.

"Oh God," he cried aloud. "You know where she is! Save her! She is Your child!"

He stumbled blindly back to his car. The other car had disappeared.

He managed to get his car turned, though it was a difficult task in that narrow lane. Then he drove wildly back to town again, trying to think just what he ought to do, trying to order the circumstances in his mind.

Of course there was a possibility that he was all wrong in his first premise. In the darkness he might have mistaken Sally or one of the nurses for Maris, and Maris might be even at that moment safe at home in her bed sleeping.

Although to his sharpened senses this seemed a most remote possibility, he decided that he had better telephone from the nearest station to the Mayberry house and find out before he made any other moves. He had to keep his head and remember that if he had made a mistake it might mean unpleasant publicity and endless embarrassment to the people he loved best in the world.

But if she was not at home where was she?

Was she in that little tramp plane, winging somewhere, through the night? And where? And dead, or alive?

Of course the police would have to know it at once if she was gone. But he would have to contact some of the family first. They might have some answer to it all.

Was Merrick really hurt, dying perhaps, somewhere? Was it conceivable that the call to come to him might have been genuine?

In that case he would have to tell Mr. Mayberry, and how he shrank from bringing more anxiety to that already harassed spirit!

Then next came the wonder who could have done this thing? Just gangsters, for ransom? Had there been a ransom note found yet?

And if not gangsters for ransom, was there any other possibility? Was it conceivable that a quiet girl like that had enemies? Was someone else perhaps in love with her? What was this Tilford Thorpe like anyway? He wished he knew. Of course Merrick's ideas of him must be taken with a grain of salt, for Merrick all too evidently hated him.

Of course Tilford Thorpe would have been the natural person to be informed first, of all that had happened, if he were still engaged to Maris. But Maris had distinctly said that the engagement was broken. Tilford Thorpe then, must be out of the picture, except as he might possibly figure in the gangsters' minds as they laid their plans for ransom.

Just then there loomed the clear red and white lights of a service station off to the left on a macadam road, and he went straight to them and demanded a telephone.

There was only one attendant just then and he was busy outside waiting on a car. He motioned toward the telephone, and Lane hurried into the little office, thankful to have it to himself for the moment.

His voice trembled as he called the familiar number, and he stood there dreading to hear the answer, wondering what the next two or three minutes would reveal. Then he heard the receiver click off at the other end and Merrick's voice, "Yes? Hello!"

"Oh, are you *home?*" he said shakily, weak with relief.

"Sure, I'm home! Where would I be? What's the idea?"

"Well, of course," said Maitland, "but something queer has happened. Is Maris there?" His voice was quivering with anxiety.

"Maris? No. We thought she'd gone out riding with you. The nurse said she heard a car at the door and Maris went out."

Lane Maitland suppressed a groan.

"Oh, then it's true! Listen, Merrick. I'm afraid she's kidnaped. I was out in the yard and a sedan drew up. A man went to your door. I thought I heard him say you'd had an accident and were dying. He said you wanted Maris right away. He said Doctor MacPherson had sent him for her. He took hold of her arm and pushed her in the car and shut the door. I called out but the car started right away. My car was there in the drive so I followed. They went out Lundy's Road, turned into the country, and ended up at a small plane in a field. I was too far away to see much, but I'm sure I saw them carrying someone, rolled in dark cloth, to the plane. It started almost immediately. I called again but the only answer I got was a shot that whizzed by. Merrick, is there anyone who would want to kidnap her, or is it just plain gangsters? We must get busy at once. I have the license number, but that's not much. The plane went north. Should the police know, or what? I'm at a filling station. Sixty-fourth and the pike. Can you give me any suggestion or shall I come straight home?"

"Good night!" said Merrick solemnly. "Are you kidding me, Lane? Haven't you got Maris there?"

"No!" said Lane sadly. "It's all true. Don't waste time. Do you think we ought to tell Thorpe before we report it to the police?"

"No!" said Merrick sharply. "Not that guy. He's no business with our troubles. Not any more. She told us this morning she'd broken the engagement. He hasn't been around for several days. But say! Wait! You don't think maybe—! Lane, I don't know but *he'd* be that mean. I wouldn't put it past him. Maybe he kidnaped her himself!"

"You don't think any man is as low as that, Merrick! Not any man who loved her!"

"Well he'd do anything to get his own way. I have an idea he wanted Maris to go on with the wedding in spite of mother's illness. I know several things they don't know I heard. He's a skunk if there ever was one!"

"Well, don't waste time. This was the wedding day, wasn't it? Would he take her off and hide her or what, do you think?"

"I don't know. Maybe take her on board the ship. Carry her off to Europe! I wouldn't be surprised. They were to sail tonight."

"What ship? What time?" asked Lane sharply.

"The *Emperor.* Midnight. They had a bridal suite or something of the sort. But how could we find out until it was too late, and what could we do if it was so?"

Merrick's voice was full of despair.

"There are always things to do. I'll phone to the ship. You phone to that bird's father and see if you can find out a thing or two. Tell him what's happened. He's likely a decent man even if his son isn't. Better try that before we go calling in the police and getting things in the paper."

"Okay. I'd like a word with that guy's papa!"

"Look out, brother. You must remember you may be talking to enemies. Well, get busy. This number is Fenwick 36498 if you need me. I'll call you as quick as I find out about the ship."

Lane Maitland went to work in a business-like way, and soon got in touch with the ship company. It did not take long. Yes, Mr. Tilford Thorpe had booked passage for himself and wife on their ship, weighing anchor that night at midnight. No, they were not as yet on board, but had sent word that morning that they would arrive early in the evening. Mrs. Thorpe was not well and wanted to have her berth ready. Did the gentleman wish to leave a message for them?

Maitland said no, sharply, and hung up. He put a shaky hand to his lips and tried to still their trembling. So, that was that! It didn't settle the matter fully, but it was at least a clue.

He looked at his watch. There was not too much time. Could he get there before it was too late? And having got there, could he do anything? Would she want him to do anything? Suppose it was only a quarrel between them and Thorpe had made it up?

With perplexities thickening about him he called up the Mayberry house and Merrick answered.

"I couldn't get the old bird," he said gloomily. "He and the mother were out. Nobody knew anything about Tilford."

"Well, they're booked on board, Mr. and *Mrs.* Tilford Thorpe, and expected to arrive soon. They said the lady wasn't so well and wanted to go to bed at once. Now, I think I'd better drive right to New York. I'm thirty miles on the way, and I think I can make it before the ship sails at midnight. I tried to get a plane, but the next one would get me there too late. They couldn't tell me about hiring a special until I got over to the field, and by the time I got there it wouldn't allow much margin. Counting all the time from flying field to dock and so on, I think it's best to drive. Not much traffic this late, and anyhow I might need the car when I get up there. I can always abandon it if it seems best."

"But you ought not to be doing all this,"protested Merrick. "I'm her brother. That's my job."

"Cut that out. You've got to stay by the house. The family have got to be protected from this as long as possible. Nobody will miss me. You tell the boys in the morning, if I'm not there, that I was called away on business and am leaving them to carry on camp and keep up discipline just as if I was there. Tell them there'll be an extra honor stripe on their shoulders if they do."

"Okay," said Merrick solemnly.

"You say your father is asleep?" went on Maitland. "That's good. Perhaps we'll know more before you have to tell him anything. Better tell Nurse Bonner the truth. You can trust her, and she will look after Lexie. My car's filled now, and I'm off. I'll phone you from New York as soon after midnight as I can make a station. So long! Cheer up! God isn't dead!"

"Maybe not," said Merrick drearily. "Oh, I say, Lane, wait a minute. What about those cops? Think I ought to let them know?"

"I guess you ought. In general that's always the first thing to do. If there's one you are sure you can trust to keep it quiet, perhaps it would be well to ask his advice. Of course it isn't necessary to tell the whole family history. Not yet, anyway, but you might say you didn't know but it would turn out just to be a practical joke put on by a friend, or something of that sort, and you will let him know just as soon as you hear from one who has gone to investigate. How would that be?"

"Okay, perhaps. I know the chief up here in our district. He'll keep it under his hat, unless he has an idea it may be gangsters. But I'll hold him off till I hear from you if possible. Would you try the old Thorpe bird again?"

"Perhaps. It might give you some idea whether the family knows about it, in which case keep away from publicity till we know more. Now, keep cool! I wish you knew how to pray!"

"Well, I useta know. I might make a stab at it in a case like this. Take care of yourself, Lane. I don't know what we'd do without you. Good bye. I've got to get busy."

They hung up and Lane jumped into his car and away northward, but poor Merrick, bewildered at the responsibilities thus thrust upon him, gave a dazed look about him and uttered his favorite word when excited:

"Gosh! Can you beat it?"

17

MARIS came back to consciousness with someone pulling off her slippers and dropping them on the floor.

What floor?

She was instantly aware of disaster, fear, terror that had been about her when she passed out. What had made her pass out? She had never fainted in her life. She had always been proud of that. Ah! Now she knew. She recalled the burly man who had lured her into that awful car, telling her Doctor MacPherson had sent for her, that Merrick had had an accident and was dying and wanted her. It was perfectly clear to her now that there must have been something crooked about the whole thing. Maybe Merrick wasn't even hurt. Maybe it was all a hoax. She had read about people being kidnaped. But why would anyone want to kidnap *her*? All her friends knew that they were not rich people and could not pay a ransom. Surely the criminal world must know that, they were said to be so well informed as to people's private lives.

Stay! They had heard of her engagement to Tilford perhaps. The Thorpes were reputed millionaires. And the underworld scarcely would know yet that the engagement was broken. She had told nobody but Lane and her family. Maybe they had heard it was her wedding night.

Her heart suddenly sank at the prospect. If that was what had happened there would be nobody to come to her rescue. Tilford of course would not be searching for her. Only her dear family would be in anguish. Her poor tired family! Oh, that must not be! Somehow she must get away without their having to suffer. It was entirely up to her.

Yet she was not alone. Almost as if a voice had spoken in her secret heart she heard those words again: "No weapon that is formed against thee shall prosper." Those words she had read in her Bible just before all this awful thing happened. No, she was not alone. Her Lord was with her, living in her!

She did not really think this all out in words, it was just a comforting consciousness that came to her as she lay quite motionless, trying to get her dazed senses back into working order.

The one who was working over her had put on some other shoes that did not belong to her. They were tight and uncomfortable. Now she was fussing about her head, lifting it a little and tucking something underneath, arranging it around her face, pulling out her hair here and there and patting it.

The sudden thought crossed her mind that perhaps they thought she was dead and were preparing her for burial. Almost she cried out, but she held herself in steady control and waited. She must not let it be known that she was conscious. She tried to be utterly relaxed and lie limp, but her heart seemed to beat so wildly that she felt it could almost be heard.

This was a woman working around her. She could hear the rustle of her dress. Once a sleeve brushed across her hand. She was arranging her drapery about her feet. Maris became aware of alien garments upon her, unaccustomed garments, fitted, long, and voluminous. It was as if her inner consciousness went out stealthily spying to convey to her the details of her situation. As if her senses had banded together within her body to feel out and inform her of everything. Her hand that lay quiet at her side came alive suddenly and informed her she was clothed in heavy smooth satin of a soft rich texture. She had a consciousness that her hair had recently been brushed and ordered pleasantly. There was something on her head, a hat or a band or coronet of some sort, and there was a sense of something soft and cloudlike near her cheek and forehead, something light as air, or was that only part of a dream? She lay there trying to think it out. And now she discovered a ring upon her finger twisted slightly, the great stone pressing against the flesh of the next finger. Cautiously she pressed her fingers closer to make sure. A ring, yes. Like her own that she had given back to Tilford. Was this just a dream?

The person who bent above her wore heavy beads about her neck and she could hear them rattle against each other as she leaned over and smoothed the satin on the far side, so of course this must be a woman. She also wore cheap unpleasant perfume that Maris thought had a musty odor. She somehow felt this person was not overly clean. Maris was glad when with a final pat to the draperies the woman walked away. She walked heavily with a quick little nipping tread, as if her shoes were too tight.

What was this place?

Her mind went back to the car in which her consciousness had gone out, and that hateful bitter rag that had been thrust into her mouth. Had this woman been along? Was it she who had sat at the far end of the seat and helped to pull her in? It was all so vague and fraught with awful fear. So now what was this place and how did they get here? She found she had no memory that would suggest it.

The woman seemed to have stepped through a door. It

must be a bathroom for there was a sound of running water. Dared she open her eyes to look around?

Cautiously she lifted her lashes just a tiny bit and then wider, in a quick sharp glance, then shut them again for the woman was returning.

But she had seen enough to show her that she was on board a ship. She had distinctly seen the portholes either side of the dresser and the outline of the room was strangely familiar. It was like the picture of the bridal suite that Tilford had shown her. Had she then been kidnaped by gangsters and were they taking her abroad where her friends could never find her? Panic seized her and she felt the little pulse in her neck begin to throb wildly. But she must not get excited. She had need for every faculty. She must keep calm. She must not appear to be awake. She must think this thing through somehow. Her very life depended on this. The ship did not seem to be in motion. Perhaps there would be a way to escape before it sailed, though that was scarcely likely if her captors were really gangsters. They would have thought out all possibilities of escape and guarded against them. This woman was likely put here as her jailer.

But how did this theory fit with the silken garments she was wearing? Why should they dress her up this way? If she could only get a good glimpse of that woman. Dared she open her eyes and peep at her?

It seemed that she was standing over by the dresser, opening a small handbag, if she could judge by the sound. Cautiously she peered through her lashes. The woman was looking into the mirror and powdering her nose. She studied her an instant before she closed her eyes again. She was a stoutish elderly woman with shingled graying hair. And now, could it be true? She was setting a small youthful hat on her head. Was she perhaps going away? Would there be a chance to escape, or would someone else come?

That terrible man, perhaps, who had pushed her into the car?

The woman was turning her head to get the effect of the hat and as she swung around toward the bed Maris closed her eyes quickly holding herself rigidly quiet, but as she did so she caught a glimpse of the dress she was wearing, and saw that it was white satin, and that that was a wedding veil she had felt about her face, and silver slippers were on her feet!

She was filled with such horror that she could scarcely keep from shuddering and crying out, as she thought of the possibilities that were before her. That awful man—! Oh, what could it all mean? And what could she do? Were they going to try to force her through some horrible marriage ceremony? She could never hope to escape in those garments. She would be marked of every eye.

Then all at once came words ringing back into her heart: "No weapon that is formed against thee shall prosper . . . the heritage of the servant of the Lord," and a quiet self-control came over her. After all, God was here. Nothing could really harm her. Nothing could happen that he could not control.

"Oh, my heavenly Father! Help me!" cried her frightened heart. And then her mind became clearer so that she could think. She hadn't got this thing straight yet. It didn't make sense. People didn't go out and kidnap poor girls and take them on ship board to marry them, or to make sport of them. There was something more to it than that.

The woman was walking about the room now, picking up a few things and putting them into a small overnight bag. She must be going to leave. But who was coming to take her place?

As the woman bent over to fasten the bag, Maris ventured another quick look, and this time she noted a pile of handsome looking baggage over by the bathroom door.

There were initials on some of the pieces. She forced herself to puzzle out the letters. "T.T." Her heart stood still. Those were Tilford's initials! Was it thinkable that Tilford would do a thing like this? Was that his ring on her finger again, and was he "exerting his authority"?

The thought came and looked her in the face as she lay there, struggling to keep her expression from being anything but absolute unconsciousness in sleep. It menaced her with as much horror as when she had thought of that awful kidnaper as a bridegroom. For if Tilford had done this thing to her he was no longer the Tilford whom she had thought she was in love with. He was a despicable tyrant, bound only to conquer and bend her to his will, and she was suddenly filled with a worse fear than before.

"The heritage!" came the words again. "The heritage of the servant of the Lord!"

"Oh, my Heavenly Father! I am Thy servant! The very humblest, the latest perhaps, and surely the very lowest of Thy servants, but still a servant. I claim Thy promise!"

The woman was walking about the room now, placing her suitcase on a chair, putting on a pair of white lacy gloves, tilting her hat a little more to the side, touching her lips with a brighter red. Maris ventured another glimpse and felt sure she was preparing to leave soon. She had glanced at her watch. She wished she knew what time it was, what ship this was. But somehow she must be ready to spring into action if the woman did leave.

But what could she do? She could never rush forth in a white satin dress and a wedding veil. Was there anything about the room that she could wear?

Beneath her lashes once more she explored the side wall next her. There were hooks and a gray tweed coat with a fur collar hanging on one. Whose coat was that? Would the woman take it with her? So she lay and thought out what she would do if she got the opportunity.

And then, all at once she became aware of a throbbing in

the heart of the ship. Was that the engine? There was a ship's bell ringing, a clear sharp sound of warning. Were they weighing anchor already? Was it too late? Oh, her precious mother, and father, and the little sick sister! What would they all think?

But the bell gave another warning resonant ring and it seemed to mean something to the other occupant of the room. She looked at her watch, and picked up her bag, glancing uneasily out the door. Then she closed the door again and came back, as if waiting for something, some signal. Oh, would she think she had to wait till someone came to take her place? Wouldn't there be even a chance to try and get away?

And then there came a voice, clear and ringing: "All ashore that's going ashore! All ashore that's going ashore!"

The woman turned and fairly ran toward the door, glancing casually at Maris there on the bed, so resolutely limp and silent, her eyes not even quivering. As quiet as if she were laid out for burial.

The woman flung open the door and went out shutting it hastily behind her. She had not locked it! The key was still on the inside! Hadn't she meant to lock it? She had not taken the coat with her. Had she forgotten it? Maris dared not stir for a second till she heard the woman's little high heels clicking down the metal edges of the safety treads on the stairs. Even then she opened her eyes most cautiously, with a sinister feeling that somehow Tilford or the other awful man had been spirited in as the woman left. If he were there, if either of them were there, she had planned she would lie utterly limp and still. She would not respond to any effort to bring her to life. It was the only mode of warfare that she could think of for one under a tyrant.

But the next instant she sprang into action. There might be only a moment more and she must do her best.

She flung the costly wedding veil from her head, wiping it from her forehead with its coronet of orange blossoms as if it were abhorrent. She sat up and clutched at the fastenings of her dress. She must get it off if she had to tear it seam from seam. Could it be the dress that Tilford's mother had ordered? How all the chapters of the story were dropping into place!

She struggled out of the dress frantically, then stooped and wrenched at the jeweled buttons of the silver slippers and kicked them from her. She could never walk in them, they were too tight! She bent and groped on the floor for her own little comfortable everyday slippers. Had that woman put them away? She had no time to search. Would she have to go in just silver stockings? Ah! Here they were! She stepped into them gratefully, and then the glitter of the ring caught her eye. Tilford's ring! She tore it from her finger and flung it on the pile of wedding finery on the bed.

Just then a man rushed by the door crying out again, "All ashore that's going ashore! Last call!" and her heart stood still with fear. Now she *had* to go, and she had no dress on, only a little white silken slip!

Wildly she seized the tweed coat from the hook on the wall and caught a whiff of horrid perfume! It was that woman's coat, and she would perhaps return for it! But this was no time to be squeamish. Maris flung it about her, thrust her arms into the sleeves, and drew the fur collar up about her face. Then she cautiously opened the door and looked out.

There was not a soul in sight. The clatter and noise of many tongues rose from a region below somewhere, people saying last things.

There were stairs close at hand, the stairs that woman must have used, but she dared not risk them. She might meet her coming back to get her coat. Wildly she fled along the gallery to another flight and dashed down. Endless stairs, they seemed, wide and low and turning on incessant landings. Would she never get to a place that would lead her off the boat?

Then suddenly as she rounded a turn she saw Tilford Thorpe just below her standing on a lower step talking earnestly with the woman who had just left her; beyond was a glimpse of the outer world, and a gangplank not far away.

Her heart contracted, and her breath came in stifled gasps. She grasped the handrail and reeled back, turning and flying up to the deck above, and back along that to another flight of steps.

Her heart was beating so wildly now that it seemed as if she could not go on, but she took a deep breath and tried to steady herself. At least she knew where they were. But could she ever hope to escape them? Was that gangplank the only path to safety? Would she have to pass under their very gaze? Was there any hope she could do so without being recognized?

"All ashore that's going ashore!" called a voice quite near, and she almost slid down the next stair she came to. A great siren set up a clamor to add to the din, and she found she was trembling in every part of her body. Even her lips were shaking.

These steps she was going down seemed endless. Perhaps she had gone too far, for they landed her amid a lot of bales and boxes and baggage; coils of rope lay in her way, the heat of a furnace came from somewhere on her right. She rushed about trying to find out where she was, and felt like a rat in a trap. A sailor came by.

"You don't belong here, lady. Look alive there! You'll get hurt. Can't you see you're in the way?"

"But isn't this the way to get ashore?" She pointed to a tilting floor that spanned a space over black sullen water.

"No! This is freight. You wantta go up the other end. Better hurry we're just weighing anchor."

Then suddenly he grabbed her and drew her out of the way of a large packing case that was being brought on board by several men.

"Lady, you'll get killed if you don't look out!" He glared at her.

"Oh, I've got to get ashore, and I'm afraid I can't get there in time. Couldn't you put me off here?" she pleaded.

The man looked at her in disgust, then called to one of the men who had just helped with the packing case.

"Here, take this fool woman ashore. She's lost her way, and they're just hauling in the gangplank."

The burly shoreman grinned and swung her up the incline. She had one awful glimpse of the dark water on either side, and then she felt the wharf beneath her feet. She was so relieved that she almost sank down right there.

But suddenly amid the noise and confusion the siren sounded again. She realized that people were all about her, calling farewells to their friends. She looked and the ship was already moving, putting stately distance between it and the dock. There were people crowding all the decks looking down, some smiling, some weeping, confetti hurtling through the air, snarls of paper ribbons like crazy rainbows littering the railings, girls snatching for them and gathering them in like trophies. The ship was gone and she had escaped! She stared for an instant with dazed eyes, unable to take it in, incapable for the moment of further action.

It was just then she saw Tilford, standing on the upper deck by the railing, staring out over the motley company on shore. In a moment more he might see her! Perhaps he could do nothing now. Yet there was no telling. He was still capable of issuing orders. She might find herself under custody! And the woman! She might be somewhere in this crowd perhaps!

Her fear redoubled, Maris turned and stole through the crowd that even in that short time since she had stood there, had milled around her, filling up the way.

Keeping her face away from the ship, she edged between the jostling people. She pushed the fur collar up about her chin, daring not to look up lest she would be looking into the eyes of her erstwhile keeper.

At last she reached the edge of the crowd, and darted away down the long shadowy reach of wharf, her frightened feet fairly flying. There were bales and boxes about in the way. She had to go between them, to weave her way in and out, but she was glad of even so much covering for her flight.

The din on the other end of the wharf seemed farther away now. There were not many people about here, everybody was up at the other end watching the ship's departure. Sudden tears of relief blinded her vision. She was almost at the end of this long wharf now. A dark street loomed ahead, a city street with unknown perils at midnight but that seemed small beside the perils already past. There were lights from an office at the right. She must avoid those, she must keep out of sight as much as possible.

Then, when she was almost minded to rest for an instant she heard footsteps behind her, quick heavy steps, like the woman who had been in her cabin, and fear leaped up in her breast again. The woman had seen the coat perhaps, and was coming after it. She would call the police. There would be another awful time. Oh, she could bear no more. She felt as if she must sink down and rest, she was so tired!

But she started to run with all her might, breathlessly, lightly in her little old slippers, keeping to the shadows as much as possible, not heeding where she went, and then all at once she stumbled on a great coil of rope and went sprawling face downward, her hands outstretched. This was the end. She could go no farther. She would just lie here and let them do what they would. She could not rise and go on!

But those footsteps were coming on now! It was a woman! She peered back fearfully, and just then the woman passed under an arc light and she thought she recognized her. It was, it must be that woman. She was hurrying. She must have seen the coat!

The place where Maris was lying was in the shadow. Yet she dared not risk staying there. Fear stimulated her waning strength, put fight into her soul once more. Her mother and Lexie at home needed her. She must not get into the clutches of kidnapers again, even though Tilford whom she dreaded most was out on that ship sailing away from her. By this time he had likely gone to his cabin, and discovered her flight. There were radios on shipboard, and Tilford's long arm was capable of reaching even to the land. Tilford never gave up a thing he had once started until he had his way.

She struggled to her feet, bruised, and sore, with a long scratch on her arm, and splinters in her hands, but fear was behind her driving her again. Her feet seemed gifted with wings, and she flew on noiselessly toward that spot of light from the windows of the office, toward the darkness of the street ahead. Which should she take? Should she go into that office and claim protection of the people there, summon the police, or should she trust to the darkness of the unknown street? Oh, the street would be safer. She could not trust that woman. She was wearing respectable clothes, she could probably summon friends. And Maris was in a strange array. Nobody would believe her, and she might be hailed to jail charged with stealing a coat!

The thought gave new momentum to her flight. She darted ahead with every ounce of strength that was in her, and not six feet from the street she came into violent collision with a man who was also sprinting, just rounding the corner from the street to the wharf. And suddenly she collapsed in his arms, the breath knocked from her body. This surely was the end!

18

BACK at the Mayberry home the mother was restless. Perhaps she felt the tenseness in the atmosphere, although Merrick had been very careful. He had called Nurse Bonner from her room just as she was preparing for a good night's rest, and downstairs out of sound from above, he had told her the situation with regard to Maris.

Nurse Bonner was wise. She did not exclaim. She took it calmly with a quick sanity that helped to steady Merrick, who was full of despair over his responsibility.

"Yes," said Nurse Bonner, "it's pretty serious of course, and we'll have to be wise about the invalids. Your father too. Don't waken him unless you have to. Wait at least until you hear from Mr. Maitland. If your father can get a full night's sleep he will be better able to bear whatever comes tomorrow, and really, he can't do any more than is being done tonight. It is imperative of course that not a breath of excitement reaches your mother. She is exceedingly sensitive to noises, even to feelings, in the household. If your father finds out tonight he will be nervous when he sees her in the morning. That must not be. She must think he's gone to his office happily, and that all

237

is well. And we won't say anything to the night nurse yet."

Merrick looked at her gratefully. Her very tones made him feel more like a man, dependable, able to handle this situation in the way it ought to be managed.

"All right," he said. "Sorry to have disturbed you, but I thought somebody ought to understand things."

"Yes," said the nurse, "and don't hesitate to call me in the night the minute you get any news. I'm used to waking at the slightest sound. It doesn't spoil my rest in the least."

"All right!" said Merrick. "I'll call you."

"I'll leave the door open and you can just step in and speak to me. I don't want to disturb any of the others."

"I'll do that," said Merrick, and went back to the telephone with a sense of comfort that somebody else knew what was going on and he wasn't entirely alone.

But in spite of all their caution the situation somehow reached its invisible fingers out and penetrated the sick room. The night nurse came tapping at Nurse Bonner's door a little later.

"I wish you'd come here a minute," she whispered. "My patient is restless and I don't like the way her pulse acts. She keeps calling for Maris. I haven't heard her do that before at all. I went to Miss Maris' door and tapped but she didn't answer. I didn't know whether I ought to waken her or not, she's looked so tired the last few days."

"Maris is out," said Nurse Bonner briskly. "I'll come!"

She threw her kimono around her and was at the bedside almost at once.

"Now see here," she said quietly, as if it were a joke, "what's the matter with this little mother?"

Mrs. Mayberry lifted troubled eyes.

"Maris!" she said piteously. "Maris!"

"Maris has gone out," said Nurse Bonner. "She went for a little ride."

The troubled eyes searched her face.

"Getting—married?" the slow lips formed the words earnestly.

"Oh, no. Nothing like that!" said the nurse.

But the eyes were still troubled, puzzled.

"Her—wedding—day—!" murmured the sick woman.

"Oh, no. Not at all. You've got mixed in your dates. Maris isn't getting married today at all. She wouldn't be married till you were able to be at the wedding. Now be a good little mother and shut your eyes and go to sleep. I'll take care of Maris when she comes and tell her you sent her your love."

She got the sick woman quieted at last and then stole in to see about Lexie, for she had left her door ajar, and now there seemed to be a lot of restless turning over and sighing.

She found the little girl crying.

"I called and called my sister and she's didn't come!" said Lexie with whispered sobs. "I vanted a dwink of vater."

"Well, that's too bad!" said Nurse Bonner. "Your sister had to go out for a little while, but she'll be back pretty soon, I guess. I'll get you the drink of water and then you'll go to sleep like a good little girl, won't you?"

"Wes."

Downstairs Merrick was having troubles of his own. A call had come from the Maitland house. The housekeeper said the little boys had waked up and were demanding Mr. Maitland. So Merrick had to call them to the telephone and give them Lane's message. They responded loyally as Lane had known they would, but their voices sounded most dejected as they said good night. It touched their older brother and he promised to be over the first thing in the morning and let them know how soon Lane would return, and perhaps they could get ready some kind of a celebration to welcome him home. They'd talk it over in the morning.

So at last the little boys went back to their beds, cheered by the thought of a festivity in the offing. They planned to pick strawberries enough for strawberry shortcake for lunch, and then wondered if Lane would object to their decorating with a lot of little flags they had found in the attic.

And Merrick reflected on what a lot of different kinds of troubles there were in this world, all at once, when life had heretofore been such a jolly affair. He decided it was all because of Tilford Thorpe and that blamed wedding.

The ship sailed out on a silver sea, and the New York harbor became a speck in the distance.

Tilford Thorpe turned from watching the shore, and with lips set with determination went to his stateroom. He was expecting to have a bad time for a few minutes with Maris. She would probably be stubborn for a while. But when she found that they were off on their honeymoon actually, and there was no turning back, she would easily come around. Maris had always been so sweet and yielding!

He hoped she would be fully recovered from the sleeping potion that had been given her, and see the immediate necessity of submitting to the marriage service for which he had arranged with the captain, to take place soon after the starting of the ship.

He ascended the steps to his suite with pleasant anticipation. He had Maris now where she couldn't gainsay him. He meant to be very kind and loving to her—after she once came to herself and realized that he had been right—just to make up for taking her away forcibly. Of course she might be a bit upset at that at first, but he would show her such a good time that she would soon forget it. He was glad he had had his mother buy those two evening dresses. They would have a gay time on board and when they got to Paris they could stock up on some really smart clothes for her. Of course she would likely be disappointed not to have her own things that she had prepared for her trousseau, but they wouldn't be much loss. Anything she would have bought would have been far below the standard of what his wife should wear, anyway.

Then he reached his stateroom and opened the door.

There on the bed lay a heap of satin and lace, tossed aside, ripped and torn, as if it had been jerked off in great haste. Half crushed at one side lay the priceless wedding veil, an heirloom in the Thorpe family and yellow with age. It drooped from the coronet of orange blossoms dejectedly, and sparkling out from its ethereal folds there lay the great diamond ring, its prisms flashing gaily with a startled air, as if surprised that it had been rejected.

Tilford stared down on it scarcely believing his senses. She had torn off the wedding dress and gone! She had flung his ring back at him again! But how was this possible? Mrs. Trilby, the woman he had hired to attend her and dress her, had told him just now that she wasn't awake yet. That it would likely be another hour before she was fully free from the sleeping tablet. Had the woman double-crossed him? Sometimes those low-down hirelings did that. Only he had been so sure of this woman. She was to receive another hundred dollars at her home if he found everything all right when he went to his stateroom! And it wasn't conceivable that Maris had bribed her, because Maris would have nothing to bribe with. Maris was penniless.

He stepped forward, incredulous, to lift the ring from the folds of lace, half believing he would yet find Maris beneath the heap of finery, but he stumbled over a little silver shoe, and plunged his arms deep into the lace and satin, the ring evading him and slithering out of sight gaily, as if it enjoyed tantalizing him.

By the time he had found the ring he was thoroughly himself and very angry, trying to plan how he could get revenge on Maris for thus evading him. He could not understand how she had managed to get away. He was sure Mrs. Trilby could not have been down on the deck more than three minutes before the ship sailed. He had himself been standing close at hand when the gangplank was hauled in. Maris had not passed him, he was positive. Besides, how could she get away without any clothes? He had told Mrs. Trilby she might have and take with her the garments Maris was wearing when they took her. She had left the wedding dress behind! She could not have gone without clothes!

He strode to the pile of baggage heaped in the corner. Not one had been disturbed. The expensive outfit that he had made his mother buy was still locked up in those suitcases, and he had the keys in his pocket. He counted everything over. Nothing disturbed. She could not have gone in such a state as that.

He tossed the things on the bed aside. Not even a sheet or blanket was gone! It was inexplicable.

She must be somewhere about, perhaps playing a practical joke on him! Well, in that case he would forgive her, of course, but it was careless of her to fling around expensive clothes and diamonds that way. He would have to teach her to be more careful. Of course she had never been accustomed to such prices as he paid for things and perhaps had not realized.

He strode to the bathroom and looked in, he pulled aside the shower curtain, then peered into a wardrobe. But no Maris appeared. She was not anywhere.

He threw open the door of his stateroom and looked outside but the galleries were alive now with people coming back to their staterooms. There was gay chatter everywhere. People laughing and talking. And he was alone! He had never been so frustrated in his life as he had by Maris Mayberry! Little puritanical hypocrite! Pretending to be so awfully good and then standing him up on his wedding at the very last minute. He would know better than to be fooled by a demure face again. She wasn't his kind of course, but he could have raised her into his class. And she was beautiful, there was no denying that.

He stormed back and forth from bed to portholes, trying to think what he should do. Somehow he meant to get it back on this little girl who had turned him down and scorned his wealth that he had intended lavishing upon her. He would think up a splendid way and take her by surprise. She hadn't heard the last of him yet by any means.

Meantime, he was out on the ocean alone and what was he going to do with himself? Well, there was a famous actress on board. He might amuse himself with her, and manage it that news of his flirtation should get back to some social column in a paper Maris would be likely to see. That would be a good beginning.

He kicked at the rich wedding gown that was trailing off on the floor. The wedding gown that his mother had paid for! It occurred to him that his mother had really made all this trouble, insisting upon that wedding gown. He would tell her so when he wrote. It did his wrathful soul good to blame it on somebody.

It also occurred to him that the captain would be expecting a summons pretty soon for the wedding he was to perform. He had better do something about it at once. So he rang for the steward and sent a note to the captain that the wedding had been called off on account of illness in the family which detained the bride at home.

Having thus disposed of the wedding, he rolled the wedding dress up in a wad along with the veil and orange blossoms and slippers and bestowed them in a suitbox which he ordered the steward to have wrapped and shipped to his home. He was resolved that he would somehow bring it about, sometime in the future, that Maris should yet wear that wedding dress and be married to him. He would take a little time off in Europe on this supposed business trip, and give her mother time to get well, or die, one or the other, and then he would come back and make Maris eat humble pie and have such a wedding as *he* should prescribe. When he once brought her thoroughly to her knees she would do what he said, and like it!

With which resolve he went downstairs to the bar and refreshed himself with several drinks. His wedding night without a bride had to be celebrated in some way. So he drank. Tomorrow he would look up that actress and forget Maris for awhile.

But somehow it was not so easy to forget Maris, and he had to take a good many drinks before the vision of her face in her wedding array faded from his thoughts, and he began to consider other phases of the subject. There for instance was all that money he had paid to the man and woman who carried out his plans. He had had to borrow it from his mother, and he didn't see how he was ever going to pay it back again. Probably dad would find it out and then there would be an awful row! Strange he had so much trouble in his life! Strange he never could have anything he wanted without a fuss.

He, who had been pampered since ever he was born!

He drank so much that he had to be helped up to his stateroom at last, and went to bed dead drunk!

And that was the night that was to have been Maris' wedding night!

19

MEANWHILE Maris, limp in the arms of an unknown man, dumb with new fear and horror, panted for her breath in the darkness and wished she could die. She was too tired to go on, and too dazed to think a way out of this awful maze of disasters into which she had so innocently walked a few hours ago.

"No weapon ... shall prosper!" came the words through her despairing mind. Was that then untrue, that promise that had so heartened her? Did God not care?

The man had recovered his balance and was looking down at her. He had been running for that ship that was so noisily sailing away from the dock. Had he missed it after coming so far? And just because some crazy woman had dashed into him and almost upset him?

Even if he dropped her right here and ran on, could he make it? But one couldn't just drop a woman like that who had fallen into his arms, and was apparently almost unconscious, and breathing painfully. She lay like a dead weight in his arms. It was not thinkable that he could lay her down here and dash on, not even for his own important errand!

He held her off a little and looked into her face, and then suddenly he exclaimed and drew her close again, as one draws something precious.

"Maris! Beloved!" he breathed, nor knew what he was saying. "Oh, my dear! Are you hurt?"

He bent over her looking into her face against his shoulder, and suddenly her eyes opened and she looked at him. Then all at once the stark terror within her eyes turned to incredulous wonder, and a great blinding joy. She clung to him, and quivered, hiding her face on his breast. His arms went around her and held her close.

"Oh, Lane!" she whispered. "Oh, Lane!" It was all she could say, and great long shudders of relief shook her slender body.

Then suddenly she remembered and grew tense again.

"Hide me! *Quick!*" she pleaded. "There was somebody after me!"

She turned her head and looked behind her, and then hid her eyes again and shuddered. She was breathless and her voice trailed off.

"There! My darling!" he said gently, patting her head as if she were a little child. "Nobody shall touch you, beloved! I'll take care of you! Come! Are you able to walk? It's only a step to my car!"

With a strong arm supporting her, her hand in his, he set her upon her feet and led her quickly out into the shadows of the street, and across to where he had left his car.

There were people coming away now, a good many of them. She could hear their footsteps, and their voices. She clutched at his arm, but he drew her around the other side of the car out of sight and put her gently in.

"Put your head back and rest," he said. "No one will see you. No one will trouble you any more. I am here to protect you."

She dropped her head back, but her eyes peered out and he saw she was still frightened. It was not until they had driven several blocks away from the wharf and left the crowd entirely behind that she began to relax and be more like herself.

He had his hands full with traffic for a few minutes, but when they reached the Holland tunnel and were speeding down the smooth way he spoke again:

"What are you afraid of, Maris? No one can get you now. They will not recognize you riding along in the car. They cannot see your face enough for that. And what could they do to you now that you are with me and I am here to protect you?"

"Oh," she said, her voice with a little tremble in it was almost between a laugh and a wail, "it's the coat! It is not mine. They might arrest me for stealing. I had to take it. There was nothing else."

He laughed.

"We can pay for the coat, or send it back. Don't worry about that. Just you rest back and shut your eyes. Aren't you too warm in that heavy coat with all that fur about your neck? Don't you want to take it off? We can fling it out of the car window when we get out of the tunnel if you want to."

"Oh, but I can't take it off," she said laughing shakily. "They took my own dress and I had to put on this coat or I never could have got away!"

Lane considered that.

"Well, now see here," he said, "I think we can remedy that. Why don't you put on my coat? I certainly don't need it this warm night. I only happened to have it along because I was hoping to take you riding. It's thin. It's only linen. It surely will be more comfortable than that heavy thing."

"But oughtn't I to send it back to the owner?"

"Do you know who the owner is?"

"No, but there might be a way of finding out. I felt some papers in the pocket when I put it on."

"Well, then we won't throw it out, but you are going to be more comfortable. Here!"

He stopped the car for a moment and slid out of his coat, handing it over to her.

"Now," he said, "take off that coat and hand it out to me. I'm going to get out and open the trunk in the back and get this coat out of your sight. If there are papers in the pocket we must guard them carefully. They might give some clue—"

He got out and Maris hastily changed into the linen coat, and handed the tweed coat through the window. When he got back in again he asked her if that was more comfortable.

"Oh, so much!" she said. "I didn't see how I was going to stand it all the way home."

"Well, now," said Lane, "I don't want to force your confidence, but it's necessary that I telephone Merrick as soon as possible. I wonder—do you want to tell me anything? I don't want you to have to dwell on unpleasant things, but Merrick is liable to have a couple of detectives out scouting right now, and he'll want to know what I've found out!"

"Oh," she said with a quick gasp, "is Merrick all right?"

"Yes, Merrick is quite all right. He's at home safe and well waiting anxiously to hear from me. If it will help you any I'll just tell you what I know. I was out in our yard looking for a ball and heard your friend drive up and tell you that yarn about Merrick. I didn't hear more than a word or two, but it was enough to worry me. I called to you as you were getting in the car that I would take you, but the door was slammed shut and the car shot away, so I followed as fast as I could. What happened next?"

"Not much that I can tell you," said Maris. "They shoved me into the seat and someone caught me in his arms, or her arms, it might have been a woman. They stuffed a bitter wet rag down my throat and I passed out.

That's all I know till I woke up on board that ship with my head going around in circles and some woman taking off my shoes. She lifted my head and fixed something under it, and when I dared open my eyes a little I found I was dressed in a heavy white satin dress, and a veil, and silver slippers. The woman smoothed down my dress and went away, and when I looked again she was powdering her nose and putting on a hat. Then she picked up things around the room and put them in her suitcase. My dress I had worn away was one of them. I think this coat belonged to her. It smells of unpleasant perfume just as she did. She must have forgotten it in her hurry. She got all ready and seemed impatient as if she were waiting for someone. She didn't look my way any more. I was terribly afraid that awful man was coming. But when the second call came to go ashore she just made a dash for the door, and I think she forgot to lock it. I was wondering how I would get out if she locked it. I wondered if the steward would let me out without asking questions if I rang. But she didn't lock it, and as soon as I heard her going down the stairs I jumped up and tore off that dress and veil and those slippers. I found my own shoes, snatched the coat from the hook on the wall and ran. I had an awful time getting off. I couldn't find the way. And once I came on Tilford and the woman talking at the foot of the steps, by the gangplank. I drew back just in time, and then got all mixed up in the freight place. But a sailor put me off there for the other gangplank had been hauled up. I had an awful time getting through the crowd, and I saw Tilford again up on deck. I was sure he would recognize me, so I ducked behind some boxes, and started to run, but I fell over a coil of rope and then I thought I heard the woman coming, so I got up and ran blindly. But when I ran into you I thought the end had come."

Lane's hand went tenderly out and folded over hers, like a blessing, it seemed to Maris.

He was quite still for a minute and then he said:

"Have you any idea who perpetrated this dastardly deed?"

His voice was husky with feeling. He was joyously conscious of that first moment when he had held her in his arms. And he didn't just know where he stood with her.

Maris didn't answer right away. She too was remembering the thrill of his arms about her, and felt a constraint. Her voice was low, almost shamed, when she finally spoke.

"I'm afraid I do," she said sadly. "I'm afraid—no, I mean I'm almost *sure*—it was Tilford Thorpe!"

Her head drooped and her eyes were downcast as if she felt she ought not to tell that, or rather as if it were her own shame she was confessing, not another's.

Lane considered that.

"What makes you think so?" he asked, his voice almost embarrassed.

"Because I saw his initials, 'T.T.,' on the baggage in the stateroom. Because we had had a discussion about a wedding dress his mother wanted me to get, and I'm almost sure it was that dress I was wearing! Because—" she hesitated and again that shamed look crossed her face, "because that woman had put *his ring* on my finger, the ring I had given back to him some days ago! Then, too, I saw him on the ship, you know."

"That's pretty conclusive evidence!" said Lane, his lips setting in a stern line. "It's hard to believe that any man from a respectable family would stoop to a thing like this. But—I won't distress you now by discussing it. The important thing is, Merrick should be told at once that you are found. I'm stopping right here to telephone. Aren't you hungry? I'll bring you a sandwich. Here's my hat. Put it on and pull it down in front if you are afraid anybody might recognize you. I won't be a minute."

Lane dashed out at a bright little wayside restaurant, and

true to his word was back in an unbelievably short time. His message to Merrick had been crisp and brief, but filled with a note of joy that pulsed over the wire to the tired brother and lifted his burden even before he took in all the words.

"Hello, Merrick! Happy ending! It's just as we thought. I've got her safe and sound and we're on our way home! No bloodshed and nobody the wiser yet when we left. Better put the quietus on the cops for the present, at least till we get there."

They were on their way again, thrilling over each other's nearness, and over Maris' swift deliverance. Eating their sandwiches and saying little as they flew along through the night.

At last Maris spoke:

"Where were you going, Lane, when I collided with you? What were you going to do?"

"I don't exactly know," he said gravely. "I was trusting the Lord to guide me. I was expecting Him to open the way as I came to it. I was on my way to catch that ship, even if I had to sail all the way across to find out if you were on it. You see, I had a flat tire on the way up or I'd have been there a full half hour before sailing time, in plenty of time to find your stateroom and go to it, ostensibly to say good bye. That was all the plan I had when I started. If I got as far as that I knew the way would open. I would be shown what to do."

"But I don't understand how you got the idea I would be there. Why did you think I would be on shipboard?"

"Why, you see I followed that car you were in and it took you to a measly little rat of an airplane, and the plane went north, that was all I had to go on. That and the license number of the car. I noticed it while the car stood before your house. But it was Merrick who suggested the ship and gave me the name and time of sailing."

"Why would Merrick think I would be on the ship?"

she asked in a puzzled tone. "*I* would never have thought of Tilford's doing a thing like that. Why, I couldn't believe it myself at first."

"I'm afraid your brother hasn't a very high idea of Mr. Thorpe," said Lane dryly.

"No," said Maris sadly, "I knew he didn't like him, but I thought it was just a prejudice that he would get over when he knew him better. Oh, if I had only realized sooner what he was! But Lane, you have been wonderful. It was marvelous for you to come all this way to find me."

"Wonderful!" said Lane. "*Won*derful?" He gave her a look in the darkness that would have told her volumes if she could have seen the full splendor of it, and then he added in a tone of deep feeling, "Why, Maris, I think I'd have died if I couldn't have gone! You don't know what you mean to me! This is no time to be talking about myself, I know, just when you are finding out the perfidy of the man you thought you were going to marry. Of course you don't want to hear anybody else talk about love now. But, Maris, I guess I've got to tell you that I love you as my very life. I don't want the knowledge of it to be a burden to you. I just want you to understand that I'm one friend who would give his life for you if necessary. Even if in the future you can never care for me, I'll go right on loving you and doing anything I can to care for you. I'll be your brother, or your friend, or just nothing but a servant for times of need if you don't want me to be closer. I want you to know that there is a strong earthly love that carries no obligations, that is yours for the taking, but you don't need to take it if you don't want it."

Lane was silent for a moment, scarcely daring to look toward her, wishing now he had waited until another time to speak. Then Maris spoke in a small voice:

"But I do want it, Lane!"

He brought the car to a sudden stop at the roadside and turned toward her.

"You *do!* Do you mean that, Maris? You're not just saying it because you are grateful for my coming after you?"

"Oh, no!" she said with a great surrender in her voice. "I love you, Lane! I've fought against it almost ever since you came back. It was your coming that made me feel there was something wrong in my feeling for Tilford. At first I was only wishing he might be like you but soon I knew that wasn't enough. I knew that you were taking his place in my heart. I struggled against it with all my might for a few days, but I wasn't able to keep my heart from thrilling every time I saw you coming across the lawn, every time I heard your voice on the telephone, every time I touched that beautiful Bible you gave me! It troubled me very much, because I was going to marry Tilford in a few days, and I knew it wasn't right for me to be thinking of you. I was very unhappy. I wanted him to be *you,* the way you used to be when we were children in school and you used to carry my books home for me and bring me candy—"

Suddenly Lane's arms went out and drew her hungrily to himself, holding her close, his lips against her hair.

"My darling!" he said softly. "My own dear girl!"

She nestled closer to him and felt that suddenly Heaven on earth was open before her.

"Go on!" he breathed. "Tell me the rest."

Her hand slipped up around his neck and she drew his head down. Softly, shyly she laid her lips against his.

"I wish there weren't any of that to tell," she said sadly. "It seems so dreadful that I should have let myself think I was in love with a man like that, when God was preparing this for me!"

"Beloved," he said, his lips against her eyelids, "don't feel that way. Tell me the rest and let's get it over with, and just be thankful God led us back together."

"I know," she said. "I am. I think even this last act was an answer to my prayer. You see Tilford had been very disagreeable about mother's illness, and about my caring for Lexie. He practically insisted I leave them both to nurses and a hired housekeeper, and stay with his mother till the wedding. And when I wouldn't he tried to exert what he called authority over me, by right of his ring that I was wearing. So I gave him back his ring. His actions then did a great deal to open my eyes to his true self, for I had never seen him cross before. He'd always had his own way. But afterward I got to thinking about his disappointment and fearing that perhaps I had not been gentle in my way of saying no. That perhaps I had no right to give back the ring when the wedding was almost at hand. I worried a lot about it, and couldn't sleep. Till at last I just asked the Lord to make it very plain to me whether He wanted me to apologize, and marry him later when mother got well, or give him up. And the answer to that was—" she paused and a shudder went through her, *"this!* This awful thing that happened tonight! It was unmistakable, but it was a terrible lesson for me to have to have."

Lane laid his lips on hers:

"Precious little girl!" he said softly. "Bless the Lord, O my soul, and forget not all His benefits!"

Maris laid her tired head on his broad shoulder, closed her eyes, and let such gladness flow over her as she never had known before. It seemed a healing tide to wipe out all the awfulness of what had gone before.

Presently she asked:

"But did Merrick ask you to come up here after me without even knowing I would be here?"

"Oh, no," said Lane, "he wanted to come himself, but I told him his job was to stick around at home and keep your mother and father from finding out there was anything the matter. But I didn't come up here without knowing there was a possibility of your being here, you know. I telephoned the ship to find out if Mr. Thorpe was booked and they answered yes, that a Mr. and *Mrs.* Tilford Thorpe were booked, and that they were expected to arrive early in the evening."

Maris gasped:

"Oh, did Tilford dare to do that! How *could* he?"

Suddenly Maris dropped her face in her hands and wept, her slender shoulders shaking with great rending sobs.

Lane gathered her into his arms again.

"Don't, beloved, don't feel that way! It is all over. Let's forget it!"

"But oh, to think I almost married a man like that, when there was you waiting for me! How can God forgive me?"

"Dear precious one, say rather how good God was to bring us together in this wonderful way! But now, Maris, I think we have talked enough. You should rest. You are worn out. And besides we should get home as quickly as possible, not only for your sake but for the sake of the family, so that you will be there and have everything normal in the morning. Now, put your head down on my shoulder and go to sleep and we'll be at home in a little while."

So Maris nestled down with her head on Lane's shoulder, and though she was so strangely happy, she fell asleep almost as soon as she closed her eyes.

20

MR. Mayberry was restless at intervals all night.

When Lane and Maris arrived they came in so quietly that not even a mouse would have been startled by them. Merrick had gone out to meet the car and bring his sister in. They walked on the grass so that their footsteps would not be heard. But in the early dawn of the morning the invalid suddenly asked out of quiet sleep:

"Has—Maris—come yet?"

"Oh, yes," said the night nurse cheerfully. "She's in her room asleep. She'll come in and see you after breakfast."

But Maris was so happy she could not stay asleep. She woke up with the sense of being surrounded by love. The love and the goodness of God in protecting her and bringing her safely home: the love of her dear family—for Merrick had given her one of his bear hugs and a genuine loving kiss. She could see he had been terribly frightened. And the great love of Lane Maitland, that seemed too good to be true.

As the morning light sifted through the maple leaves out on the lawn and the birds sang their silver notes in the tops of all the trees around, her heart swelled with thanksgiving and wonder that God had opened up a new world to her, and made her life jubilant with love.

She went into her mother's room in a fresh little pink and white dress with white frills down the front, one of the pretty little frocks she had purchased first for her trousseau. Why shouldn't the pretty things be worn now and gladden the family?

Most unexpectedly her mother's eyes rested upon the dress, and then her glance went to Maris' face, radiant with a quiet smile.

"Are—you—married—yet, Maris?" She asked the question in the slow way she had been speaking ever since she had been taken sick, but there was an anxious breathlessness in the end of the words as if the answer would mean everything to her.

Maris hadn't heard her talk much since her illness. There had been that sweet sad smile the last few days, but nothing more. Now she looked at her mother astonished, but quickly rallied and her eyes lit with a whimsical light as she answered sweetly, "Oh, no, mother dear. Not married. Just Maris yet."

The mother was silent watching her wistfully.

"Tilford kept you out so late—last—night—!" The voice trailed off wearily.

"But I wasn't with Tilford last night, mother," said Maris with a lilt in her voice. "I was with Lane Maitland."

"Oh!" said the mother with relief.

Then a moment later a shadow came into her eyes:

"You—put off—your—wedding—for—me! I'm—sorry!"

"But I'm glad, mother!" She stooped and kissed her mother.

"Dear!" the mother murmured softly. Then, with an effort:

"You—mustn't wait—any longer! Tell Tilford—I'm sorry—delay. Go on—with—wedding!"

Maris smiled tenderly at her mother, and then leaned down and said softly:

"But mother, I'm not marrying Tilford at all. I found I didn't love him enough. Are you sorry?"

A great joy dawned on the mother's anxious face.

"I'm—*glad!*" she smiled. "Now,—I can—go to sleep!"

And she drew a deep breath and closed her eyes.

Maris felt as if she were walking on air as she went downstairs to speak to Lane who stood hungrily at the door signaling her with his eyes.

An hour later the father came downstairs, joy shining from every wrinkle in his kindly face.

"Mother is decidedly better," he said to Maris. "The nurse says she's having the best sleep yet!"

Later in the morning when the doctor came he confirmed the nurse's word that his patient was decidedly better.

Then he went over to see Lexie and said the quarantine could be removed in a couple of days and the little girl would soon be able to go out in the yard in the sunshine.

Gwyneth had gone to her teacher's home and taken her examinations. The little boys were reported as having been exemplary in the matter of maintaining discipline in camp during the rest of the night, and were spending the morning sewing two very crooked yellow stripes to their sleeves. They had cut them from a piece of yellow cambric the housekeeper had hunted up from the attic trunks.

So Maris was very happy as she went about her morning duties. The fear of the night before seemed like a bad dream. Now and again she paused as she passed by the window that looked into the garden. Across on the Maitland lawn Lane was having a game of handball with the boys. Her eyes grew dreamy and sweet as she lifted her heart to Heaven in thanksgiving for her marvelous deliverance, and God's great loving kindness to her who had been so stupid and indifferent to the things that should have been so plain to her.

And her heart went singing:

"Oh, Lane, Lane! How wonderful that he and I are to spend our days together! Why didn't I know that Tilford would never bring me true happiness?"

The little boys finished their game of ball and retired to the garden benches under the hemlocks where Lane had set up a miniature school room. And when they were deep in their studies with enticing promises for the afternoon if they knew their lessons well, Lane betook himself to the garage and looked up those papers in Mrs. Trilby's pocket.

That evening he showed them to Merrick and Maris.

"Here is evidence that will conclusively put a stop to any more interference with Maris," he said as he brought them out of an official looking envelope. "They are two letters written by Tilford Thorpe to this woman, Mrs. Trilby, the first giving her detailed directions about arraying Maris in those wedding things, even to the ring on her finger. The second one deals with the amount of sleeping potion to be administered. They are signed T. Thorpe. Do you know the handwriting, Maris?"

Maris took the papers in trembling hands and read them through, growing very white as she read.

"Yes," she said looking up with quick tears in her eyes, "that's his handwriting!" Then she took out her handkerchief and brushed the tears away.

"Oh, it makes me so ashamed!" she said.

"It's not your shame, sister, it's his!" burst forth Merrick.

Lane gave her a tender smile.

"I wouldn't have troubled you with this," he said, "but I felt you should identify the handwriting. These letters are important. With your permission I am putting them into a safe deposit box in the bank, Maris, in your name, and instructing my lawyer to write a letter to Mr. Thorpe saying that the letters are in safe keeping and will not be used against him as long as he does not trouble you, but if at any time in the future he attempts to annoy you again your family will immediately take steps to let his actions be widely known. That will save you from further worry about the matter, and will at the same time be fair to the young man's family."

"He ought to be strung up!" said Merrick viciously. "He ought to be hanged for kidnaping. But of course I suppose you are right."

"Will father have to know?" asked Maris anxiously.

"No, I shouldn't think so. At least not now," said Lane. "Now, Maris, let's forget it and be happy. God sends sunshine after rain, and rainbows in our clouds. Mother is better, I hear. Let's thank God and sing hallelujah in our hearts!"

"Okay!" said Merrick fervently, and got up and walked away to hide his emotion.

When a few more days had gone by so many happy things were happening that Maris almost forgot that she had been kidnaped and been through frightful tortures of horror before she escaped. Only at night sometimes she would waken with a strange terror possessing her, and think for a minute she was lying on that bed on shipboard. Then all the awful nightmare would return, and she would have to go over every terrible second of the experience and try to think how she might have prevented it all in the first place. And she found that the only way she could dispel the thoughts was to pray.

But the days were too happy now, to allow such nightmares to continue when the morning came. Lane was sure to be over before the sun was very high, to draw her away for a few minutes to the hemlock retreat just across the hedge, where they might have a few words together alone.

And mother was getting well. The doctor jubilantly

admitted it. He said that if she continued to improve she would be able to go off for a few weeks' rest with father, and then she would be as good as new. Of course the nurse must go along to make sure she did not overdo, and to watch her pulse and blood pressure and diet and sleep and a few other minor points.

He said this down at the front door early one evening to the assembled family, Lane included, and Lane watched their expressions of joy and relief as they heard.

But his eyes lingered longest on the father's face. There had come an instant radiance at the news, of course, but then there had succeeded a look of gravity, almost a troubled look, as the proposed trip was mentioned. It was the first time the father had heard of that trip seriously, and Lane knew he couldn't see how it was going to be managed.

After the doctor was gone Lane slipped his arm through Mr. Mayberry's and drew him along the path.

"Come over here to my refuge among the hemlocks a little while. There's something I want to ask you. You come too, Merrick. I want to talk something over with you both."

The father hesitated. He felt he had a great deal to think about just then, ways and means for this trip, which of course had to be if the doctor wanted it.

But he didn't like to refuse Lane. Lane who had been so kind to them all, taking care of the little boys, and helping in countless ways beside, so he allowed himself to be led over to the hemlocks. And Merrick came bringing up the rear, trying to think how he could get a little extra money to help out with.

When they were all comfortably seated with the sweet darkness about them, and the soft slant of moonbeams peeping restfully through the dark lacework of branches, Lane spoke:

"Mr. Mayberry, I'm going to butt in on something that isn't my business. I hope you won't resent it."

"Why, of course not, Lane," said Mr. Mayberry genially. "You've certainly earned the right to talk anything over in this family without feeling you are butting in. I'm sure whatever you suggest will be well worth listening to."

"Thank you, Mr. Mayberry. Well, then, here goes. Hear me through to the end before you jump to conclusions. I heard you tell the doctor just now that you didn't see how you could get away from your business to accompany your wife on this trip the doctor wants her to have—"

"Yes," said the troubled father, passing a thin hand over his furrowed brow, "it's quite impossible just now. I've been away from the office quite a good deal since mother has been sick, and I'm not at all pleased with the way things are going down there. My assistant is well meaning, I guess, but his judgment is not always as good as it should be. It is really imperative that I should be in the office for the next few weeks, unless I am willing to let my business go to the wall."

"Yes, Mr. Mayberry. I was afraid you might feel that way. I've known from one or two things you have said that you were troubled about the business. But you see we all feel that it is also quite imperative for your wife's full recovery that you be with her while she is recuperating. I am sure the doctor feels that the trip without you would not be of the lasting benefit that it would if you were along. It would be better to have even your business go to the wall than to have Mrs. Mayberry do so, wouldn't it?"

"Of course!" said the harassed father with a sigh. "But how am I to finance the trip at all if my business goes to the wall? And how are we to live afterwards?"

"Well, now that's just what I want to talk about. Perhaps I've given more thought to it all than you will feel I had a right to," said Lane pleasantly. "In the first place about that trip. I know a way that that can be accomplished for practically nothing. I've inherited from an old aunt a lovely old place in the mountains of Virginia, where the air is fine, and the neighborhood is so still you can almost hear the clouds go by. It has plenty of big airy rooms, thoroughly furnished, and nobody is there but the housekeeper who used to companion my aunt before she died. She's all alone with the old colored cook who is past master at her trade of tempting appetites. I'm under obligation by the terms of the will to keep the place up as long as Mrs. Morton lives, even if I didn't love it myself. So it's there, and empty, and ready for your occupancy as long as you and Mrs. Mayberry and the nurse want to stay. And you wouldn't need to feel under obligation to me, you know, for you'd only be returning the visit I made at your house when I had that long siege of typhoid fever once. How long was it I stayed with you? Four months I think it was, and I probably wouldn't have been living today if your wife hadn't nursed me, and then fed me afterwards till I was able to go back to work. And you didn't charge me a cent's worth of board either, though I think I ate you out of house and home when I got better."

"But we loved to have you, son! And your father was my best friend for years!"

"Exactly so," said Lane waxing more earnest. "And that's just why I claim the right to step in now and return the hospitality. And it isn't as though it will cost me anything, either, for it won't. Mrs. Morton has a garden with everything needful in it for food, and a cow, and a lot of chickens, and there's an old gardener who attends to it all. It's there anyway, and plenty for a lot more than use it. So much for the trip. And of course I'll take you all down in my car! That goes without saying!"

"Well," said Mr. Mayberry. "That's wonderful! Why, Lane, I can't say thank you enough! Why, of course I'll accept that! It lifts a great burden off my shoulders. You are a dear lad! Your father's own son! But, about my business—"

"Yes, about your business, Mr. Mayberry," said Lane quickly, "I was just coming to that. Maybe you'll think this is preposterous. I don't know, but perhaps when you think it over it won't seem quite so impossible as you think. You see I'm out of a job for the summer, that is when my detention camp is over, of course." He laughed. "You may think I'm very presumptuous, but I was going to propose that you let Merrick and me come in and help you out, at least while you are gone. Merrick tells me that his job ends on Saturday. Of course he hasn't had experience in your office, but he's your son, and would naturally guard your interests, and could be manager, at least in name. And as for me, I've had a good bit of experience right along the lines of your business for the past three years out west. To tell you the truth, while I have two offers for fall, I'm not really satisfied about either of them. I have been waiting till things quieted down so that I could talk business with you. That's really one reason I came back here. You see I've always wanted to be *in* business, not just to be working for somebody else. I've a few thousands to put in, and if you would be willing to try me out there's nothing I'd rather do than be in business with you. I hope you don't think I'm too audacious."

"Audacious! Presumptuous! My dear boy, you are overwhelming! I can't think of anything more ideal than what you have proposed. But I couldn't think of having you put money into my poor little struggling business. It used, of course, to be good and thriving, but the depression has knocked out the foundation from under it. I couldn't think of allowing you to risk money—"

"I don't feel it is any great risk," broke in Lane. "Frankly I've studied over this thing for some time, and I know more about your business than you are aware of. I'm certain that a bit of money just now, and one change in personnel that I have in mind, would put that business on its feet. Don't you feel so yourself?"

"Yes, I do!" said the broken man, his voice shaken with feeling. "Even a *little* money would help. But I couldn't let *you* take the risk—"

"There, now!" said Lane waving his hand, "I don't want to hear any more about that. It wouldn't be you *letting,* it would be me *putting* my money in your concern. And that's what I want to do. You see I don't know anybody in this wide world I'd rather be tied up with than you and Merrick. But even if you don't want me permanently, I figure that in the two weeks before the doctor lets your wife go away, Merrick and I could come down every day to the office and get to know enough about affairs to carry on while you are gone. Could you trust us that much?"

"Trust you?" said Mr. Mayberry. *"Trust* you? Well, I should say! But boy, you don't know how hard pressed I've been. I'm ashamed to tell you just how things stand. There have been three distinct times this last three years that I didn't know from day to day whether I was going to be sold out by the sheriff or not. But please God, He's always seen me through, so far. I'm not entirely down and out yet, but I'm so far near the edge again that I wouldn't dare let anyone else put his money in with me."

"Aw, say, dad, whyn't you make him a full partner and I'll be the office boy, and let old Morgan go work for somebody else? I'll bet he's the one Lane wants to kick out, anyway." He grinned at Lane's look of evident approval. "And you say he's always kicking for a higher salary and threatening to go to Chicago. Let him go! I can learn. I'll bet it won't take me two weeks to get onto enough to keep the old boat afloat while you go off with mother on a second honeymoon."

They talked long, till the moon slipped down toward

the rim of the west, its beams crept away across the lawn, and the world was very still and sweet.

Mr. Mayberry lay back in the big chair, and let himself relax for the first time in months. At last he turned to Lane with a deep sigh of gratitude.

"You don't know what relief you have given me, son!" he said. "To tell the truth I was hard pressed today. I didn't know which way to turn. Morgan got very ugly this morning. He says he has an offer from Chicago at almost twice the salary, and I didn't see just how I was to get along without somebody, yet I could not offer him more salary. But now, it looks to me as if we might weather it. Now I can tell him in the morning that he can accept that Chicago offer and go as soon as he likes." There was eagerness and a new hope in his voice.

"Yes, but dad, you better not let him go till Lane has been over his books. I never did trust that bird! You can't tell what he's pulled off."

"Well, we'll look into that, too! I haven't been so sure myself." Then he laid his hand on Lane's shoulder.

"I shall never forget this night," he said earnestly. "I shall never forget what you have done for me. You are like a real son. Merrick and I both feel so, don't we, boy?"

"Sure do!" said Merrick with a husky choke in his voice.

And as they walked through the shadows back to their respective homes, Lane was thinking in his heart that it wouldn't be long before he was a son indeed. But he wouldn't tell them just yet, not till he and Maris together could tell both mother and father.

21

IN the morning Mr. Mayberry and Lane went down to the office. Monday Merrick was through his job on the bus and went along. They went joyously, like three boys, and Maris stood in the door with a glad light in her eyes and watched them go. Everything seemed so wonderful! It was sweet to see the three men she loved going off together in that fellowship in a common cause. All eager for the same end.

Lexie was out of quarantine now, and the boys were allowed to come home. They came in shyly, but with a new assured air. They were still cadets and on their honor to keep discipline, which discipline now included silence in or around the house. They walked almost reverently, mindful that God was answering their nightly prayers. The first morning after they had slept at home Maris found them in their rooms, quietly, precisely making their beds.

"Sure! We always do that!" said Alec with a grown-up air. "That's part of our daily routine!"

Gwyneth was very happy. She was out of quarantine in time to attend commencement, and she returned from a visit to her teacher with the joyous news that she had passed in all her studies.

The mother was well enough now to have the children tiptoe in every morning silently and kiss her hand, and watch for her smile.

"Can't I even tell her I've had the measles?" asked Lexie eagerly.

"Not yet, dear. She would just worry over how much we had been through without her, and think we were keeping a lot more things from her."

Maris herself was very happy. Lane was so wonderful! He satisfied her heart so fully! How had she ever imagined Tilford was anything at all to her? Oh, God was so good to her!

Quite swiftly the days went by, till the morning came when Lane was to drive the father and mother down to Virginia.

They kept everything very quiet till the last minute, though it was hard to keep the excitement out of the atmosphere.

It was Merrick who picked his little mother up and carried her down in his strong young arms to the comfortable place that had been prepared for her in the back seat, with the nurse close by her in one of the little middle seats, and her husband in front with Lane who was driving.

The mother gave the children a feeble wave of the hand and a tender smile, as they stood grouped around Maris, with Merrick protectingly just at the side, and then they were gone.

And suddenly Gwyneth's eyes filled with tears.

"Sister, isn't our mother ever coming back again?"

"Why, of course, dear child. We hope she'll come back very soon and be as well and strong as she ever was," said Maris slipping a comforting arm around the little girl's shoulders, and then Lexie came stealing close to her on the other side, and wriggled her hand into Maris'. And suddenly Maris felt how very dear they all were, and how dependent just now upon her, and her heart thrilled with gladness that she was right here with them in their need, and not careering through Europe with a sulky selfish man, spending money for things that were not real and vital to her heart's joy. How good God had been to her!

And her eyes followed down the road, where she could still glimpse the outline of Lane's head and shoulder as he drove the car so steadily, bearing her mother away to rest and refreshment. What a lover, who loved her people also, and would always be one with her in her love for them. One who would never be trying to wean her away from them, nor complain when they needed her. Ah, this was going to be true union of soul!

And all at once she saw that Tilford had only wanted her because he thought she was beautiful, and would grace his home. How much he had harped on her beauty, until she herself had almost believed in it too, though she knew now that mere loveliness of youthful outline and coloring were a poor foundation on which to build the happiness of a lifetime.

"Muvver tumin' back," echoed Lexie with dreamy eyes. "I want muvver to turn wight awound and tum back now. I *wove* muvver."

"Well, muvver can't come right back," said Maris briskly. "We've got quite a lot to do to get mother's room all fixed up pretty and new before she gets back. How would you like to help?"

"Oh, wes, wes!" cried Lexie dancing up and down. "Vat can I do?"

"Well, how would you like to make a lovely motto to pin on the outside of her door for her to see the first thing before she goes into her room? I'll find you a nice big piece of cardboard and you can have your new colored crayons and your stencils and color a letter every day till it's done. Would you like that?"

"Oh, goody, goody," said Lexie. "Wes, I would like dat. What would I say on the motto?"

"Well, you'll have to sit down and think about that. You want to get the very best words of course. You could say 'Welcome,' or 'Welcome Home,' or if you don't get too tired working you might say 'Welcome home, mother dear!'"

"Wes!" said the little girl with shining eyes.

"What about father!" said Gwyneth sharply. "We'll be glad to see father, too. You might make one for father, Alec."

"Aw, naw, that's girl's work!" declared Alec loftily. "Lexie can put father too. 'And father' she can say. I'm going to paint baseboards. I can do that real well, Lane said. You just put sheets of paper down on the floor very close to the wall, and then you hold your brush just so, and paint very carefully. I learned how all right. I can do 'em swell. You want mother's baseboards painted, don't you, Maris?"

"Why of course!" said Maris smiling. "We'll all work at that room. I suppose you could paint the doors, couldn't you, Eric?"

"Oh, sure! I did all the doors of the kitchen over at the other house. You just go over and look at 'em."

"What can I do, sister?" asked Gwyneth in an aggrieved tone.

"Well, there are windows to wash, and new curtains to make. Oh, we'll find a lot for you and me to do."

"Seems as if we ought to manage some new wall paper," said Merrick as he picked up his hat and started toward the door to go to the office, himself the sole proprietor of the business until Lane returned.

"Yes, I was thinking of that. I wasn't sure whether we ought to spend the money just now. Of course, the paper itself won't cost much, it's the putting on. I wish I knew how. I believe I could manage it."

"No! You've got enough to do. I know a fellow who's a paper hanger, and he's out of a job just now. He'll do it cheap. I've still got a little of my bus salary left. I'll stand for the work if you'll get the paper, Maris."

"All right. We'll go down and choose it just as soon as we get the day's work out of the way."

So they scattered to make their beds, with happy voices and smiling eyes, and the first wrench of the departure of father and mother was over. The children plunged gaily into activities. Beds were made as by magic, furniture was dusted and garments picked up and put in place.

"Why couldn't we paint the cellar windows?" demanded the boys. "We can get some paint. I know what kind Lane got. We got some money we earned. I can get Lane's brushes. He won't mind."

So the boys went to work at the cellar windows, and quiet reigned in the yard, save for a gay whistle now and then.

Gwyneth took to washing the first floor windows, with a little help now and then from Sally, and presently the boys finished the cellar windows and began on the first story ones, finishing a whole window before Maris got around to notice and protest. But she found they had really done it well. Lane's coaching had not been altogether in vain, for of course they had had a lot of practice on Lane's house.

When Merrick came home at night he stared at the improvement with wide eyes.

"Say, fellas, that's great work! I might take a hand myself after dinner. Got any paint left? Okay! How about my putting up the old ladder and doing the front gable before dark? Say, we can change the face of the old mansion if we go about it right. Great work! I'm with you, lads!"

Meantime in the house Maris was superintending a

crayon motto by Lexie, and a new bureau scarf that Gwyneth was cross-stitching intermittently with window washing.

The next two or three days went swiftly, and by the time Lane returned there was a distinct difference in the look of the old house, although of course there was still plenty left to be done.

Lane reported that the mother had borne the journey well, and was enjoying the new surroundings, and the nurse felt it was going to make a great change in her in a short time.

Then they all settled down to a regular program, work, interspersed with more work of a different kind.

Lane entered right into everything. He and Merrick were very conscientious about the office, and talked eagerly about their "prospects." He came back in the evening to do his part toward the painting, as interested as the rest in making the old house renew its youth.

After it got too dark to paint the two young men would frequently call up Mr. Mayberry on the telephone and consult him about the business, carefully planning their questions so that they would be calculated to reassure him rather than to worry.

But there was always a few minutes at the end of the evening when Maris and Lane would manage a quiet talk together, sometimes a bit of a walk in the moonlight, sometimes a few minutes sitting among the hemlocks. Though Merrick didn't give them much time alone. It hadn't occurred to him they would want it. He was all full of the business, and talked with Lane constantly, trying to plan ahead for his father.

It was almost as if they had always been together in family interests.

"Good night, Lane," said Merrick one night, "you act just as if you really belonged to the family!" And then suddenly he caught a glance between Maris and Lane, a glance of radiancy.

"Perhaps I do," said Lane dryly.

"Well, you certainly belong a lot more than ever that poor fish of a Tilford did," said Merrick. "I certainly wish you had been around before he ever moved to town."

"Well, I was," grinned Lane, with another sly glance at Maris. "Have you forgotten?"

"No, I haven't forgotten," said Merrick, "but I was just trying to figure out how Maris ever had anything to do with that half-baked jelly-fish after she'd once seen you."

Lane reached over in the soft darkness and caught Maris' hand silently, giving it a gentle squeeze.

"Yes?" said Lane comically. "I've often wondered about that myself. How about it, Maris?"

"You're getting much too personal," said Maris jumping up. "Let's go and take a walk, Lane."

So they walked away into the shadows and left Merrick to wonder, and to speculate, and to wish that Lane were really his brother so that there would be no more need to worry as to what would happen when Tilford got back, and mother got well.

Then the very next day Mr. Thorpe came to call on Maris.

Luckily no one but Maris knew him, so there was no excitement about it. Sally merely announced to her that a gentleman in the parlor wanted to see her. So Maris washed the paint off her nose and one eyebrow and went down stairs. A book agent, she thought it might be. She was well into the living room before she recognized him.

He arose almost shyly, watching her come, and held out an apologetic hand tentatively.

"Perhaps you wish I hadn't come," he said softly. "I wouldn't blame you at all if you did."

Maris in a sudden rebound of pity reached out her hand

and grasped his, giving him a shy, half frightened smile. It wasn't any of it his fault, of course.

"You see I've just found out what Tilford did, and I've come to apologize. Of course I know no apology can ever atone for a thing like that, and I'm not going to try to excuse my son. He did a very terrible thing. He oughtn't to have done it. My only consolation is that it was instigated by his love for you—at least I sincerely hope that was the reason—although my knowledge of his life thus far might make it just as possible that it was done purely to have his own way. I have to be honest and state that that might have had a great deal to do with it. You perhaps do not know, could not realize, that Tilford has always had his own way, and cannot brook being crossed in anything, even if he only *thinks* he wants it. Though I sincerely trust that this time it was because he really wanted you that he dared to do this dreadful thing. But that is no excuse whatever for his having committed a crime, for it was a crime to try and kidnap you and force you to marry him. So I have come to you to make what amends are possible. I scarcely dare ask you to forgive my son. Of course it is his place to ask, not mine, but as his father I must ask you that for my own respite. I have never suffered such anguish as since I knew what my boy dared to do."

Suddenly Maris put out her hand.

"Please don't, Mr. Thorpe," she said gently. "It was not your doing, I am sure of that. And as for forgiving your son, I can forgive of course, and I will. But I must tell you honestly that I can never marry him. You see, even before he attempted to force me to do what he wanted at a time when I did not feel free from home obligations, I discovered that I never had really loved him enough to marry him. And even if he had not hopelessly put himself where I would never dare to trust him again, there was a bigger barrier than that separating us."

"I am not surprised," said the old man with a deep sigh. "Indeed, I must admit that I was absolutely amazed that Tilford had been able to secure the love of such a wonderful girl as you are. I felt that you had great depth of character, great sweetness, and rare culture. I can only grieve that you are not to be a part of our family. But I knew all the time you were too good for my boy, and he would only bring you sorrow. For your sake I am glad you found out in time. You have something almost Heavenly about you, something—God-given, I would call it, and I feel that through my son you have been greatly dishonored by his attempt to carry you away to a foreign land without your consent. So I have come to humbly offer my apologies and beg you to understand that I knew nothing of the plan or I would certainly have made it impossible before the indignity was put upon you. I want you to know that I personally deeply regret the whole matter, and long to have your forgiveness."

"Why, of course, Mr. Thorpe," said Maris earnestly. "I never connected you with it in any way. And I am entirely willing to forgive what has been done, with the understanding that Tilford and I are to be henceforth strangers. God forgives. Why should not I? Perhaps I was to blame in the first place for having let Tilford think I loved him. Perhaps I did not understand my own heart at first."

"You are a very wonderful little girl," said the old man, deeply moved. "You have something that I wish we all had. You have a God that I wish was mine."

"Oh, Mr. Thorpe, I am sure you can have my God. He is glad to accept everyone who comes to Him through His Son Jesus Christ. He loves you. He sent His Son to die for you, and I know He longs to have fellowship with you."

"It may be so!" sighed the old man humbly. "I only wish it might be."

"But it is so!" insisted Maris eagerly. "I know for I have

just been finding out what He has wanted for a long time to be to me, and I was so full of the world I would not let Him. Wait! Let me show you!"

Maris reached over and picked up her New Testament that she had been reading just before dinner.

"Here it is," she said eagerly, handing him the little book. "Won't you take this home with you and study it? It is God's own word to you. You have only to believe it, and trust Him. Here—" she turned down a page, pointing to a marked verse: " 'God so loved the world that He gave His only begotten Son, that whosoever believeth in Him should not perish but have everlasting life.' "

"And here—" she added fluttering the leaves over a little farther to Revelation: " 'Behold I stand at the door and knock: if any man hear my voice, and open the door, I will come in to him and will sup with him, and he with me.' "

She handed him the book.

"Keep it," she said, "I have another. You'll find it is wonderful if you will just give yourself to the study of it."

He looked at her wonderingly, with a kind of worship in his eyes.

"Thank you," he said brokenly. "I only wish God could have granted me the gift of such a daughter as you would have been. I only wish I might have brought up my son to be worthy of you. But, no matter. I don't wish to distress you. I shall always look upon you as one I could have loved deeply as a daughter. But I know you are right in your decision. May God greatly bless you, and may you some-time be able to forget the shameful way in which my son treated you."

He turned to go out the door, and then, fingering the leaves of the Testament, he looked back at her again:

"I shall—always—treasure—this little book. I shall study it because you have given it to me. I hope—I shall some day find your God, and get to know Him. I thank you," he said brokenly.

Then with his head bowed and tears blurring his eyes he went out the door and slowly, sadly down the walk to his car.

Maris stood in the doorway and watched him, tears coming into her eyes. Poor lonely old man! He was the only one of the Thorpe family she could have loved and honored! Would he find the Lord in the little book she had given him? She must pray that the Lord would lead him in His own way to peace and rest in Himself.

"Well, I suppose that old bird came to try and patch things up with you and his precious son, didn't he?"

It was Merrick's voice just behind her that spoke, with a keen dislike in his tone.

Maris turned and Merrick caught the glint of tears in her eyes.

"Yes, and you're just softy enough to be caught by it, too, I'll warrant," he challenged her.

"No, Merrick," she said brushing the tears away from her face. "You're all wrong. He didn't come to patch it up at all. He came to apologize."

"Aw, bologny! That was just his line. He knew he'd get you that way. Good night! I thought you'd had lesson enough. I didn't think you'd fall for that fellow again, the poor weak simp!"

"Stop!" said Maris sharply. "Don't talk that way any more, Merrick. I'm not falling for anybody. I'm just sorry for that father. He's ashamed of his son!"

"Yes, in a pig's eye he is! Whyn't he bring him up right then? Whyn't he teach him a few plain morals I'd like to know? Why does he think you've gotta stand for all his mistakes?"

"Oh, but he doesn't!" said Maris. "I told him plainly I had found out I never really loved his son. I told him I never could trust him again, even if I loved him."

"Aw, *hooey!*" muttered Merrick. "You'll fall again when that guy gets back from Europe You fell before for a pretty face and a languid air, and I suppose you'll fall again. Mother'll get well and then haveta get sick all over again worryin' about ya. Good night! What's the use of painting the house and fixing things up if you're going through the same performance again? I'm sick of it all!"

Maris glanced up in distress and there stood Lane, looking from one to the other.

"Oh, Lane!" said Maris in relief. "Tell Merrick—about us! Make him understand how silly he is."

Lane stepped over and put a strong arm around Maris.

"What's it all about, sweetheart?" he asked, and then bowed his head over her and kissed her gently.

"Why, you see, Mr. Thorpe, it seems, has just found out about things and he is terribly ashamed and he came to ask my pardon for what his son had done. And Merrick won't believe but what I'm going to run away to Europe and marry Tilford in spite of everything. You'd better tell him the truth."

Lane gathered Maris' free hand into his.

"All right, here goes! Listen, fella, you're making a big mistake. Your sister is not going to marry Tilford Thorpe because she's already fallen for somebody else. It's true Maris is going to be married sometime, as soon as it seems wise taking everything into account, but it's me she's going to marry, and not Tilford Thorpe. So, now, if you've anything to say against that, speak now or forever after hold your peace! We'd have told you some time ago, if we hadn't felt we ought to tell your father and mother first of all. But since you had to get the high-strikes about that poor sorrowful old man perhaps it's just as well to make it all plain right now."

Merrick's face was a study as he listened to Lane. Amazement, incredulity, dawning belief, overwhelming joy succeeding one another quickly.

"Oh, but I say, Lane," he exclaimed huskily, "this is too good to be true! This is the greatest thing ever! Say, I don't deserve this! I'm a chump if there ever was one. I—ask your pardon, Maris! I ought to have known you had more sense than I supposed!"

They had an evening of rejoicing as they worked away together more one in spirit than they had ever seemed to be before.

"Say, I wish dad and mother knew about it!" said Merrick as he put the finishing touches to the door into his mother's room. "Do you know, I believe that would do more than anything else to cure mother. Why don't you and Maris run down and tell them?"

"She might not like it," said Lane with a troubled look.

"*Like* it!" said Merrick. "My eye! What do you think my mother is? Don't you know she's been worried sick lest Maris'll go back to that dud Tilford?"

Maris gave him a quick glance.

"I wish I'd known that, Merrick. It might have opened my eyes sooner," said Maris with a sigh.

"Well, I doubt it," said Merrick. "If you couldn't see how mother felt without anybody telling you, nothing would have done any good. Let's just be glad you've got them open now."

"Well, how about it, Maris? Will you take a run down with me for a day and tell your mother?" asked Lane eagerly.

"I'd love to," said Maris wistfully, "but it would worry her terribly to have me go away and leave the children."

"Nonsense!" said Merrick. "Why can't you get that night nurse to come here for a couple of days till you get back? The kids love her, and she makes them mind like anybody's mother."

And so at last it was settled that if the night nurse could be prevailed upon to look after the children Maris and Lane would drive down early Saturday morning, and stay over Sunday, or part of Sunday, and break the news gently.

Then work went merrily on. The little boys and the two

little girls entered eagerly into the plan of trying to get the house in order for mother, and were terribly pleased to have the night nurse in charge. They felt quite grown up and important to be left behind, and so Maris and Lane got ready for their expedition with great joy in their hearts, and such a light in their faces that Gwyneth told her sister, "Why, Maris, you look as if you had morning in your eyes!"

But it was not until their visit was completed, when with the blessing of the happy parents upon them both they started back home, that they fully realized the great joy of belonging to one another. If Tilford could have caught a glimpse of their faces during that Sunday afternoon that they took their homeward way, he would have known instantly that the idle dream of finally marrying Maris after all, which he still cherished now and again between his various flirtations would never be realized. For there was something gorgeous and glorious, something really eternal in quality, in the joy of their glances, that was almost blinding to an observer.

"Now," said Maris Monday morning after breakfast, "we've got to get to work and finish this house at once, for mother declares she is in a great hurry to get home, and the nurse said she was sure she would soon be able to return."

So the happy children scurried through their breakfast and got to work, finding no task too hard for their eager fingers. And the two young men hurried down town to the office to try and bring business up to the promises Lane had made.

22

THE wedding was early in October.

Maris hadn't been willing to let her mother have so much excitement sooner, although she had come back home three weeks before with a flush of health on her cheeks, and a joy in her eyes that made it seem almost absurd to be treating her like an invalid. But both Maris and Lane felt that everything should be quiet and calm, and that the mother should have first consideration.

But this was to be no hectic wedding, and best of all there was no heartbreak behind it.

Invitations?

Maris only laughed when Gwyneth reproached her for having burned up the other ones.

"They cost so much, Maris," said the little girl. "You know you said they did! You could just have changed the date on them," she suggested frugally.

"Yes, but you forget that there is one other item, most important, that would have had to be changed also, little sister," said Maris blithely. "The name of the bridegroom happens to be a different one, you know!"

"Oh, that's so!" said Gwyneth astonished. "Well,

couldn't we have got a rubber stamp and stamped them with the other name?"

"It isn't being done, little sister!" said the bride gaily, and then sat down and laughed till she cried. A rubber stamp over Tilford Thorpe's name! What would Tilford say to that?

There was some talk of having the wedding in the garden, just quietly, "for mother's sake" they said. But after the consideration they all agreed that even if there were but very few invited it would be more or less of an excitement to carry on the whole of a wedding at home, and mother would insist on being into it all.

So Lane and Maris talked it over and brought their decision to the parents for approval.

"We're going to have it in the church," said Maris, "and then stop at the end of the wide aisle by the door and shake hands with any of our friends who come."

"That will be sweet," said the mother with shining eyes. "Well, if that is settled we ought to order the invitations at once and get right to work addressing them. There won't be quite as many as there were before, but it always takes time, and I suppose you want them to be mailed, of course, at exactly the right time."

"We're not going to have invitations!" said Maris calmly.

"Well, but *every*body has invitations!" said Gwyneth in horror.

"No," said Maris brightly, "not everybody. *We* don't."

"But aren't you going to let anybody come? What's the use of me being maid of honor if nobody's there? We might just as well have it here at home, just the family."

"Oh, yes, we're going to let people come, anybody who wants to."

"But how will they know?"

"We're going to have it announced in church!"

"Maris Mayberry! How funny! Nobody does that! And

suppose the people didn't go to that church? Suppose they lived in some other town?" burst out Gwyneth again.

"Oh, if there's anybody we're particular about, like people we know real well, we'll either write them notes, or just call them on the phone, and say: Maris is going to be married Thursday morning, at twelve o'clock in the church and we'll be glad to have you with us if you find it convenient."

"Maris, do you mean it?" Gwyneth's eyes were large with wonder.

"Why, surely, dear. Why do we have to go through all that burden of sending out expensive invitations for people to throw in the waste basket? It's all right, of course, if you have money to burn, or if you are noted public characters, but we're not going to try to put on a big show for people to see, so why should we go to all that formality and trouble?"

"My dear," said the mother with a relieved smile, "how wonderful of you to take an attitude like that. It seems to make the marriage ceremony more sacred, when there is not so much fuss and fashion. You know, dear, that's the way your father and I were married. In the church just informally, with all our dear friends, and then just a little supper for the family."

"Yes," said Maris happily, "and Sally is going to cook that supper! Yes, mother dear, no expensive caterers this time! I want everything as different as can be from the way we planned it before. I talked with Sally about it before you came home and she thinks she can do it. She's got a sister and niece who will help, and a couple of brothers for waiters. We're having creamed chicken in little pattie shells, and Sally's best potato salad. She'll make that the day before, of course. And little hot biscuits with butter in them, piping hot, and that delicious concoction she makes out of grapes and melons. The ice cream will come from Shallups, and be in molds of fruit and flowers, and there will be nuts and candies of course. But the wedding cake is all made. Sally made it while you were away, rich and black with fruit, her old recipe. It's great. She made a tiny one so we could sample it. And it's put away in the big tin box to mellow. Now, doesn't that sound good, mother?"

"Wonderful!" said the mother lying back in her chair with a great sigh of relief. "I see I shan't have to do a single thing except look pretty and act stylish."

"That's it, mother! You've caught the idea exactly," cried Maris jumping up to kiss her mother.

So the quiet preparations for the wedding went steadily forward and did not interfere with so much as a wink of the mother's afternoon naps, or other resting time. Oh, she wrote a few notes to her most intimate friends, but that was all, and smiled and said to her husband, "It's really the way a right-minded wedding should be anyway. You and I never felt badly that we didn't spend all we had on frills and folderols. When you have real love it doesn't matter much what else is lacking."

And her grayhaired lover agreed with her and kissed her tenderly.

So the days went by and the wedding morning came.

Maris hadn't invited a single one of her fashionable friends who were to have had a part in the first-planned wedding. But she had written a sweet reserved little note to Mr. Thorpe, Senior, letting him know that she was to be married.

Merrick and the little boys had driven out to a woods that belonged to the Maitland property, and selected and cut a small wilderness of lovely juniper trees. These had been brought to the church and set up about the altar till they made a lovely background for a myriad of tall wonderful pink and white chrysanthemums that stood in stately grace on either side.

And there was a dear old friend of Mrs. Mayberry's,

whitehaired now, and not in active service, but who could still make marvelous music on the organ. It was she who played tender old melodies, and then the wedding march.

Merrick was best man, tall and good looking in his new dark blue serge. He looked very grown up and attractive beside the handsome bridegroom, standing at the head of the aisle.

Lexie in her pink organdy and Alec in a brief white linen suit marched up the aisle heading the procession, and carrying baskets of pink roses which they were to scatter in front of the bride as she came back down the aisle.

Then came Gwyneth, in her treasured pale blue chiffon, taking careful stately steps and holding her wonderful armful of pink roses and delphiniums. Gwynnie held her head as if this were at least a million-dollar wedding. She was enjoying every step to the last degree.

But the eyes of the church full of dear old friends were upon the bride, as she came up the aisle on the arm of her father.

She was wearing the lovely organdy dress that her mother had made, and she looked so sweet that the bridegroom feasted his soul upon her loveliness, and wondered how it came about that God had thought him worthy of so fair a bride. And back in the corner among the shadows, half hidden by a group of small juniper trees, sat an old tired sorrowful man who had almost been her father-in-law. He was watching her keenly, sadly, as she looked up into her own father's tender face with a gay and gallant smile. He studied her simple lovely attire and wondered what his wife had meant by saying that Maris did not know how to dress, and wanted to wear a dowdy home-made affair to their son's wedding. She seemed to him like his ideal of an angel, with her white roses and lilies of the valley in her arm, and the soft mist of bridal veil about her face.

He marveled at the tender beauty of the service, so unique and cognizant of the presence of God in their midst, and he sadly acknowledged to himself that Tilford would never have fitted a service like this, wherein the Presence and guidance of the Lord Christ was invoked for this new household that was being set up. Yet he was humbly thankful in his heart that this lovely bride that was not his daughter had taken time and thought to speak the words and pass on the eternal burning message in God's Word, so that he too could understand what was here going on.

Half way across the ocean came a great floating palace of a boat, bearing on board the lad who would have been the bridegroom if he had been worthy. And sometimes he went gaily among his kind, trifling with brittle hearts, and sometimes he sat apart and planned how he would go back and lay siege to Maris' heart once more.

But Maris was marching down that flower paved aisle, with her hand resting on her dear bridegroom's arm, and her face alight with a love that Tilford Thorpe had never been able to bring to her eyes.

A happy lovely wedding it was, and when they reached the back of the church they paused there, and grouped the family about them, and received happy wishes and congratulations, many of them from humble plain people who loved them. Maris' heart thrilled with the beauty of it all, and it came to her that that other wedding, even though it might have been held in the same church, with costlier flowers about and richer people filling the pews, could never have brought her half the joy and blessing that she found here among plain, loving, simple people who loved the Lord.

"This is the heritage of the servant of the Lord" kept ringing over and over in her head above the sound of old Aunt Mehitable's tender gay organ melodies.

She spoke of it to Lane after they were back in the car

alone together, Merrick having taken the family home ahead of them and brought the car back. She told Lane how that sentence had rung over and over in her ears the night she was escaping, and how it had come today to finish out the ceremony.

Lane smiled tenderly.

"That's the best heritage any soul could have," he said. "It will hold good throughout the years. I could ask for nothing greater for a dowry for my precious wife. 'No weapon that is formed against thee shall prosper; and every tongue that shall rise against thee in judgment thou shalt condemn. This is the heritage of the servants of the Lord.'"

Said Maris, thoughtfully, as she laid a gentle finger on a fragrant lily of the valley. "One ought to walk very courageously with a heritage like that! We must never, never get careless and forget how wonderfully God worked to bring us together again, and how He has saved us!"

Lane's eyes were full of understanding as he watched her, and he murmured softly:

"God grant that we may never forget what He has done for us!"

And then the car turned into their own street, and Maris looking up suddenly saw the house in its new coat of paint as it were for the first time.

"Oh, look, Lane!" she exclaimed, "isn't it wonderful? The house! It looks so clean and beautiful!"

"Yes," said Lane admiringly, "the dear old house! I think I love it just as much as our own!"

"The dear old houses," echoed Maris softly, "I love them both!"

Lane's fingers curled softly about hers, and then the car drew up at the curb, and, there they all were out in front waiting to welcome them! Hand in hand they got out and went in to their beloved family.

"'This is the heritage—!'" murmured Maris in almost a

whisper as together they mounted the steps and smiled at one another.

"'Of the servants of the Lord,'" finished Lane. "I'm glad we're that, aren't you?"

About the Author

Grace Livingston Hill is well known as one of the most prolific writers of romantic fiction. Her personal life was fraught with joys and sorrows not unlike those experienced by many of her fictional heroines.

Born in Wellsville, New York, Grace nearly died during the first hours of life. But her loving parents and friends turned to God in prayer. She survived miraculously; thus her thankful father named her Grace.

Grace was always close to her father, a Presbyterian minister, and her mother, a published writer. It was from them that she learned the art of storytelling. When Grace was twelve, a close aunt surprised her with a hardbound, illustrated copy of one of Grace's stories. This was the beginning of Grace's journey into being a published author.

In 1892 Grace married Fred Hill, a young minister, and they soon had two lovely young daughters. Then came 1901, a difficult year for Grace—the year when, within months of each other, both her father and husband died. Suddenly Grace had to find a new place to live (her home was owned by the church where her husband had been pastor). It was a struggle for Grace to raise her young daughters alone, but through everything she kept writing. In 1902 she produced *The Angel of His Presence, The Story of a Whim,* and *An Unwilling Guest.* In 1903 her two books *According to the Pattern* and *Because of Stephen* were published.

It wasn't long before Grace was a well-known author, but she wanted to go beyond just entertaining her readers. She soon included the message of God's salvation through Jesus Christ in each of her books. For Grace, the most important thing she did was not write books but share the message of salvation, a message she felt God wanted her to share through the abilities he had given her.

In all, Grace Livingston Hill wrote more than one hundred books, all of which have sold thousands of copies and have touched the lives of readers around the world with their message of "enduring love" and the true way to lasting happiness: a relationship with God through his Son, Jesus Christ.

In an interview shortly before her death, Grace's devotion to her Lord still shone clear. She commented that whatever she had accomplished had been God's doing. She was only his servant, one who had tried to follow his teaching in all her thoughts and writing.